New Gods

Robin Triggs

This novel is entirely a work of fiction. The names, characters and incidents portrayed in it are the product of the author's imagination. Any resemblance to actual persons, living or dead, or events or localities is entirely coincidental.

Paperback Edition 2021
ISBN: 9798497390452

Copyright © Robin Triggs 2021

Robin Triggs asserts the moral right to be identified as the author of this work. All rights reserved in all media. No part of this publication may be reproduced, stored in a retrieval system, or transmitted, in any form, or by any means, electronic, mechanical, photocopying, recording or otherwise, without the prior written permission of the author and/or publisher.

Cover art by Shellie Horst

New Gods

Robin Triggs

Also by the author:

Night Shift
Human Resources

For Jen and Lyra, as always

...Static... A crackling, whistling roar... Vision slowly filtering – and then suddenly resolved...

A slum: the camera jerks around, shows you a forest of crude buildings. There is no order. The shacks fall into each other, rubbish litters the dirt streets. But this isn't a shanty; rather its descendent. It's a palimpsest, a polyglot of styles, of years, of building, rebuilding; cannibalisation of a thousand different materials and styles. This is rubble and dust...

A voice, sudden and uncomfortably close, barks in an unfamiliar language. The camera spins and blurs again; down a mud street it finally focuses on a unit of soldiers. A dozen or so men armed with rifles. They're walking – not marching, this is no parade-ground drill – but neither are they diving for cover. Company logo on their chests, on their guns. Behind them, maybe another thirty yards back, come the bulldozers. They roll inexorably on, smashing walls on their blades, carving a highway of crushed brick and mangled iron and powdered glass.

The camera pans again and there are more shouts. Now you see a crowd of men – and women, and children – facing the soldiers. They are unarmed, but they are resisting. Indian or Bangladeshi; there are scraps of writing, unfamiliar text; there are more shouts, screams. And yes, there are men with weapons there too: blue-capped soldiers nervously trying to herd the civilians back.

You watch as a man leaves this group and advances towards the bulldozers. He is waving, shouting towards the Company men. His voice is lost beneath the roar of engines. His words are swallowed by the crash of masonry and he coughs as dust billows around him. He spreads his arms wide: stop. He pauses and sets his gun on the ground before walking forwards still further. His face is pale, his Adam's apple bobs as he swallows.

The Company men pause, and, though the camera is unstable and the focus swoops in and out, you can see the tension etched in their faces. Their sergeant advances to meet the leader of the blue-caps. Sergeant waves expansively. Move aside. We are coming through. There is nothing more to say.

Blue-cap shakes his head. He gestures behind him, to the civilians, then to encompass the slum around them. He is speaking, shouting. He is begging.

The sergeant does not care. He pushes the man aside and Blue-cap's colleagues step forwards, then halt as the Company troops bring their weapons to bear. Blue-cap is still begging. And all the while the bulldozers are closing in, behind them a storm of dust like a waterfall. Now you can see that the drivers are all masked. They're horribly robotic without their eyes.

Another burst of static, a blurring; more voices from behind the camera. A microsecond of blackness and then an almost vertiginous movement; you are running, camera showing the ground, showing feet – the cameraman is not alone, and this small group is ducking behind walls, scattering, scampering down alleys, through abandoned kitchens, kicking over pots and scrambling through windows. They pause. Words are said. You are afraid. You peer around a corner, zoom out and in and realise you're looking at the same scene from a different angle. But the dynamic has shifted. Now the blue-caps are backing off, the Company man advancing in a line, weapons held steady before them. The blue-cap leader tries again. He is almost crying – dust or emotion? – as he pleads.

You are rocked: the camera spins. Focus. In the background a bulldozer has exploded. Gas bottle? IED? Debris rains down. Spin again: the civilians are cheering. Some kneel to pray. A boy scampers forwards and grabs a section of caterpillar track, a souvenir. Some chant, inaudible over the din that surrounds you.

You turn back to the soldiers. The Company sergeant now has the blue-cap pinned against a wall. Blue-cap is speaking quickly. He gestures to the bulldozers, now drawn up just a few yards behind the confrontation. Again Blue-cap is begging. Stop. Stop, please. Talk to us. He waves to the civilians, tears in his eyes.

The sergeant's face is hard. He is in control. He speaks in short bursts. We have our orders. We will not stop. We are coming through. This town is being erased.

The voices around you are as much part of the background as the terracotta sky.

Blue-cap's face changes. Now he looks dazed, unbelieving. His mouth falls open. He shakes his head weakly, swallows. Camera zooms in tight on his eyes (brown), just for a moment, then out again. Company-man turns away from Blue-Cap, releases the pressure on his shoulder. He signals the bulldozers to continue their advance. Blue-cap is stunned. He staggers out of the sergeant's grasp and into the middle of the road. He faces the bulldozers, head turning this way and that. And then a Company soldier steps smartly forwards, whips the butt of his rifle across Blue-cap's face. He falls. Blood drips onto the rutted track. The defenders raise their weapons. The Company troops respond in kind. The bulldozers growl.

You jerk round again, back to the civilians – the ones who are losing their homes and everything they can't carry. A man is running forwards. He is young. His clothes are rags. He is carrying – my God, he's carrying a sword. Where the hell did he get that?

The man's eyes are too wide, too white. His mouth is distorted in a feral snarl, saliva spinning off his beard. Dust eddies around his bare ankles as he raises the weapon to cleave...

He is shot before he gets within a dozen paces of the enemy. A red bloom erupts from his shoulder; the sword flies from his hand. He falls backwards, spinning madly in the dirt as if his blood is pushing his body in tight little spirals, legs flexing madly, scrambling in a crimson razor-dance.

This is the first bullet fired. No-one knows who made the shot.

The bulldozers are moving again.

Blue-cap makes on final effort to make peace. He is pushed aside. The Company men have had enough. They advance, ignoring the weapons pointed at their chests. Stones fly, the civilians, the peasants, resisting the only way they can. The missiles rattle off body-armour, off helmets, off the blades of the bulldozers. The camera spins again; there is so much to take in, you can't see it all.

So you miss the next shot.

Blue-cap is dead, a neat little hole in his forehead. His face still bears a look of shock, of disbelief. The Company soldiers walk calmly over his body.

Then the bulldozers grind him into a bloody smear in the dirt.

More shooting. More UN soldiers drop. The slum-dwellers are fair game too.

The cameraman is backing off; dragged away, you think, by his companions. But he keeps the lens pointed –

– static again, the picture breaking up –

– civilians screaming. Women crying, children wailing, the timeless sounds of panic. There is no mistaking terror.

And the staccato snap of bullets, cutting through the avalanche of collapsing buildings. Bulldozers dig their blades into flesh and masonry without prejudice.

The camera spins; you see bare feet. The battle is lost. You are fleeing.

But there is still time for one last look back. Now you can see only Company soldiers amidst the rubble.

Company soldiers and the dead and the dying.

One

The train looked strange with only two carriages behind it, almost like it was a worm cut in two, spasming along its final journey through the ice-desert that was Antarctica. Even that second carriage was a surprise. We were only expecting the one. I wondered idly what – who – it contained. But the engine was sputtering to a halt and I had no more time to think. My men took up their positions. Two ranks, one either side of the doorway to the first carriage, facing each other. They stood and waited; their green-scaled warmsuits made them look identical, both men and women uniform with their shock-baton held at their sides.

I stood with Augustin, the prison warden, by the gates. They were already open. Where my officers left off, gaolers took their places, lining the walls of the corridor within – down into the courtyard and the depths of the prison proper.

The door to the first carriage cracked open. I brought myself to attention, was aware of my men gripping their batons tighter, shifting slightly. Sergeant Bartelli oversaw one flank, Officer Guder the other.

The first person out of the carriage was a UN security man, identifiable by the markings on his suit. He surveyed our security arrangements, then strode down the passage formed by my officers towards myself and Augustin. We advanced to meet him.

"Sergeant Nordvelt? Warden Augustin?" It was a

woman, not a man. She had a deep, confident voice. "You're ready to receive the prisoners?"

"We're ready," I said stiffly.

"I need to confirm your identities. Masks off, please."

I grimaced at her manner but complied; I took off my face-mask, unclipping the fastenings then pulling the whole front-section away. My skin tingled as the blood-vessels in my cheeks contracted, and then I was left with a sense of numbness as the cold grasped me hard.

The UN woman nodded and, frowning at the old scar on my forehead, brought up a hand-held iris-scanner to first me, then Augustin. She checked the results and nodded again. "Good. Now me."

She removed her own mask, and, despite her training and her expectations, she blanched as the cold hit her. I scanned her eyes with my reader. Captain Agnetha Gísladóttir. Confirmed. And though recent events had made me a little less confident in such technology, I had no reason for doubt here.

She hurried to cover herself back up. "Okay. Let's get this over with. You ready?"

"We're ready."

"Right, let's bring them out, then."

* * *

Fifteen people; fourteen men and one woman. War criminals all. All had declared their innocence in The Hague. All had been found guilty of some of the most horrific crimes carried out under cover of the Resource Wars that had swept the world some thirty years ago.

Genocide. Massacres of innocents. Even, it was rumoured in some cases, cannibalism.

None of us could see the criminal's faces. But we all knew them well enough. Chief of Security Albert Francis had made sure we'd studied them in depth – and that had made for some uncomfortable viewing and a questioning of whether humanity was worth all the effort we were undertaking to preserve ourselves. Why else were we in Antarctica at all?

My biggest fear was not that they'd attempt a breakout – although I did keep scanning the horizon for anyone mad enough to attempt to rescue them – but that some of my officers, or some of Augustin's wardens, might attack them, or at least heckle them.

But only the wind bore comment.

The last two out of the carriage were the ones that were unable to walk unaided. First Diziao, hobbling with the aid of a cane and with a nurse on either side. Then N'Gepi, his huge, bloated body wheeled out on a hospital bed. It hadn't been possible to get him in a suit; instead a sort of mobile heat-curtain had been installed around him, and his bed, and the three attendants that pushed the trolley and carried his drip.

Through the curtain I could see his distended rolls of flesh, a yellowish sheen to his sweating skin.

The security team that had accompanied these monsters now followed them into the jail, as did Guder's squad. They were to ensure the prisoners reached their cells safely and without any little accidents along the way.

The prison doors slid closed behind the last of them. They should have clanged shut, but they didn't. There was barely a sound as they sealed.

But by then I was staring at the door to the second carriage – the one I hadn't been expecting. Whilst all attention had been on the prisoners this had opened and some passengers had emerged. Three of them. They were standing on the sheet ice and watching the show.

Two of them gave me no clues as to their names, ages, races – anything. All I could tell from their suited forms was that they were tall, both of them.

The third wasn't wearing a warmsuit. He was barely wearing any clothes at all, save for a tight-fitting white shirt that revealed the impressive musculature of his arms and chest and ordinary jeans and boots. Sunglasses hid his eyes.

I gaped at him. Though it had been three years since I'd last seen him, I knew him instantly.

This was impossible.

Mikhail Petrovic. Back in Antarctica and showing no ill effects from an incident which shattered his back and burnt away the majority of his skin.

And showing no discomfort from his exposure to the freezing conditions.

* * *

My mind was spinning as I rode back to town. I'd left Guder and half my team at the jail, just in case. Their place in the bus had been taken by the UN security team who'd accompanied the prisoners.

Mikhail Petrovic. Back in Australis.

The last I'd seen of him he'd been lying in a hospital bed in Tierra Del Fuego.

And I'd been the one who'd broken him.

"Don't worry," Gísladóttir said suddenly, snapping me out of my reverie. "They won't get out. They're going to die in this hell-hole."

I looked round at her, surprised. As ranking officers, we'd got the seats at the very front of the bus. "Who are?"

My mind was full of images of the original Australis crew.

She looked at me oddly. "The criminals, of course. Who did you think I was meaning?"

I shook my head. "Nothing... Nothing."

"You looked perturbed. I assumed it was because these monsters," she said, jerking her head back in the direction from which we'd come, "are now your problem." Her cropped blonde hair barely moved.

"Tell me," I said, trying to hide my sudden urgency. "Tell me, what do you know of the people who came with you? In the other carriage?"

Gísladóttir gave me a puzzled look. "Why you want to know about them?"

"I... I wasn't expecting anyone but you and the prisoners."

"Neither were we," she said. She sounded more relaxed now, head back against its rest, staring out at the road in front of us. I'd still not seen her smile. "They were waiting for us at O'Higgins when we were disembarked. It was only then I was told they would be accompanying us to Australis. Must be pretty important to get a whole carriage for three men. There was plenty room in with us and the prisoners. That man must be made of iron to stand this cold, you reckon? With no suit? You saw him?"

"Mm." I nodded.

"Don't know how he stands it. I come from a cold land, but I wouldn't go out there without a suit, right?"

"But they must have said something to you – shown you some authorisation?"

"Oh, yeah, yeah," she said dismissively. "Company officials – no business of mine. I just know they were to accompany us to Australis. Nothing more."

I nodded and tried to return to my musings.

"So what's there to do in this city of yours?" Gísladóttir

asked. "My men were a long time on that God-forsaken boat. And the train was hardly a barrel of geese either. Is anything actually to do in this new miracle-city? Or is as barren and dull as all this?" she said with a wave that encompassed the entire continent.

I frowned. "There are bars," I said stiffly. "There's the garden, and a sports-hall, and theatres..."

"Mm," she said, disinterested. "Well, we shouldn't be here long anyway. We'll be gone in a few days."

Finally she lapsed into silence and I could get back to my thoughts.

Mikhail Petrovic. Back in Australis and in some apparently exalted company. I had no idea what to make of that.

He'd looked in good shape, though; he'd put on a lot of muscle somewhere along the line.

I wondered if the rest of the original crew knew anything – Fergie, maybe, or Max, or Maggie. I'd have to call them – they'd want to know. I was suddenly impatient; I urged the coach onwards.

How *had* Mikhail been able to stand the freezing conditions unprotected?

Two

The first thing Mikhail did was to save lives.

I remembered the alarm, the panic, my ill thought-through response. A fire in the medical centre. Bartelli, Guder and myself running to aid the trapped – no matter that we were ill-equipped and the professionals were on their way.

The fire had started on the fourth level. We were past the epicentre now, up on the second floor. I grabbed one of the extinguishers from the niche beside the doors. Guder grabbed a second and Bartelli took an axe. We looked like some rebel militia with our hastily-covered faces and weapons in hands.

I didn't give myself time to second-guess, to acknowledge the ache in my legs. I glanced at the others then took a deep breath. I held the extinguisher in one hand and covered my face with the other. Then I shouldered the door open.

Fire roared like a desert lion, starving and furious and desperate.

We found our first group of survivors shortly after, deep in black oily smoke, past corridors with blistering murals. A group of three, two medics and a civilian,

"To me," I called into the darkness.

"No, this way," Guder contradicted sharply.

"You sure?"

"This way!" he shouted again.

There are times you just have to trust and hope. I crawled towards his voice, fumbling over legs and arms, trying to urge people along without the use of sight. My head ached like a bastard. "Keep talking, Guder! All of you follow his voice!"

Those ten or so yards' crawl seemed to take forever, but suddenly we were through a door and the air became a little clearer. One by one we dragged through – six of us, now – and collapsed, coughing up black lumps whilst our eyes streamed uncontrollably.

When my vision had cleared I took stock. Guder had brought us back the way we'd come, into the stairwell. Unable to form words, I patted his leg by way of thanks, then looked over those we'd rescued. One of the medics was cradling his arm; his slumped shoulder indicated a broken collarbone.

"We've got to," Guder said weakly, "we've got to go upstairs. It's our only option."

"But we can't get out there, the storm's still blowing," the civilian said.

"There'll be suits," Guder pointed out. "We get to the vestibule, we have a chance."

Beside me I could hear someone retching. I fought open my eyes just in time to see the injured medic throwing up what seemed to be a slick of tar.

I let Guder drag me to unsteady feet. Bartelli was on his haunches, leant against the wall. Guder was right; we couldn't stay here, not with the fire steadily climbing towards us.

The air wasn't so foul on the top floor. But even the floor-panels were smoking; the heat underneath must have been intense. We shambled along, supporting each other. We were making progress; not so long, now until we could drink in that blissful, frozen Antarctic air. Better an ice-storm than this pollution.

The injured medic wept as we went on. My legs felt like they were made of glass, my arms of stone. My head throbbed with every beat of the heart. The extinguisher I carried had barely weighed anything, it seemed, when I'd first grabbed it. Now it felt like I was trying to carry a black hole.

And all the while we were finding others, lost and alone. Our little band was now twelve-strong. People chased upstairs by the smoke.

It was typical of me. I'd damn well rushed in like a fool, trying to save lives and be the hero. Now our lives were at risk and it was all my fault.

We staggered, limped and fell through another set of doors, past caring what was on the other side. To my open-mouthed astonishment I found the entry to the vestibule a mere dozen yards away. The vestibule, warmsuits, then out into the freshest air in the world.

The only problem was the fire that blocked the way.

Wearily I shook the tears out of my eyes, saw the floor-panels black beneath the flames. So unfair! We'd come all this way only to face this wall of flame right before the exit. Plastics belched fumes that stank like cat's piss; we were all coughing and wheezing so much that I barely noticed anymore.

I hauled my extinguisher upright; struggled with the pin, then ripped it out. I pointed the thing in vaguely the right direction and pulled the trigger.

I'd had my training. In this underground world, and with such a hostile environment outside, all security staff had been drilled in fire-management. But the training was a far remove from the real thing. I hadn't been exhausted when I'd practiced. I hadn't had to fight the buck and rise of the extinguisher. I'd not expected to miss, the white chemical cloud expanding in the air rather than at the base of the inferno. I rapidly adjusted my aim but not before the the cloud had billowed back to cover me in a pale white powder.

The fire weakened, smothered, but too soon my extinguisher was empty. And then part of the floor fell away, sending a new sheet of flame roaring upwards.

I felt Guder push up alongside me, fumbling with the tag of his extinguisher. Smouldering debris rained down on us all, specking our skin with pinpricks of pain. I tried to roll away to give Guder room, but my hand was stuck to the frosted sides of my extinguisher. I screamed as my skin ripped away, my voice swallowed by the roar of the flames.

Guder squeezed the jaws of his extinguisher. A blizzard of blue-white powder erupted from the nozzle and blew back the heat and the smoke, gave us a little oasis of sweet air.

But in moments his weapon was empty and the flames advanced again.

And then the vestibule door opened.

The influx of fresh, cold air was almost as much a torture as the rank fumes we'd become accustomed to. Just as quickly we adjusted, clean air filling my lungs like the first breath of life.

But the fresh breeze had also enraged the fire and it came howling back at us. Almost everything I could see now was aflame; roof, floor, benches – even the walls seemed to be burning. I cast around wildly before settling on the figure now visible in the vestibule doorway. I gasped as he raised two extinguishers, one in each hand; and then he disappeared in a haze of gas and foam. Again I choked as I inhaled a lungful of carbon dioxide. Then the clouds drifted away and the path before us was – well, it wasn't clear, but it was a hell of a lot better.

"Quickly," the man yelled. "To me! Jump!"

I scrambled to my feet, light-headed and aching all over.

"Quickly!" he shouted again.

I dragged Guder up, pushed him forwards. Then the injured medic, and...

One by one they leapt over the missing floor-sections, to be caught and pushed onwards by the big man in the doorway.

Soon only Bartelli and I remained, smoke once more thickening around us. He still had his axe grasped in one hand. I reached out to shove him forwards and screamed as my raw fingers brushed his shoulder. He got the message, though. He lumbered into the smoke and made the jump.

One last look around and then I ran too. I leapt blind and stumbled into waiting arms. And now, past the flames and into fresher air, I felt true cold. Through my streaming eyes I saw the exterior door was open but I could make out little beyond, the ice-storm reducing visibility to only a few feet.

"Now," a voice in my ear yelled, "into the warmsuits."

Blurred figures around me were doing just that. Into my burning hands were pressed mask and suit and numbly, automatically, I tried to fumble them on.

It was only then, with my head pounding, my lungs raw, that I could begin to comprehend what I'd known since I first saw him.

Our rescuer, our saviour; unsuited and standing like an old comic-book god. Our saviour, Mikhail Petrovic.

Now I stood in an office that used to be mine, not quite looking at my new boss – new as of a month ago – coughed up smoke and contemplated my demotion. When the news came in that Albert Francis had been appointed over me – well, I'd been touched by the support.

Most of that support was now whole-heartedly behind the new boss.

I couldn't blame them. My colleagues just got on with

their jobs because that's the human way. And I was under no illusions about the power of my own charisma. Francis, with his easy smiles and the occasional outbursts of temper, had proven himself more understandable – more human – than I'd ever been.

I still felt numb. Almost as if I was in denial, though I'd had enough time to get used to the idea.

First the visit from Chief of Operations Ricardo Baurus, the Mayor, telling me that, what with the continued growth of Australis (nearly a hundred thousand now) questions have been asked... ordered to review security arrangements... very sorry... you have to reapply...

Then the agonies of writing and rewriting and rewriting and starting again, telling and re-telling my life story with particular relevance to...

The message informing me that they were pleased to inform me I had an interview on this date at this time... Please bring...

And then, of course, the interview itself, and we all know how that went.

Mr Nordvelt, please meet Mr Albert Francis, the new Chief of Security at Australis. A big man, dark of skin and white of hair, liver-spots on his wrinkled hands. A big man and a big personality.

At least I'd been allowed to keep my apartment, even though it was now above my grade. I'd been granted the position of Senior Sergeant almost as an afterthought.

Francis stirred behind his desk, though his didn't look up from the report he'd been reading. "I suppose I should commend you. You did your best. Not your fault the fire-suppression system failed."

"I was wondering how the fire started," I said. The hand I'd injured was itching. I closed and opened it, feeling the wound-pad soft against my skin. "And, yes, why the sprinklers didn't work."

"We're looking into it. That's not your concern, though."

"No?"

"This Petrovic – he's an old friend of yours, isn't he?" he asked.

I considered. "I think 'friend' would be pushing it a little." I had, after all, nearly killed the man. *Dragging his broken body out of the maelstrom of fire, his screams echoing in and out of my broken, half-melted mask… and then the heartbreaking realisation of what had caused the explosion in the first place…* Memories of a different fire, a different time.

"Why's he here, Nordvelt?"

"Sir?"

"How on Earth did he manage to drag two heavy fire-extinguishers through an ice-storm? Hell, how can he be outside at all without a suit? It's not right."

I said nothing. I had nothing to say.

"The men he arrived with," Francis went on. "Know anything of them?"

"Not a thing. Sir."

Francis scowled at me. I kept forgetting to give him the respect he thought he was due. "I want you to find out what's going on. I want to know who they are. I want to know why they're here. And why now."

"Sir. May I ask why?"

"No you bloody well may not!" he barked, before answering anyway. "It's a mystery and I don't like mysteries."

I stopped myself from asking how he'd ended up in charge of a security team if he didn't like mysteries.

"Three men manage to get emergency transport across Antarctica? Their own carriage on a top-security land-train? Have papers that makes a whole UN security team look the other way? It's not right, Nordvelt. Nothing good will come of this, you mark my words."

"And you want me to…"

"Find out who the hell they are. You know Petrovic. You have your friends, the crew from the original mining project. Talk. Ask questions. I know you think of yourself as a detective – go do some damn detecting."

"You think they might be from Oversight?" Oversight was the rogue, murderous offshoot of Human Resources that most people thought of as a fantasy. I knew better.

Francis shook his head. "It's not Oversight's style. They've still got their man on the Committee – not that he can do anything, not after you exposed him. He's a busted flush."

"What, then?"

"That's what I want you to find out! Leave the fire investigation to the experts. Go tell me what Petrovic is doing here."

"He's not broken any laws," I pointed out.

"Yet. He's not broken any laws yet."

"But you're asking me to spy on him."

"I want you to ask your friend what's brought him back to Antarctica and who his friends are. That's not too much to ask, is it?"

* * *

Bartelli was at the desk we shared when I came out of Francis' office. He flexed his moustache by way of a greeting before returning to his screen. I sat heavily beside him, spilling hot coffee over my wound-pad as I set the glass in front of me. I sighed and grabbed a tissue to mop up the spill.

"How's the boss?" Bartelli asked.

"The usual. Just likes to bark."

"Anything I should know?"

"He doesn't want me to look into the cause of the fire."

"No, I just got a message from him. Wants me to prepare an initial response."

I began to answer but was overtaken by a fit of coughing. My smoke-inhalation had been treated in the aftermath but still I was hawking up black phlegm. My eyes streamed as I finally managed to breathe again. When I could see, could swallow back the dirt, Bartelli was holding out a glass of water for me. I took it gratefully.

Which reminded me, I needed to write up Bartelli and Guder for a commendation.

"Anything interesting in the evidence so far?" I asked when I could speak again.

"I thought you were not to bother with that," Bartelli said, the hint of a smile behind the unruly moustache.

I gave him a look.

"The evidence-scanners have been run, we have the data from those. But the investigation's barely begun yet."

"Any indication of why the sprinklers didn't work?"

"Oh yes. That we know."

"Well?" I took a swig of water.

"The sprinklers didn't work, *signore*, because they had been turned off."

I sprayed the water over the compscreen in front of me.

Three

The original crew of Australis base – the mining base that preceded the city – had been thirteen-strong. Eleven survived that first winter. Eight of us were still here – eight, plus Mikhail. I was the last of them to arrive at Abi's restaurant.

Mikhail, taller than in my memory, was talking with Dmitri near the service hatch. The Ukrainian beamed with delight as the blond man slapped him on the shoulder.

They were all there, lounging against the bar and around a pillar. Mikhail and Dmitri, the big men (and had Mikhail always been as broad as the Ukrainian?); Fergie and his permafrown; Nigerian beauty Max and little Weng – taller than hydroponicist Maggie, in fact, but slighter and much, much quieter. And there was Abi, the Libyan, the owner of the restaurant, smiling softly and nodding. Next to him Keegan wore the colourful, almost gaudy clothing that was becoming increasingly popular in the city.

They greeted me with handshakes and smiles, and I felt myself relaxing. Until I saw Mikhail's face.

He was scowling at me. Blue eyes boring into me, distaste in his expression.

I looked away to acknowledge a word from Keegan, and when I glanced back to Mikhail the look was gone.

* * *

"So how are things here?" Mikhail asked of the group. "How's your work? Are you happy?"

Fergie made a dismissive noise. "Work? Ach, let's no' talk about work. Work's annoying and frustrating. Let's not talk about that tonight."

"Don't listen to him," Max said affectionately. "It's fine. Everything's fine here. Come on, Mikhail, we want to hear about *you*."

"Seriously? You don't think the Committee are idiots?"

"Hah! Now you're speaking my language, pal," Fergie grunted.

"Why do you say that?" Max asked.

Mikhail took another sip of beer. "Well, just from a personal level, you've all been pushed aside, haven't you? Had people appointed above you, people who aren't as qualified as you. I mean, you were all on the original base for a reason, right? You're the best. So why have all these middle-managers been pushed above you? I mean, look at Holloway," he said with a nod to Maggie, to Weng and Keegan. "Okay, he's a decent scientist – so I'm told – but what does he know about Antarctica? The three of you have such expertise, but does he use it? Nah, you've been pushed aside and forgotten. Right?"

Maggie was nodding slowly. She flicked her eyes up to mine and I wondered just how much she'd worked out. I knew a few secrets about Holloway. There was more to him than science.

"I mean, even Anders here – he kept his post for a while, but now? Must hurt to be demoted, ain't that right, killer?"

That was barbed. I recoiled, and before I could recover he'd moved on.

"See, there's strange stuff going on behind the scenes. This mayor of yours, Baurus. Some real politicking went on to get him placed in charge here. And the rest of them – Holloway, Prashad, Garcia-Lomax. They're not experts, they're politicians."

I frowned, covering my confusion by taking a sip of beer. This wasn't what I'd expected, not at all. Although we'd found a table big enough for the group, were all sitting together with drinks in front of us, I wasn't comfortable.

I winced as a burst of laughter from a nearby group hit precisely the wrong pitch and reverberated off the fixtures.

"But that still doesn't explain what you're *doing* here, Mikhail," Maggie said.

"What, I can't just come to visit old friends?" he grinned, then laughed at her sceptical expression. "I've got a new job, that's the reason."

"You're going to stay in Australis?" Dmitri asked.

"For a little while, at least. Over the winter. I'm working with Benitez Ferraldi – you've heard of him?"

Heads shook around the table.

"You will do. He's a high-up in the Company, a big man. I probably shouldn't tell you, but he's here to carry out an inspection."

Dmitri frowned. "An inspection of what? The prison?" It was the logical conclusion.

But Mikhail was shaking his head. "Not the prison – well, in part, but Ferraldi is going to be looking at the whole project."

"The whole... the whole Australis project?" Dmitri said into the resulting pause.

Mikhail laughed, dispelling the tension and almost drowning out the noise at the bar. "Don't worry, friends, the project is safe – there's no way this can be closed now, not when you've accomplished so much! It's hardly a secret that the Company's already reliant on the minerals we get from Antarctica–"

"No' to mention being a dumping ground for all the excess population the world over," Fergie put in.

Mikhail acknowledged the comment with a tip of his drink. "No, the project's safe. Ferraldi and I are here to make sure the Committee is working well. Making the right decisions, you know what I mean."

Maggie nodded silently. Fergie muttered his agreement.

"So you're acting as what – Oversight?" I asked with a frown. I shouldn't have mentioned it but Oversight had been on my mind recently.

"If you like." Mikhail shrugged. "I mean, not like that conspiracy-theory mob that we all know from the movies." His eyes contained a warning as they flicked up to mine, and then the expression was gone as he took in the rest of the group. "But it's our job – Ferraldi's, really, I'm just an aide – to make sure Baurus and his cronies are up to the job – hey, watch out!"

A man from the neighbouring table had staggered over and crashed into Mikhail's side. Beer spilled onto his head, and from Mikhail's own glass drink rained onto the surface, onto Dmitri.

"Watch yursel'" the stranger slurred and drew back, his feet unsteady beneath him.

Abi was first to his feet – his bar, his responsibility – but the rest of us weren't far behind.

Mikhail shoved the drunk off him, pushing with a force I'd not have thought possible for someone half-way from their seat. The man staggered backwards into his friends; they'd been coming to – to assist, to calm or to look for trouble? – but their momentum was stalled. They grabbed and steadied their man. Rivulets of beer slicked his beard.

"Hey," one of the group cried, "what d'you think you're doing?"

"Yeah, he was –"

"Just get away from us," Mikhail interrupted sharply. "Get this idiot out of here."

"Who're you calling an idiot?" the drunk man snapped back. He stepped forward, fists raised.

"Call security," I muttered to Maggie, then stepped forwards to get in front of the drunkard.

He was a big man. Bit of a paunch, but more muscle than fat. He looked to be in his thirties. Most of the group behind him were younger; I counted six people, men and women. Fleeting impressions, but there was something in their eyes...

I spread my hands in an attempt to calm the situation. "Come on, now, this is a restaurant–"

"You think you're better than me, is that it? You want some of me?" the drunk bellowed. He was still speaking to Mikhail, but now I was in the way it was me he tried to shove.

I was ready for it. As he pushed at me I grabbed at his wrists; I got my grip okay on one arm but he broke free with barely a grunt.

And then something struck me on the side of the head. I staggered, the room spinning round me. I felt, rather than saw, Dmitri and Mikhail shove past me. The sounds of fighting seemed to come from a long way away. Someone pulled me back into a chair. Giddily I raised a hand just about my ear and it came back bloody.

By the time I could focus again, the fight was over. Mikhail, Dmitri and Fergie were standing proud and defiant amidst broken glass and overturned chairs. The drunkard, still yelling, was being dragged towards the exit by his cronies. A crowd of shocked onlookers had gathered in a loose circle around the scene.

I sighed deeply. "Bollocks," I said.

Abi crouched by me, looked in my eyes. "Anders, my

friend," he said. "There seems to be a disturbance every time you're here. Maybe you, like them," he said with a glance towards the drunkards and the ghost of a smile on his lips, "need to be barred from this place."

Four

Not much chance to get more out of Mikhail after that. Checks for concussion (it was, apparently, a bottle that had been used on me), a ride home on one of the little tuktuk-like electric vehicles that served as internal transport, then painkillers and bed. When I went in to work next morning, past the arts-committee-approved murals that added a little individuality to the otherwise indeterminate corridors, it was with the sense of both a job and personal matters unresolved.

But even distracted as I was I couldn't miss the atmosphere in the security centre. Half the officers, it seemed, had either disappeared or were keeping their heads down. The other half were rushing around frantically, seemingly with no clear plan or direction; datapads were being waved around like shields. And above it all was Francis. He was standing in front of the open door to his office, grey, thinning hair almost like a halo above his wobbling jowls. I'd never seen such fury in his face before. It was enough to stop me in my tracks.

"Nordvelt!" he yelled as soon as he'd clocked me. "About bloody time you got in. Get over here. Now!"

Jawad, the dispatcher, scurried past me as I made the long walk. He shot me a sympathetic glance as he went.

"My office," Francis snapped unnecessarily.

When I got inside Francis was pacing.

"Have you heard?" he said as I shut the door.

"Heard what?"

He gave me a sharp look, as if he thought I might have been winding him up. He examined my face carefully, then deflated a little and leaned back against his desk. "It's not too well known yet, then," he said in a quieter voice.

"What is? Isn't?"

"We've received – no, somebody's posted –" He was interrupted by a shout from through the door behind me. Francis frowned and tried again. "Somebody's released a video on the servers," he growled. "It's *supposed* to show –"

"Where's Nordvelt?" someone bellowed from through the wall. "Where is he?"

I tried not to wince.

"Well, you *are* Mr Popular today, aren't you, Nordvelt?" Francis said.

I was saved having to answer by the door behind me being shoved into my back. I stumbled forwards and spun round to see Shakil Mithu in the doorway. Mithu was an old acquaintance of mine; a troublemaker, if you wanted to be uncharitable, and for a while prime suspect in the murder of his wife.

He had once been big and broad but grief had reduced him. Now he looked gangly and awkward.

He also hated me and, right now, his whole being radiated anger. He was almost snorting, bull-like with fury. He levelled a finger, uncomfortably steady, at me.

"How dare you, Nordvelt?" Mithu snapped. "How dare you? How long have you known? How long have you been lying to me?"

All I could do was shake my head.

"Now hold on there – it's–" Francis began.

"I'm not talking to you, fat man," Mithu cut him off, still without taking his eyes off me. "How about it, Nordvelt? You thought you'd got me tamed? You thought The Exiles were done? I promise you, Nordvelt, you thought we were bad before? You've seen nothing!"

I shook my head again, looking through his glasses into fierce brown eyes. I saw only hardness.

"That's enough," Francis snapped. "It's Mithu, isn't it? Guder, Jackson, breach of the peace is Breach of Contract. Get him to the cells!"

"I don't give a damn what you do to me," Mithu almost howled. "I don't give a damn, you hear me?" He gave Francis a look of such contempt that even he took a small step back.

Behind Mithu I saw officers in the doorway. Jackson, lacking the imagination to be afraid, laid a hand on his shoulder.

The tall man spun round, knocking her arm away. Shoulders rising and falling with his breaths, he occupied the doorway and dared anyone to challenge him.

I finally gathered my feet, my brain. "Shakil," I said. "Shakil, don't –"

Suddenly he was facing me again, just two big strides and he was in my face, towering over me. I could feel his breath on my cheek, see every pore in his face. "Don't you ever," he said with a coldness and intensity that it took all my will to stand up to, "don't you ever call me that again. *You never use my first name again, pig*! I'm going to break you, Nordvelt. You and everyone you know. I'm going to take this city down brick by brick, I'm going –"

"That's enough," Francis interrupted. "That's enough. Jackson, Guder, get in here and cuff this man, Get him to a cell. Now!"

Mithu didn't resist. He held his arms behind his back like a good little employee. But not once did he take his eyes off me. Not once did the hate fade from his eyes.

I didn't realise I was holding my breath until he was out of the office, out of sight.

"You really do have a way with people, don't you Nordvelt?" Francis said as he crossed to the door, watched Mithu being escorted away. "Well." Mithu's interruption seemed to have taken the anger out of him. "It's hardly surprising. The Exiles – that's the separatist group you had so much trouble with in the summer, isn't it?"

I nodded. "They were sent here against their will and have been agitating to get home ever since. But they've been quiet recently. Look, Francis – sir – what the hell is going on? What's this all about?"

"You really don't know? Well, sergeant, last night a video was released onto the Australis servers."

"What sort of video?"

"A very, very nasty one. One that I was hoping to keep from people like our friend Mithu. One that at this very moment I'm trying to remove from public access. One that I'm trying to trace right as we speak." He smiled unpleasantly. "One that I think is going to take up far too much of my valuable time. So why not go and have a look for yourself, Nordvelt? I don't need to send you a link. Don't even need to tell you what to look for. You'll find it in seconds. Go and watch, and then we'll see what can be done."

* * *

The servers were the soul of Australis, someone cleverer than me once said. They were the democracy in a nation of employees. Unmoderated and in theory free of Company intervention, they were the voice of the people.

The Australis intranet could be accessed by everybody who lived there, and whilst it was not a good career move to criticise one's boss or be *too* vocal about the Company's failings, there were no limits on contents. Provided there was nothing too illegal, too obvious.

The forums were abuzz. Loud with horror. Cold with anger.

Yeah, Francis had been right. It took mere seconds for me to find the video he'd been talking about.

I leaned back in my chair and rubbed my chin. The clip was tagged as 'Company massacre' and the comments below were almost all warnings. Not suitable for children. Do not watch if you're easily upset. Oh My God.

I started the playback.

A hum of static filled my ears and I hastily turned down the volume. The picture crackled in and out for a second before gradually resolving.

I had no idea where it took place. The rag-tag architecture could have been from anywhere around the world. There were little hints… the language sounded Indian – Bengali, Hindi, Gujarati – to my untutored ears; what little vegetation there was suggested a warm climate. A hazy sun beat down but the shadows were short. The sky seemed filled with dust.

Slum clearance. That's what I was witnessing.

God alone only knew who was filming this. A group of shanty-dwellers, that was the best guess; the shaky image kept flitting around and catching odd glimpses of legs, arms, torsos. Words came and went in the background. Sharp cries, yells, muttered words that, in this language I didn't understand, quickly became mere counterpoints to the soundtrack of heavy engines and falling masonry.

This almost first-person view was unnerving. I kept wanting to take control, to steer the camera. I wanted to get a bigger perspective. To find out where I was, to be *introduced* to the characters. But I was a passenger; just along for the ride.

I was watching a confrontation between Company soldiers and UN troops.

I'm a Company man. Spent my whole life protected – raised, fed, then employed by the Company. After my father's… after my parents were taken from me, the Company took me in. Yeah, I've had questions; I've had problems with my employers. But I was loyal. I'd never put any stock in conspiracy theories, in the tales of Company abuse.

My jaw dropped with the horror of what I was seeing.

The Company soldiers, advancing with bulldozers at their rear, were trying to clear the settlement (and with no greater perspective, no words, it was astonishing how clear the message came across). There were still residents, mounting some kind of protest down the rutted mud road to my right. They were defended – was that correct? – by a group of UN soldiers easily recognisable in their blue helmets.

That wasn't how it should have been. The settlement should have been entirely cleared before the bulldozers rolled in. The people should have been found housing, given opportunities, incorporated into the Company world. That was how we were told it worked.

And yet there the people were. The inevitable conclusion was that this was a forced eviction.

Behind the bulldozers was a shroud of dust, the mangled ruins of what had been houses just visible through the haze. The heavy machines advanced steadily, crawling onwards, consuming whole buildings and spitting out their remains behind them.

Ahead the Company troops had stopped. The camera spun momentarily, focus came, went, came again. A UN soldier had advanced, had the nerve to try and check the advance. He looked scared, his face pale – and so, so young. He held his arms wide, unarmed.

Slum clearance was hardly an unknown phenomenon, but – but not like this. The people should have been long gone. There should be no need for a UN presence.

I felt sick, my stomach tight.

The people with the camera were running now and for a moment all I could see was a collage of mud-brick walls, corrugated iron sheets, dirty feet, bare legs, arms. Then it calmed again – momentarily, before an explosion shattered equilibrium. One of the bulldozers had gone up. The civilians cheered; I think some of the group with the camera were cheering too. Had they mined the settlement? Debris rained down on the slum.

Now the sergeant – dust-covered stripes on his shoulder – had the UN man pinned against a wall, gun to his throat. The Company man yelled something in his face. The blue-cap shook his head wildly, eyes open wide, entreating, begging. He got nothing. He looked stunned, disbelieving. He seemed to give up, then, and the sergeant released him, turned back to beckon his men – and the remaining bulldozers – onwards.

There was a shout, and yells off-screen. The camera turned quickly, and in the blur of movement I saw a figure running forwards. He disappeared off-picture for a moment before the camera found him again.

A bare-footed warrior; dark-skinned, throat vibrating with some sort of ululating war-cry.

He was carrying a sword – an antique piece of thin metal, red with rust.

A bullet lifted him off his feet, his war-cry mutating into an almost-scream as blood pulsed from his shoulder. He spun in the dust, feet beating up clouds around him as his muscles flexed and flensed – and as if in some infernal disco he gyrated madly.

I barely heard the voices around the camera now. The foreign tones seemed to match my feelings exactly. Dead tones, numbed with fear and horror.

The view changed again, away from the twitching flesh-bomb and back to the Company soldiers. They pushed the UN man aside and resumed their advance. The roar of the bulldozers changed cadence as the engines jerked forwards.

The peasants (is it cruel of me to think of them so?) threw rubbish, debris at the soldiers. I saw what looked like the wheel of a toddler's buggy skim off a helmet; a rock caught another on the knee. There's so much to see, so much to take in. It was so frustrating to only see what the cameraman allowed. I wanted to see it *properly*, to truly understand.

So I missed the second shot. The one that killed the UN soldier who'd stood so bravely.

The camera found his body, still, almost peaceful on the ground. His eyes were still open, face set in an expression of surprise. A neat red hole had been drilled between his eyes.

The witnesses are running again, the picture breaking up, falling back into static. There was just enough cohesion left for me to see the bulldozers reduce the corpse to an apologetic pulp in the dust. At least the noise of the engines masked the snapping of bones that my imagination couldn't help but overlay

I felt sick.

And just before the video ended I was sure I could see more UN soldiers falling, and civilians too, and then the gang fled and static finally crackled into black.

Slowly I returned to my surroundings. I was sweating like I had a fever, both cold and hot. I wiped my brow with the rough fabric of my sleeve.

I didn't know what to do, what to think. Numbness crept

through me.

This video was filmed a long way away. That was clear. I wondered if it was now playing all across the world. Enough that it was freely available here. I'd already seen how it galvanised the Exiles, they with their terrorist methods. How many other groups would be motivated to bite the hands that fed them? How many more resentments would be drawn out for examination?

And what if this was just the tip of the iceberg? What about all the other clearances, where there was no UN presence, no-one to agitate for the rights of the inhabitants? What was to stop the Company from simply running the bulldozers through occupied houses at night – or worse, things (*flames, poison, gas, bombs...*) my imagination flicked at me but dared not linger on.

I sat at my desk for a good five minutes, not doing anything, barely even thinking. I knew it would take days before I could forget the image of the bulldozer crushing that corpse into the dirt.

I tapped my stylus on the desk for a moment, then went down to see Mithu.

Five

He ignored me when I walked into his cell. He'd glanced up when I entered, but now Mithu just sat on his bad and stared at the wall.

I made sure the door had locked behind me and stood as far from the cot on which Mithu sat as I could get.

I cleared my throat. I wasn't sure what to say. The words "I'm sorry," fell weakly from my mouth.

"You're sorry," Mithu said with contempt. He still wouldn't face me.

"I didn't –"

"You didn't know?" Mithu cut in. "You didn't know? You didn't care? You didn't want to see!"

I shook my head.

"I hate the Company. I've hated it since I was a child. I hate the people who sold me and sent me here, to this prison," he spat. "But you? In you I almost..." He looked at me, now. Fury screamed from his eyes. "I almost trusted you. I was taken in by you, I admit it. What happened to your promises to get me home, huh?"

"I never –"

"You never promised anything, yeah. I know. I see that now. You just made me *believe*. I told Kaiser to ask for you if ever I got in trouble. *I gave my son hope* and you've smashed it again. Thank you, Nordvelt. Thank you, boy. You know what you are? You're just a stupid naïve child, making promises you can never hope to make good."

My hand went to my chin. "I didn't…"

"Yes?"

"I didn't know anything of this," I said, cursing the weakness of my words. "I promise you, I never –"

"*You never looked!*" he yelled, suddenly on his feet. "I told you! I told you that we – and others – were moved across continents on the say-so of the corrupt and the careless! Did you look? Did you think any more of my words after you'd given us your reassurance? Did you even try, Mr Policeman Nordvelt?"

He saw his answer in my silence. He snarled and turned away again. "How long will I be here?" he asked.

"I don't know. Francis is in charge now. He ordered your arrest, and, given your record – and because this time you've pissed him off personally – I'd imagine he'll invoke Breach of Contract. Public order is part of your contract. He'll try and make you take an anger-management course or something."

"Francis is a fat streak of piss," Mithu said with a curl of the lip. "He has nothing. I'll be out of here in a day."

"Maybe."

"Kaiser is at school. If I'm not out when it closes…"

"I'll see that he's okay."

"Like I have any faith in you, boy? Give me my datapad. I'll sort it myself."

"I'll do what I can," I said.

"That really reassures me."

"How is Kaiser?"

Mithu glared at me over the rim of his glasses. "He is a good boy," He said almost reluctantly.

"He's doing well in class? How old is he now, fifteen?"

"He's smart, like his mother was. Computer science, chemistry, electronics – he already outshines his father."

"You must be proud."

"It's no business of yours, Nordvelt."

* * *

I went for a walk out into the Strip, the main thoroughfare of the city. It was supposed to be flamboyant, even gaudy, a place for shopping, for leisure, for culture. It'd always just felt a little desperate to me, with its Company-sponsored art-installations vying with the special offers emblazoned over the competing 'independent' coffee outlets, whose boulevard chess sets were about as close to a scene as Australis got.

I bought a drink and sat in one of the atria, where a side-road crossed. The city didn't have enough curves for my liking, but curves were inefficient and a ruthless grid system prevailed.

It was the consequence of building a city underground. The costs were high enough without adding unnecessary aesthetic quirks.

It was quiet. Usually people would linger here, drink and chat and socialise. Nobody was out today; I had the bench to myself. Those people who passed through did so quickly, head down or shooting furtive glances around them. The owner of the coffee-cart looked bored and glum.

I burnt my lip on the hot liquid and swore quietly to myself.

What was I supposed to be doing now? Researching Mikhail and his boss – what had he called him? Benitez Ferraldi, that was it – I supposed. But that seemed to have faded into deep insignificance after the video. Did I want to be part of an organisation that sanctioned massacres? I mean, if this video was true, how could I stand quiescent? I put up with the great monoculture because it at least pretended to diversity. The murals, the art – they were all evidence of the pretence at multiculturalism. Everyone knew it was all determined by committees and panels but the lie mattered.

But what if it was really nothing but lie? All this benevolence a mask for unfettered capitalism – profit at any cost? It would be a betrayal of all I'd ever stood for, all I'd ever stood up and said that the Company was. Where did I stand now?

I couldn't imagine not being part of the Company. I'd been part of the system since I was a child – and most people alive today had been part of it their whole lives. There had never been an alternative. And it wasn't like I was being asked to swallow terrible privations for an ideology. The Company was for people like me. The ordinary Company citizen. I was safer for it, secure with a guaranteed job placement, with guaranteed rations and a guaranteed residence. My self-interest was clear.

Could I stand by, cleave to my own, if non-Coms were being executed for no other crime than for being poor? What kind of a man would that make me? The thought was enough to make me feel sick.

I pulled out my pad and flicked idly through the pages. Yes, there were the deniers, claiming the video was a fake. And those that claimed that they'd seen such things, and far worse, and the people were fools for allowing such a monolithic organisation to rise to prominence in the first place.

I shook my head and checked my messages.

There I found a warning.

Nordvelt, the message read. *A cache of weapons has been hidden in level 12 aisle 36 of engineering supplies warehouse 4. A group is planning armed rebellion. They will retrieve the equipment today at 11:00.*

A Friend.

I sat perplexed, mystified. Armed rebellion? Weapons? (And my mind immediately went back to the video I'd watched; the Company soldiers marching forwards together, bringing guns to bear on civilians...) Had Mithu and the Exiles been spending the quiet months assembling an arsenal?

I checked the time. Barely nine o'clock. I forwarded the message to Jawad; this was more than just I could handle alone.

I got up and tossed my coffee cup into the recycling; headed out to investigate this message – no matter that I'd passed it on, I needed to check myself – when my datapad cheeped.

It was Weng. Little Weng, the most vulnerable of the original Australis crew. And it was a live call, not just text.

"Anders," she said quickly, "are you there?"

"I'm here, Weng."

She was clearly upset. She kept shooting glances behind her, her delicate make-up smudged with tears. I stopped in my tracks. "Anders, please –"

An inaudible shout came from behind and once again she turned away.

"Weng, what's wrong? Where are you?"

"I'm at work – listen, you must come, you must bring help –"

"What's happening, love? Are you okay? Are you in danger?"

She swallowed and shook her head. "I – I am fine. There is a protest. They are marching on Holloway's office!"

"Who are, Weng? What's going *on*?"

"Just come, Anders, please," she begged. "It's not right, it's not right..."

I turned, already calculating my route, and marched

straight back past the coffee-cart I'd just patronised. "I'm on my way. Just hang tight, okay? I'll be fifteen minutes."

Jawad had been informed of the threat. He'd send someone to engineering. They didn't need me.

Besides, Weng was a friend.

Six

I scurried through corridors, up stairs, out to the edge of the city where the scientific department was based.

Weng's office was on one of the higher floors, far, far from the centre of power. She'd never been one for politicking and I felt she preferred it that way; doing her diligent best to map the geology of a continent.

I never got to her. The quickest way was to run straight past the offices of Holloway and his inner circle, and it was there I was brought up short. Or, to be more accurate, it was the noise I heard fifty yards back that slowed me to a walk.

It wasn't quite right to call it a mob. It was a protest. Organised – there were even placards and digital displays hoisted to display a shifting selection of slogans.

It wasn't jam-packed; there was still space to weave through. I made my way through the throng.

The protest was centred outside Holloway's office, right in the middle of the building. There were the banners: A New Government for Australis; Allied Thinkers' Union. And before them was a tiny woman, who must have been invisible to most of the crowd, addressing them with an amplifier.

"...we want an end to the high-handed exploitation of our skills! We want a proper debate on what the Company needs – what the planet needs! We need an Executive Committee that listens to the people!"

It was Maggie Ling. Beside her was Keegan. And I was

sure that was Dax Bhinde, one of the Exiles' leaders, just on the edge of the crowd.

I let my mouth hang open. Never in my wildest dreams had I imagined Maggie and Keegan as being the leaders of a protest like this.

It was Bhinde who saw me first. As Maggie finished her polemic and handed the amplifier to another, he whispered to the man next to him before hurrying other to me.

I knew Bhinde of old. I had no reason to trust the young, handsome Bangladeshi.

"Mister Nordvelt," he said with a careful smile, his voice cutting easily beneath the amplified distortion of the main speaker. "What brings you here?"

"I could ask the same of you," I said. "You're not a member of the Allied Thinkers' Union, are you?"

"And why shouldn't I be? But you're right. I was... just passing."

"What's going on here?" I craned over his shoulder.

"More evidence of Company misrule. Even the 'brightest and the best' are unhappy with Baurus, it seems. Ferraldi will certainly have a lot to put in his report."

"What do you know of Ferraldi?"

"He's reached out to the Exiles. Wants to talk to us.

"Why?"

A flash of anger crossed his face. "You think he shouldn't—"

"No, sorry." I held my hands up in apology. "Of course you – and he – can talk to whoever you like. But how did he hear of the Exiles?"

"Haven't you heard? Ferraldi wants to talk to everyone."

"But why are you here? Why now?"

"As I said, I was just passing."

I thought of Francis and his mistrust of Ferraldi's mission. "Are you here to stir up trouble? Is that why Ferraldi's here?

To disrupt operations?"

Bhinde looked shocked. "Mr Nordvelt, Mr Ferraldi is a Company executive. Why on Earth would he want to disrupt the smooth operation of Australis?"

"But there are many reasons you would."

He shook his head nervously, tried another smile. "We… I'm past that now, Mr Nordvelt. I mean, I still want… still hope to go home. Yeah, I'm hoping to talk to Ferraldi. But all I'd tell him is truth. The Exiles—"

He broke off as the door to Holloway's offices opened behind Maggie, Keegan, and the other speakers, and the large figure of Francis slipped out. He was backed by a nervous looking Officer Finch. The crowd quietened expectantly. Bhinde half-turned to watch but kept glancing nervously at me.

Finch shut the door behind him and cast around the crowd. Francis, great blusterer as he was, looked more annoyed than afraid.

Maggie walked up to him, looking even smaller in comparison, but she held herself straight and proud.

I didn't hear the words they spoke. I tried to get closer but there were too many people between us.

But I could read their faces. I could see the frowns they both wore; see first Francis, then Maggie, shake their heads. Maggie spoke and Francis interrupted. Keegan leaned in with the occasional word, but clearly Maggie was the leader here. A few more words, then Maggie gestured behind her and received the amplifier. She turned back to the crowd.

"Ladies and gentlemen," she said, "We've been invited to meet with Holloway tomorrow to discuss our grievances–"

I watched Francis as she spoke. I saw him lift his pad and stare at it angrily. Then his face fall. The annoyance that he seemed to carry with him slowly vanished. In its place came shock. Shock, with perhaps just a little note of fear.

A bead of sweat trickled down his forehead.

Bhinde was trying to get my attention; all around me people were murmuring to themselves, shuffling, discontent.

Francis turned his back of the protestors and muttered a few words to Finch. He hurried his bulk back through the door and disappeared.

Finch stayed where he was, his face white.

I had already turned and was hurrying away from the crowd when I got the call.

"This is Sergeant Jawad to all available personnel. All available personnel report to Block Sixteen, Level Twelve immediately. Repeat, all—"

I earned a few reproving looks as I shoved my way free. I didn't care. I felt cold, bloodless. I had to get respond to the call, get to Block sixteen as quickly as I could.

Block Sixteen – the engineering supplies warehouse.

* * *

The warehouse had only half as many levels as the other blocks, but was dug just as deep. Each floor was two stories high, the better for storing *materiel*.

The seals on the door had been broken. A fine breath of smoke was seeping out into the corridor. Alarms were wailing, echoing through my head and making me feel a little unbalanced.

I was the first here – at this entrance, at least. Who know the city better than me?

I sidled up to the door and used my foot to edge it open. A dark cloud rolled out but cleared quickly.

It took me a moment to remember what I was hearing. It'd been years since I'd last been in a rainstorm – it would've been the trip to Brasilia in the summer after my first winter in Antarctica. It never rains on Australis.

I risked a look inside, but on that first inspection I couldn't see much. The sprinklers, deactivated in the medical unit, were in full force here. Already the fire was dying down.

I stepped cautiously through the door.

It was gloomy in the warehouse. Above me, far above, strip-lights flickered erratically, casting deep shadows that turned the room into an infernal backdrop, somehow hyper-real. Shelves, high shelves, massive fixtures that had been bolted to the floor and filled with tonnes and tonnes of heavy equipment, had been tossed aside. Splintered fans, shattered housings, told me that air-conditioning units had been stored nearby. Shards of metal littered the ground; electrical components lay saturated. Boxes like tombstones were strewn on the floor.

I was drenched in an instant, the artificial rain splashing off my head and running unchecked round my eyes, down my cheeks. The smells of smoke and static were crushed by the weight of the water.

The epicentre of – of whatever had happened seemed to be about two dozen yards ahead; the few remaining flames were smoking there.

I squelched forwards slowly.

A brass plate caught my eye beneath the slick of water. *Aisle 36.*

The sound of the alarms echoed madly across the great space. I crept forwards. There was a great crash to my right; one whole rack of shelving, bent beyond its centre of gravity, had given way, shedding another few million credits' worth of equipment as it fell.

I slowly released my breath. If that had fallen the other way then I'd be dead.

The fire was out now. Wiping great pools of water from my eyes I went forwards, creating a bow-wave with my feet. I nearly fell forwards as the alarm suddenly cut out. I'd almost been leaning into it; I caught my feet, sending a thin spray into the air.

In the sudden quiet I could hear a noise. A soft whimpering, a crying. To my right...

And then the peace was shattered by voices behind: Francis, his voice carrying above others.

"Police!" he yelled. "Who's in there? Identify yourself now!"

"It's me, sir," I called back. To my left, maybe ten more yards... I stumbled on something soft then moved on.

"Nordvelt? What's happ—"

"Quiet! Please!"

There... there! "Jackson? Jackson, is that you?" I hurried forwards to kneel by the figure slumped awkwardly against an upturned truck, the sort used to jack-up heavy loads.

Her uniform had been split along the front. I bit down vomit as I saw the sheen, tasted the smell of blood, the sickening sight of her intestines spilling out onto her lap. One leg was twisted horribly back on itself. One arm... one of her arms was missing.

"Commander, it's Jackson!" I shouted. "She's... she's hurt – badly."

I heard feet splashing towards me; I heard Francis calling for assistance. I heard these things, and more, but I didn't turn round. I crawled forwards, reached a hand to the dying woman's cheek. "Jackson," I said, "Jackson. It's Nordvelt – can you hear me?"

Her head lolled forwards and in the swaying light I saw a look of recognition in her eyes. I think she even tried a smile, but the muscles on one side of her face wouldn't work.

"Hello, Sergeant," she breathed.

"Oh, fuck," someone muttered at my side. I spared a glance; it was Rampaul, ashen faced, staring down at the broken body before him.

"Oh, fuck," he said again. "Oh, fuck me."

"Staunch her arm," I snapped.

"How?" He seemed frozen – horror-struck, I supposed.

"Use your damn shirt! Snap out of it, Rampaul – this woman's going to die if you don't help her!"

He blanched and came to, quickly whipping off his top and crouching by Jackson's side.

"Jackson, can you hear me?" I said.

"I... I can't feel any pain," she said. "I can't... that's not right, is it?" She smiled again, almost blissfully. Her eyes started to close.

"Jackson! Jackson, wake up!" I could feel more people at my back, then a hand on my shoulder.

"Out of the way, sir," someone said. "We'll look after her."

Medical. Thank God. I stepped aside, but kept my eyes on Jackson, reached out with my good hand to rest a hand on her cheek.

Suddenly the sprinklers cut out. Now the room was filled with refracted voices and a million tiny drips as water pooled off shelves and racks of material.

"Jackson," I asked, "Were you alone? You didn't come down here on your own, did you?"

Rampaul's shirt, already crimson, was twisted clumsily on her stump. He watched on as a team of medics, talking in their own special code, set a stretcher next to her and began sizing up her body.

Jackson began to cry. I took her hand – her only hand. She lacked the strength to grip properly. "G-Guder..."

Her eyes were seeing through me now. I turned, still holding her wet hand, to see where she was looking.

Towards the epicentre.

The medics got her on the stretcher. One of them gave her an injection even as two others hoisted her up. They gently pushed my hand away and she was gone.

I stood, lost in a moment of horror.

Then: "Torches! Bring me torches!"

But I didn't need them. It only took me a few seconds before I noticed an irregular lump, half-submerged, half-pinned beneath a great steel girder.

He must have died quickly.

He'd lost both legs and the bottom half of his belly. Viscera trailed into the water like some nightmare work of art.

The girder had taken off the top of his head. All that was left of his face was the surprised twist to his mouth.

Seven

I sat in the corridor, blanket around my shoulders. I hugged my legs and stared at the floor. Rampaul was beside me but he might as well have been on a different continent. Feet rattled past us, and noise, and voices I recognised but didn't attempt to place.

After a few minutes I started to shiver. But even that wasn't enough to rouse me from my fugue state.

I kept my eyes open. Didn't want to close them for fear of seeing.

Eventually – time didn't mean much, just then – Francis sent me home. Although he spoke with his customary authority, some deep part of me watched the way he turned and twisted his datapad in his hands.

I found myself in my room. I stripped off, fumbling with my wet clothes. I left them where they were on the floor. I stood, naked, as if I needed someone to tell me what to do. I sat. I stared at the wall. I got up and limped to the shower. I still couldn't stop shivering, no matter how long I stood in there, leant against the tiles. My legs felt unsafe so I sat, then lay on the floor, letting the water rain down on me like it had in the warehouse...

I'd seen more guts – literal, honest to gods intestines – today than... than I ever had before. I imagined, almost fantasised, slitting open my own belly and stroking my insides. I retched, dry-heaved. Still I trembled.

I'd seen dead bodies before. Some have caused me long-term trauma, I knew that – been told many times. But I'd never seen bodies *disassembled* so.

I closed my eyes and wept.

Don't know if I was in there for ten minutes or ten hours. When I dressed again (clean clothes, so smooth, so soft against the skin) I still couldn't settle. So I went to work.

The security centre was subdued, sombre. It was getting towards the end of the day (where had the time gone?), but there were still more people in there than usual. Like me, it seemed that in their shock, as rumour spread, Guder's colleagues wanted to be here today. People were only absent if they were on patrol, or asleep, or…

Or in hospital. Or dead.

Bartelli wasn't there. I walked through the hall as if in a dream, sharing nothing words and nods of the head with the people I passed. They seemed as absent as I, as if we were in the presence of some all-powerful, wrathful deity who could strike us down at any moment; so we all kept out heads down, strived not to be noticed.

My feet, I realised, were carrying me to Francis' office.

I hesitated on the threshold, knocked and went in.

Francis looked no better than I felt. The permanent frustration that seemed to lurk beneath his skin wasn't there. He slumped at his desk, an old-fashioned pen in his fat fingers. He looked up at me with heavy eyes and blinked.

"Nordvelt," he said. "What are you doing here? You should be at home."

"So should you."

He shook his head as if trying to dislodge a fly.

"Jackson should pull through," he said.

I sighed, so grateful. *There but for the grace of God…*

"There… there'll be a ceremony for Guder tomorrow," he went on. "All policemen not on duty will attend."

I nodded. I… I hadn't known Guder well. I'd just known

him as a quiet, conscientious man with a solid head on his shoulders (*but not on his shoulders anymore*). I shuddered and drew a deep breath. Of course I would attend the ceremony. He was a colleague, and whilst I didn't buy the idea of the security team as a family, I had to go.

"Have we any idea what happened down there?" I heard myself asking.

Francis sighed and shook his head. "We've very little solid info at the moment. What with fire and flood and all that damn wreckage it'll be days before we get an absolute picture."

"Initial impressions?"

"It was murder."

Of course it was.

Francis drew a deep breath, inflating himself back to something like his normal form. "Initial impressions, you said? Well, *my* initial impression is that someone set a trap for Guder. Some sort of explosive. Either proximity-sensored or timed or a tripwire. Something like that. It'll be days before we know for sure. But that's where the evidence's pointing at the moment."

I nodded distractedly. *A trap for Guder? Why Guder? A trap for* me*? The warning was sent to me…*

Suddenly Francis was on his feet, knuckles on the desk in front of him. He stared down at me with fierce intensity. "Nordvelt, it's time for us to stop pratting about. We all know who's behind this, right? It's time to *do* something about it."

"What do you mean?" I asked, taken aback.

"Don't be a damn idiot. It's Ferraldi, isn't it? Who else would want to cause all this trouble? Who else wants to paint this place in a bad light?"

"You think Ferraldi killed Guder?"

"Not *him*," he said impatiently. "Not actually *him*. One of his goons. That bodyguard of his. Or your friend Petrovic."

"Mikhail wouldn't do that," I said, unsure.

"One of his allies then – that Mithu – he hates us, right? Or his man Dax Bhinde."

I shook my head – not in negation, just in an attempt to fit all these names, these patterns Francis was suggesting, into place in my mind.

"I told you to find out what Petrovic was up to. I need that sped up. Whatever you've done so far, it's not enough. Get out there now, you hear me, and get me some solid info."

"We need to get evidence from the crime-scene," I said. "Trace the explosives, fingerprint all the fragments–"

"No." It wasn't a shout but it might as well have been. Francis' tone was enough to make me actually look at him, see him for the first time. "No, Nordvelt, that's not your concern. I'll handle that. Your orders are to infiltrate Ferraldi's circle."

"We have no indication that Ferraldi's anything to do with this–"

"I don't care! I don't give a damn. If he's nothing to do with this, great. But we still need to find out what he *is* up to."

"Why? What's the big deal? What's more important that finding Guder's murderer?"

Francis sighed. "First, Ferraldi might be that murderer. Second, you should know that he's already met with me, with Garcia-Lomax, Unity, Holloway… the whole Executive Committee. The same thing with all of us. He's making vague promises, insinuations. He wants to take over the city. He wants Baurus out. Vague promises." He waved a hand. "Threats. Look, Nordvelt, we need to get active. Go and get a coupla bugs from stores. Go and plant Ferraldi's office. And Mithu's apartment, and–"

"We can't just go round spying on everyone," I broke in. "We've no reason to spy on Mithu, no probable cause at all! We've no grounds—"

"You think I give a flying fuck about probable cause? We make the damn laws here! Someone murdered Guder! There's a clear threat to us all and I'm not gonna sit back and let Ferraldi destroy everything we've built!"

"I did not come to Australis to help build a police state," I said, ice on my lips. I stared into Francis' pudgy brown eyes.

My boss, so tired and weak just a few moments ago, drew himself up to his full height. He was a big man, tall as well as heavy-set. He looked as if he wanted to take a swing at me. "If you're not prepared to obey orders, Nordvelt, I'll find someone who is. You're hardly irreplaceable. I reckon Jawad would make a good sergeant, don't you?" He smiled cruelly.

I took a deep breath, tried not to recoil from his jabs. Part of me spent a moment sizing up the best ways to take him down non-lethally. How much I could *hurt* him…

I didn't move.

"Well, Nordvelt? What's it to be? Plant a few little bugs for me, mm?"

"I'll take the bugs. I'll see what I can do."

"Good boy. Now get out. I've got to write to Guder's partner."

"Sir?"

"Nordvelt?"

"Guder was due a commendation for his role in the medical centre fire — he was instrumental in getting those civilians out safe —"

"And you."

"And me."

"So you want…"

"He should still get that commendation. He helped save

lives. He should —"

"I'll see he gets a damn medal." Francis spoke gruffly and for a moment I thought he was being sarcastic. Then I caught the little hitch in his voice, the shimmer in his eyes, and I realised he was being nothing but honest and direct.

"Thank you, sir," I said.

"Anything else? No? Get the hell out then, Nordvelt!"

* * *

I went back home. I was tired, so tired — but I couldn't sleep yet. My brain was too full.

I slumped into a seat and rested my pad on my knees. I flicked idly through a few routine pages; checked for messages before going onto the servers.

I'd expected to see reports of the bombing and there were indeed some 'fatal explosion' posts. But I'd almost forgotten that there'd been a political protest today. The forums reminded me in short order; a whirlwind of reports and comments. 'March for change' read headline. 'Pressure on the Committee' another.

I didn't want to read further. Didn't want to see Baurus' statement, no doubt drafted for him by civilian liaison Garcia-Lomax. I couldn't avoid the pictures though. So many people had captured stills of the event. Pages and pages of videos...

Hold on a second. Hold one damn second.

I scrolled back up. Magnified one particular image...

That was the man from the bar-fight in the background. I recognised his bushy beard, his broad chest. A strong man, by the looks of it. A bear.

I swept the pad clear and logged into the official security

net. Just a few seconds to scan my fingertips and iris patterns before entering the passcode – the latter a recent inconvenience added after the discovery of tools that could fake biometrics. Then I ran an image search, a simple tool to compare the moment I'd isolated against ID records of all citizens of Australis.

What had I said to Francis about not wanting to be part of a police state? What a hypocrite I was.

His image didn't match that of any known resident of Australis.

I gaped at the screen for a moment. What were the possibilities here? That he'd arrived on a land-train and not been processed properly (a fourth member of Ferraldi's team? Possible): that he'd had enough reconstructive surgery to fool the image search; that he was a member of Gísladóttir's squad.

Captain Gísladóttir's soldiers weren't part of the Australis database but they were on the 'guest list' system of approved users. I ran a second search through that and got a match instantly. Private Leon Lewinskiy. So one mystery solved.

But why was he at a protest against the Executive Committee? Why was he there, holding a placard with the legend 'Baurus out'? Why was he encouraging people to join in anti-Company chanting?

What on earth did he care? He'd only been in Australis for a matter of days.

I was beginning to stiffen up. I stretched, fighting overtense muscles. And I wondered: is he acting under orders? Does Gísladóttir have an objective beyond getting the prisoners here safely?

At least she – and her men – should be on the next land-train out in just a few days.

My datapad cheeped. It was Jawad.

"Sir," he said. "I'm sorry to disturb you, but we've got reports of a disturbance two floors down from you. Can you check it out?"

"I'm off duty," I protested. "Can't someone else do it?"

"Everyone's tied up," he said. "We've been very busy."

I sighed. "Send me the details."

And back to work I went.

Eight

I'd hoped to sleep in next morning but I was woken early. Blearily I stumbled through my living room, dressing gown covering my modesty. Wasn't awake enough to check who it was before opening the door. And it took me a few seconds blinking in the artificial light of the corridor before it really clicked who it was.

"Weng?"

The small Chinese girl stood almost perfectly still on my doorstep, staring up at me with an unreadable expression on her face.

She said nothing. I blinked at her.

"Do you want to come in?"

She nodded and walked past me, through the vestibule and into the main room. I followed, slowly gathering my wits.

"Take a seat?"

She shook her head. I was used to her silences, wasn't offended. Weng was part of the original Australis crew, the thirteen people of whom only eleven were still alive. Small, proud Weng – scarred, like we all were, by what she'd been through during the long months in the mining base, she'd almost been hiding since we'd all been reassigned within the city. Certainly I saw her infrequently; it had taken Mikhail's sudden arrival to bring her out of whatever geological project she'd buried herself in.

"What's on your mind, Weng? Would you like a drink?"

She shook her head and for a moment it looked as if she wasn't going to answer. But I knew how to be patient.

"We have been invited," she said in her quiet voice, her English heavily accented. "The Australis crew. We've been invited."

"To what?"

"To see Ferraldi. Tomorrow night. After the lecture —"

"Wait, what lecture? Ferraldi is giving a lecture?"

Weng shook her head in impatience.

"I'm sorry, but... I've been busy." Busy. How weak that sounded. I thought of Guder there with a girder where his head should have been. I thought of Jackson with her guts hanging out. "Busy," I said again, uselessly.

Maybe Weng read something in my face. The impatience went. "Mikhail has booked out one of the auditoria for a talk tomorrow. One o'clock. There's... talk... on the forums. Rumours. It's thought he'll explain who Ferraldi is and why they're here. And then in the evening there's a drinks reception for invited guests."

"And we're on the list?"

She nodded.

"Why?"

She frowned, a slight shake of the head telling me I'd asked the wrong question.

"Why are you telling me?"

"Are you going?"

"I... I don't know. I didn't know anything about it until you said."

She looked me up and down, taking in my dressing gown, my barely-focussed eyes and the bags beneath. "I am... scared," she said, voice barely wavering.

"Of what?"

She looked away. "You know what happened to me," she said in barely more than a whisper. "You know no-one cared when de Villiers... when he used me."

De Villiers. Commander of the original Australis mining base, the precursor to the city. Anton de Villiers, deceased. "I know what happened," I said gently.

"I do not trust people who say they have all the answers. Not any more. I do not trust Ferraldi."

"Not even with Mikhail at his side?"

She gave me a look. I wasn't sure what it meant. "Mikhail is not the man I remember."

"Have you spoken to the others? To Maggie, or...?"

"They don't want to hear. They are... discontent."

"With Baurus?"

"With the whole Committee. With the way the Australis project is being run."

"And you're not?"

"We all got what we deserve," she said, eyes suddenly blazing. "We all deserved to be fired, to be left to starve. We all saw wrongdoing, and we all looked the other way. We deserve what we got."

There was a moment's silence. "What do you want me to do?" I asked eventually.

"I want you on my side."

"I'm touched, but... but I can't tell the others what to do."

"Just don't change."

Silence fell again. I stared at her, trying to gauge her, trying to see what she really meant. Inscrutable wasn't the word. She bowed her head, letting her long black hair cover her face.

Then, suddenly, she strode up to me and kissed me brutally on the lips.

And then she left without another word.

I stared at the closed door, raised a hand to my mouth and stared at the trace of blood on my fingers.

I put a coffee on and went to get in the shower.

* * *

It must have been Garcia-Lomax on the Executive Committee who pushed for the twice-yearly equinoxes to be made into holidays. Must have been. I couldn't imagine Baurus, or cold, nasal, Professor Holloway suggesting it. Or Albert Francis. Too humourless the lot of them.

Garcia-Lomax or not, the idea was a good one. Something uniquely Australisian; was it too much of a stretch to see it as the start of a local culture? Probably, but still. A day off work before the Night Shift officially began. Maybe one day some advertising expert would convince us all to celebrate in a certain way, with piñatas or turkey dinners or with tacky greetings card, but for now it was just a time to spend a few extra credits on the little things that people did when they didn't have to go down the mines, or to the factories, or whatever.

And with the bars and restaurants doing good business it was a surprise to see so many people in the auditorium. Mikhail had become something of a celebrity, obviously, after his dramatic rescue of those trapped in the medical centre inferno. And because everybody, these days, was a journalist, everyone wanted to be first to report on his address. The hall may have been relatively intimate, but it was still crammed with, I guessed, a couple of hundred people.

I was already regretting coming. I should have been out searching for Guder's killer (and I was fresh from a memorial ceremony that was really just a lot of us cops standing uncomfortably whilst Francis told us what a good officer

Guder had been and a chaplain read something that went straight over my head), not wasting my time in a lecture like this. But I was already trapped in a bank of seats, no matter that I'd chosen to sit at the back. And anyway, being here was in line with what Francis had ordered me to do. Find out what Mikhail and Ferraldi were up to.

"Mr Nordvelt. Mind if I join you?"

It was Unity, the UN representative to the Executive Committee. She flashed me the brief smile. Friends? Maybe. Not an enemy, at least. At least not today.

I watched in awe as she persuaded – with barely a word – an entire row of people move along to give her a seat.

They were still shifting as the lights dimmed. The buzz of so many voices faded.

Mikhail Petrovic, carefully picked out by the stage lighting, walked confidently out from the wings and up to the podium. He took off his sunglasses to reveal his blue eyes and smiled warmly, his already pronounced cheekbones accentuated by the spotlight.

"Ladies and gentlemen, good afternoon," he said. He didn't need amplification. His voice carried clearly to all corners of the auditorium. "I'd like to thank you for giving up your valuable free time to be here tonight.

"I know you're expecting me to talk about my involvement in the rescue a few days ago, and I will. I'll do my best to answer any questions you might have. But before I get to that, I'd like to talk to you about Australis. This city, the place you all call home.

"I want you to know the truth."

He paused and cleared his throat. The room was quiet, but not silent. There seemed to be a collective shifting, an internal asking of where Mikhail was going with this.

"Have you ever wondered," he went on, "why you're here? Not in a big cosmic religious sense, but in the practical here-and-now? Do you ever think why the Company is interested in paying to have a city here?"

"Because the Company wants rid of us!" a man's voice came from across the room.

I frowned and strained to see who'd called out. The Exiles: that was their position. Was there going to be trouble? I glanced to the exits, wondered how quick security could get here.

But Mikhail just nodded and took it in his stride. "That's part of it, yes – for some of you, from some nations. But I was meaning more about what the Company wants."

"Money!" someone else cried.

Mikhail surfed on the tiny wave of laughter with a smile. "Of course," he said over its death-throes, "of course. But more than that. The Company wants the future." He paused and took a sip of water. "The Company specifically wants two things: the coal, oil and rare-Earth metals that can be found here; and it wants science. Ever since the establishment of the very first Company base in Antarctica, scientists around the world have been studying the bacteria that thrive here. Now, pardon me if that sounds a little esoteric – or boring, even." He gave another smile.

Had he always been this charming, this good at addressing a crowd? Someone must have coached him, I thought. Why would they do that? Not just for this; his performance spoke of practice and of surefire confidence.

"Bacteria can survive in these temperatures because they have something like a natural antifreeze in their blood. And finally I can announce to you that our scientists have succeeded – they've managed to find what, in their DNA, creates this effect.

"Two, nearly three years ago, my body was shattered in a... an industrial accident." He spoke quietly now, and – impossible, I know – it seemed as if he was now pointedly avoiding looking at me. "It was here in Antarctica. By all rights I should have died – should at least have spent the rest of my life in a wheelchair. But the Company took me and put me back together. They used unique, experimental procedures to stitch the nerves, the muscles, together in my back. They gave me a new job, retrained me, made me stronger, more capable, than I ever was before.

"We can now give all this to you. And it won't take an industrial accident to make it happen.

"And more – more than all this. I am here to tell you that I am the first person ever to have my blood-cells altered in the light of the research into Antarctic bacteria – research that's taken place in this very city! For those of you who've seen me walking in the wastes, who've wondered how I can go outside without a warmsuit, here is your answer. I literally have anti-freeze in my blood."

Why did this make me shift in my seat? This was just science, this was just progress. Was I jealous? Inferior?

"And you can have it all too."

A muttering, a wonderment, spread around the hall. A dozen different tongues low in confusion, surprise, amazement. And fifty different reports would already be burrowing their way through the servers and into the forums. Soon nobody in the city would be unaware of what was going on here tonight – and then the arguments would really begin. What did he mean? Could we be superhuman? What were the limits? Why give us that tease and not say more?

"And now, ladies and gentlemen, I'd like to introduce you to my colleague, my friend. Ladies and gentlemen – Benitez Ferraldi."

There was some applause as the man walked across the stage to join Mikhail at the lectern, but mostly there was confusion. This wasn't a name that meant anything to anyone here.

I studied Ferraldi as he shook Mikhail's hand warmly and set himself to speak. He was tall – not quite as tall as Mikhail but somehow seemed even taller. He was so thin, that was it. Thin and bald, his high domed head almost making him look like a Grand Vizier from some book of Arabian fairytales. His eyes were deep-set, the spotlight making them almost invisible in shadow.

"Thank you, Mr Petrovic – Mikhail," Ferraldi said slowly, his voice having a slight creak to it. He put me in mind of a bird, a vulture.

To the side of the stage I saw a third man, almost in the wings. He was watching the crowd, watching carefully. I immediately pegged him as a soldier, or perhaps a bodyguard. When he moved – and that wasn't often – it was with a dancer's grace.

"Ladies and gentlemen," Ferraldi continued, "it falls to me to explain who I am, and what myself and my friend Mr Petrovic are doing here. The truth of the matter is that we are here of behalf of the Company to investigate the way Australis is being run. Think of us as troubleshooters." He smiled slowly and I got the distinct impression that it wasn't something he was used to doing. "Questions have been raised at the very highest levels. Make no mistake, the Company cares for the people of Australis. We want this community to grow, to prosper, to unite. We want you to be happy and healthy.

"And we are unsure whether the current leadership will give you the framework to thrive."

I leaned over to Unity. "Did you know anything of this?" I whispered.

She shook her head. "I am a mere United Nations observer," she murmured. "The Company would not inform me of anything they see as a purely internal matter."

"Mikhail here has undergone a simple surgical procedure to make him able to survive the harsh conditions you live in," Ferraldi continued. "Would it not have made more sense to wait until this procedure had been perfected before bringing you all out here?"

He took a sip of water, held his glass up momentarily; in the spotlight it became a miniature supernova. The room was silent.

"More serious, perhaps," he said in that slow, almost grating, tone, "is the fire that destroyed your medical facility. We are all so lucky that no lives were lost in that inferno. I'm sure we are hugely grateful to the brave members of our fire-response team, and to the members of the security team who risked their lives to help evacuate the top floors. Can we have a round of applause for them, please?"

The clapping that followed was rather desultory but was still enough to make me squirm. For a moment it seemed that Ferraldi was looking straight at me, a twist of what might have been a smile on his lips.

"But," he said, firmly squashing any lingering applause, "we have to ask ourselves some questions. How did the fire start? Why did the fire prevention systems fail? Why should we rely on heroes to save us when we should be guaranteed safety wherever we are in this wonderful new city?

"Chief Operations Officer Baurus – The Mayor, as many of you know him – has questions to answer. Aside from the fire, we are aware that many complaints have been made. About all the fights in the bars – licensed and unlicensed, which is a question in itself – and about thefts. About the way that labour is used and managed. About your homes and communities.

"I will be putting all these questions to the Mayor. And I can promise you that –"

"What about the Exiles?" someone shouted from the side of the room. "When will you be sending us home?"

I craned my neck to see who'd called out, half got to my feet. But the auditorium was dark. And I didn't recognise the voice – it certainly wasn't Mithu or his associate Dax Bhinde.

Ferraldi grimaced, pausing for a moment to let the murmuring subside. When he spoke it was slowly, picking his words with care. "I had hoped... I am aware of your complaints," he said. "I did not want to address them in this forum. I am not fully cognisant of the situation. But I can assure you that I my team will gladly hear your stories. We will... look into it. And I can promise you that we will be demanding answers from the Mayor!"

That brought another round of applause; more enthusiastic, this audience, than I'd have expected.

I looked at Mikhail, standing easily at his new master's side. Nodding and smiling.

I became to feel a chasm falling away somewhere inside me. But for the life of me I couldn't see why I felt so uncomfortable.

* * *

Unity was bothered by Ferraldi's speech. I could tell, although perhaps no-one else would have been able to. A little narrowing of her eyes, perhaps. The cast of the very tips of her lips. The way she looked into the distance with a little more *intensity* than usual.

The sort of changes that seem to be from a person's aura rather than from anything more tangible.

And it was that, rather than from any real insight into his words, that worried me about Ferraldi. Maybe Francis had been right. Maybe watching Ferraldi was more important than catching a murderer. There are, after all, big crimes and small crimes and sometimes there are crimes so big they just look like everyday business to the people underneath.

I went back to the security office, docked my datapad and checked the news on the servers. They were all full of Ferraldi's speech. As I had been in the auditorium, I was surprised by the warmth with which it had been received. Aside from the news that Mikhail had anti-freeze in his blood, I hadn't thought that Ferraldi had said that much of interest.

Now it seemed that everyone in the city had issues with Baurus. If Ferraldi truly was going to meet with the people and hear their complaints then he had a long winter ahead of him.

And yes, there were the Exiles – Mithu and Bhinde, the handsome young thug, and their allies, all demanding that they be sent home immediately. But who were all these first-time commentators suddenly agreeing with him and denouncing the Executive Committee?

I suspected bots or similar hired hands. And that was a troubling thought; access to the servers was via fingerprint- or iris-scan; creating fake identities should have been impossible.

Well, that was someone else's problem. Let Baurus, Francis and the rest lose their sleep over it. I was just a sergeant.

I was about to put my headphones on and ask my pad to play me something a little folky whilst I wrote up my report of the lecture when Gísladóttir strode in. She looked round the room, searching for someone – me? I stood.

"Gísladóttir? Captain – what are you doing here? I thought you'd be getting your people together ready to head out."

She looked at me with hard blue-grey eyes full of resentment. She walked over and sat in Bartelli's vacant seat, no asking. She looked disdainfully around at my meagre desk and the lack of humanity there. "The land-train has been cancelled," she said.

"Take a seat," I said, unable to formulate anything better.

She glared at me, then shook her head, cropped blonde hair moving with a microsecond's delay. "Two days ago we heard the weather delayed our transport until yesterday. Yesterday we're told the land-train's broken down. Now the ice-storm is worse so no transport. We're stuck here. Me and my men, stuck here for the whole damn winter."

"I'm sorry," I stammered, not knowing what else I could say.

She dismissed my apology with a wave of a hand. "Not your fault. I don't know whose stupid idea it was for us to come down at this time of year anyway. Stupid. Now we're stuck here."

"I'm not quite sure…"

"Nah, nah, don't worry, sergeant. I'm not here to moan at you – we all know you're not on the Committee anymore."

I felt myself redden slightly.

"But I thought you might help. We've been in temporary accommodation so far. If we're staying longer can you sort out something more permanent for my boys?"

"I'll speak to–"

"And – I don't know, I don't like the idea of my team having nothing to do for the next six months. Is there any way you can fix us some work? Can we get sworn in as special constables, or whatever you have in this model village? I know, see, I know what it's like when soldiers get bored. It's not good. Trust me, I know"

I thought of Private Lewinskiy and his presence at the

protest. I thought of mentioning it. I thought *no transport home? How very convenient.* And the thought of her men in a position of authority here and how convenient *that* might be. "I'll have to speak to Francis," I said. "But I'm not sure..."

"You get us anything, anything at all, I'll be grateful."

I nodded hesitantly. "I'll see what I can do. But I can't—"

"You can't promise anything, I know," she said glumly. "But you will try?"

"I'll try."

Nine

I stood in the entranceway and looked around self-consciously. I felt stiff, restricted, in my smart clothes. A drinks party was hardly my scene.

I shouldn't have been here. I should have been investigating the murder. I'd managed to get a look at the preliminary forensic reports – an explosive device, a probable tripwire detonation. I'd compared it to the report on the medical centre fire but that seemed to have been caused by an incendiary grenade, of all things. Similar, but not enough to prove it was the same person responsible.

I was working on neither case. Instead I was standing in a doorway and contemplating a cocktail party.

"Shift your ass there, copper," a rough voice came in my ear.

I glanced back to see Fergie, grinning and looking surprisingly dapper In his suit.

"Good to see you here, Nordvelt. Wasn't sure you'd turn up for this sort o' thing. Come on, no point being here if we've not got a drink."

As he hustled me over to the improvised bar I looked over the crowd. A select group, around three dozen, maybe one or two more. Towards the back of the room there was even a quartet playing; I couldn't have told you if they were good or what they were playing; my ignorance in classical music is almost unparalleled. I began to wonder where Ferraldi had found the musicians before I suddenly realised that it was my own Sergeant Bartelli on one of the violins, moustache twitching over the strings.

That was something of a shock. But Fergie hurried me onwards.

Many of the old crew were there; Dmitri gave me a wave, and there was Maggie, and there –

And there was Mithu. And there was Kaiser. And there was Dax Bhinde.

Why invite the Exiles? Why mix us?

The others there seemed to be similarly diverse. I recognised a few engineers, a few scientists... And of course there was Mikhail; tall, handsome Mikhail who seemed to have acquired a... a *presence* I'd never seen in him before. A phalanx of girls of many different races seemed to have attached themselves to him.

And then, as I took a glass of orange from a broad-shouldered waiter, Unity was at my shoulder.

"Mr Nordvelt," she said with a critical stare. "You are not drinking?"

"Unity. Maybe I'll have a drink later, but for now..."

"You want to keep all your senses about you?" She smiled faintly.

I shrugged, the heavy fabric of my jacket constricting. I could not read her. How much was there behind her words? What was I actually doing here?

Where was Ferraldi?

"Do you know what all this is in aid of?" I asked instead.

She shrugged with casual elegance. "Ferraldi is hoping to seduce you."

"To...?"

But before she could say anything else, there was Mikhail himself. He slapped me roughly on the shoulder and grinned. His eyes did not smile. "Anders! My old friend. And Miss Unity." He bowed imperfectly, almost comically. Maybe that had been the effect he was after. "Would you please excuse us, Madam? I'd like a word with Anders, if you don't mind. There are some people I'd like him to meet."

Unity lowered her head in concession. Her smile hadn't reached her eyes either.

Mikhail delicately steered me away. "I know you're suspicious, Anders. You've no reason to trust Benitez, have you?" he said as we went. "But believe me when I tell you we mean you no harm. If you have nothing but good to say about Baurus and the way he's running the city, that's fine…"

It became apparent that he was leading me towards a knot of people; maybe three or four intimates, then another circle surrounding and listening carefully.

"I hear your concerns, Mr Bhinde, and I sympathise."

It was Benitez Ferraldi. Of course it was. I could see his bald head clearly, almost at the centre of the group. Most of the people around him seemed to be Bangladeshi, and it didn't take long for me to draw certain conclusions.

His bodyguard was standing a pace or so behind him, unobtrusive as ever. I couldn't place his origin, his nut-brown skin hard to pin to even a continent.

"You want me to speak to Ferraldi?" I asked Mikhail.

He shook his head. "I don't think, old friend, that Benitez will have anything to say to you that you couldn't work out for yourself. Just listen."

"For what?"

"Just listen."

"…is sympathy?" Bhinde was saying. "We need something done! We need action!"

"You understand that I'm in no position to make decisions. There is no action I can take until I've reported back to my superiors." Ferraldi spoke firmly, assertively. But the creak in his voice also carried understanding, almost as if he was talking to a favoured son who'd asked some boon.

"This is intolerable," a new voice snapped. Mithu. "How long do you expect us to wait? We've been waiting years already!"

"Nothing can happen until sunrise – six months – that's definite. I hope to have completed my investigation by then. Then my report will be sent. My superiors are expecting this and have already arranged a meeting. A response should come shortly after that."

Mithu scoffed, but enough heads were nodding amongst the gathered for me to know that this had been accepted as a reasonable time-frame.

"So what you're saying is that if Baurus is removed then we will be sent home?"

It took me a moment to realise who'd said this. The voice sounded young; a young man. Kaiser. I felt a brief flare of anger – at Mithu, perhaps, for bringing him here.

Ferraldi smiled and shook his head sadly. "I can't say anything but 'perhaps'. I can make recommendations, but I can do no more than that."

Again I felt Mikhail's hand on my shoulder. He indicated we should move away and, with one last look at the still-discussing group, I went with him. He led me back to the temporary tables where the waiters gathered and took a beer.

"So what was that about?" I asked.

Mikhail sampled his drink before answering. When he spoke he didn't look at me but stared out into the crowd. "Those people. The Exiles. You've had trouble with them, haven't you?"

I shrugged. "There were some acts of sabotage. They set up a sort of journal – an old-fashioned printed thing, you know?"

Mikhail was nodding as if he knew all of this.

"It's gone quiet over the last few months, though. A few demonstrations – flash mobs, that sort of thing. Staged protests. Nothing we can't handle."

"Now you've got Maggie and Keegan leading protests against Holloway."

There was no point in denying it. "Nothing we can't handle."

Mikhail grinned. I felt a sudden surge of anger towards him.

"You should know, Anders, that we've got *access*. One of the first things we do on a mission like this – we go into the security files and get a record of all incidents since – well, ever."

"We?" I asked. "You've done this before?"

I was gratified by the momentary reddening of his cheeks. "Well, not me, no. Him. Benitez." He smiled a little sheepishly. "Anyway, don't underestimate him, Anders. We know what's been going on in Australis..." He lowered his voice. "We know about the murder of Mithu's wife. We know about the involvement of Oversight. We know what's happened here – what's happened to you."

I stared into my juice and wished it was beer. I wished I could punch the sympathetic smile right off his face, no consequences. "What's your point?" I said quietly.

"The situation with the Exiles should have been handled much better, right from the start."

"We've done our best –"

"Not you. You've been doing everything right. It's the Committee we've got a problem with."

There's that 'we' again. Did he mean Ferraldi? Was he just meaning himself? Or was he trying to wrap me inside his world-bubble?

"What do you want me to do about it?"

Mikhail held up his hands in a gesture of peace. "I don't

want anything of you, Anders. I just want you to see things as they really are. I don't want you up there defending that which shouldn't be defended."

I stared out into the hubbub of the reception, into the mix of familiar and unfamiliar faces. I wondered if that was the point – the mixing, I mean.

"Look there," Mikhail said. "You see Maggie?"

I found her, the tiny woman clutching a glass of wine and laughing, crows' feet dancing around her eyes.

"You think it's fair that she's ignored?" Mikhail went on. "Such a brain, a *genius* – out working on parks and recreation, or whatever Holloway's got her doing. You don't consider that a waste?"

"She committed crimes –"

"She hurt no-one. Okay, you think she should be supervised? Should be watched? Maybe. But to waste that talent is the biggest crime here."

I absorbed this in silence.

"Or what of Fergie?" Now Mikhail gently steered me round, his hand so gentle on my back that I barely noticed it.

I found Ferguson talking with blond-haired Keegan. Fergie was scowling, but I could tell from Keegan's grin that some jest was passing between them.

"Fergie's an ornery bastard, but does anyone here know mining better than him? Or Dmitri? And how's Prashad using them? As little more than labourers."

"Okay, enough," I said firmly. "I know what you're getting at. And it seems you know better than me the situation here. So what do you want me to do? What do you – what does your *master* want of me, Mikhail?"

If Mikhail was upset by my little display of petulance then he showed nothing. "We want you to join us, Anders," he said.

"Join you?"

"It'd be a great help if we had someone we could rely on in the security department."

I stared at him. "I'm still not sure what you actually want me to do."

"Nothing. Nothing at all. Just tell us what's going on. Let us know if Francis is up to the job. Report to us, so we can add it to our report to Brasilia."

"That's all?"

"That's all." He grinned, blue eyes shining.

"Anders Nordvelt."

I looked up to see that Ferraldi had shed his audience of Exiles and was coming over. Ignoring the dark looks Kaiser Mithu was giving me, I shook Ferraldi's hand. His grip was confident, his skin cool, just approaching the paperiness of age. The bodyguard grinned at me over his master's shoulder.

"So," Ferraldi said. "Mr Nordvelt — Anders — I've been wanting to meet you for some time. I think it's only fair to let you know that I'm one of the few people who know the real story of what happened at the old base. Shocking, the way you were... Shocking."

I tried to smile but found I couldn't quite make the muscles work.

"I also know the, ah, the *full* story of Lata Mithu's death."

"Mikhail said." I cleared my throat. My words sounded gauche after his smoothness.

"Seems you've had more than your fair share of manipulation," Ferraldi said, his voice low. "And then to be demoted on top of all your... misadventures. It really doesn't seem fair. Not to me."

I shrugged uncomfortably and took a drink. "Thank you," I managed. "But..."

"But it is not something you want to talk about. Not right now, and not to a stranger like myself. Let me just set your mind at rest." He leaned closer. "I know of Oversight. We are nothing like them, nothing to do with them. We're from HQ and we're auditors, nothing more, nothing less." He smiled again and I felt myself begin to relax. He was a reassuring presence, this Ferraldi. And that, perversely, was enough to remind me to be on my guard.

"To be sure, I'd like to hear about your past, if you ever want to talk about it, but right now I'd like to talk to you about the Exiles."

"You seemed to be handling them well enough on your own."

"Their side of the story is valuable. I would have your perspective as well."

Mikhail leaned in. "You see, Anders, we're here to make sure that Australis is being run properly. To make sure that we're building the right sort of community. We want to make sure Baurus and the rest of the Committee are doing their jobs properly."

"We know you were the main player into the investigation into the Exiles." Ferraldi said. "I gather – reading between the lines – that you had a certain amount of... sympathy with their cause. Tell me – is that still the case?"

I tried to marshal my thoughts. *Why does he want to know this? Is this man an ally or an enemy? How much do I want to tell him?*

What do I really think about the Exiles?

"Why do you travel with a bodyguard?" I asked.

Beside me I felt Mikhail stiffen, but Ferraldi just smiled. "Ah, there's the professional," he chuckled. "We tell Collins to keep a low profile, but one good man can always spot another." He glanced over his shoulder, then took a sip of wine. "Truth is, Anders, there's no mystery there. All members of the Executive Operations Committee – the auditors – operate with a bodyguard. Maybe it's outdated, but there've been too many examples of – well, shall we call them accidents? – happening to people like me. Don't worry about Collins. He might try and shark you at cards but he's not interested in our affairs beyond his next paycheck."

There was a pause. A waiter circulated with drinks and canapes. I took neither.

"Auditors?" I said.

Ferraldi nodded. "Troubleshooters. That's what we are. We go out into different zones of operations with the authority to make changes – to replace ineffective leadership–"

"Why you *and* Oversight? You're describing exactly what they do."

Ferraldi chewed carefully on a blini before answering. "You're right. There is overlap. And I'm trusting you not to repeat this to anyone, you understand. I'm only telling you this because I know what you went through with Nascimento and all that surrounded the Lata Mithu investigation."

I nodded, glancing round to see if anyone might be listening in. The circumstances surrounding the deaths was classified. And I personally wanted as few people to know of it as possible.

"Oversight does not officially exist," Ferraldi said. "And, despite all the stories that paint them as heroes, it's not a body I approve of. They're... well, it's true that the aims are the same – to make the Company run efficiently and to maintain a course beneficial for both the organisation and for humanity as a whole. But we – Executive Operations – are overt and legal. Oversight are neither. We have limits and morals. They do not. We are rivals on a parallel course."

"So how will you deal with Holloway?" Professor Holloway, on Australis' Executive Committee as head of science, was also an agent of Oversight. This had all come out a few months ago, though only myself, Mayor Baurus and Dr Gabriel – and maybe Bartelli, though we'd never discussed it – knew this.

"I will do absolutely nothing," Ferraldi said. "He lost all his power with exposure. I'll only deal with him if he causes trouble. I will trust Collins to watch my back whilst I face resolutely forwards."

I nodded. Politics. A game I'd never really learnt how to play.

"The Exiles, Anders?" Ferraldi prompted.

"Mm? Oh, right." I weighed my glass in the air. "It seems... they had – have – a case. They were forced to come here, that seems well enough established."

Ferraldi nodded encouragingly. "That's not Baurus' fault, of course. I'm not looking into that. But do you think things should have been handled differently here? In Australis."

"I don't know the whole story. I don't know what Garcia-Lomax and Baurus said to them. But things have calmed down recently. We've not had much unrest."

"It does you credit that you're still loyal to the mayor – even after your demotion," Ferraldi said with a smile and a momentary narrowing of the eyes.

"I'm not trying to be loyal or disloyal. Just honest."

"It must have hurt, though. Losing your job when you'd done nothing wrong. You'd just caught a murderer."

I gave a weak smile that segued into a shrug. I stared down at my drink. Surely a beer wouldn't hurt? Or a brandy, my spirit of choice.

"Tell me," Mikhail asked in a heavy attempt to be light. "What's Francis like? Do you get on with him?"

"He's good at his job," I said, trying not to sound as awkward as I felt. "I don't we'll ever see exactly eye-to-eye..."

"And why's that?" Ferraldi put in.

"Just a personality difference. He's more... more gung-ho, I suppose you could say. More direct."

"And you think that's a bad thing?"

I looked up at him in surprise. "No. Not at all. I envy him his confidence."

"But don't you think you could do a better job than him?" Mikhail prompted gently.

I sighed, looked first Mikhail, then Ferraldi, in the eye. "It's sounding as if you're about to offer me my old position back – as a bribe, perhaps," I said.

A look of – of almost anger flashed across Mikhail's face, but Ferraldi just laughed. "Well, well, and you say Francis is more direct than you! He must be straight and true indeed if that's the case. Listen, Anders," he said. "We're here to see if Australis is being run properly. That means finding out how the members of the Executive Committee are doing their jobs. If they don't meet Company standards then they'll be replaced. And, should Francis go, I would imagine that you will have a chance to re-interview. But that's something I can't say, and wouldn't have a hand in anyway. I just write a report – with Mikhail's help, of course – and send it off to our superiors. It's they who make the final decisions, not us. If I were to make you any promises then I'd be a liar."

"But you can make some... strong recommendations."

"Of course. It's why we're here."

I chewed my lip.

"Look, Anders, I can understand you have no reason to trust me. No reason to trust anyone – the UN, the Company – you've had it from both sides," Ferraldi said earnestly. "But you know Mikhail. You know you can trust him. And he trusts me. All we want is what's best for Australis. You can believe us when we tell you that. Look, here – this is where

I'm making my base, my office." He scribbled an address down on a scrap of paper. "You're welcome anytime. Come and talk with me."

Ten

I could hear the sharpening of the axes.

They must have known what they were doing. *Let us know if Francis is up to the job*. An open invitation to carve that axe into his back.

It couldn't just be me. Were they asking the entire population to exhume their old vendettas?

Not for the first time I felt terribly uncomfortable. I looked round for Unity but she was nowhere to be seen. Everyone else I knew looked to be having far too much fun for me to intrude. So I slipped away; quietly, unseen. I left not by the main entrance but by the service exit.

As the door shut I felt a tremendous sense of relief, of clean air, the background of chatter and Bartelli's quartet instantly extinguished.

There were a few broad-shouldered waiters in the corridor, talking quietly, joking. They gave me curious looks as I leaned back and breathed, but they said nothing.

I straightened, opened up my chest, and figured out the best way back to my quarters from here. Going back through the reception was not an option I wished to consider.

Another waiter came through a door at the far end of the corridor, carrying a fresh tray of wine glasses on a silver tray.

I looked at him. He looked at me. His eyes grew wide.

Private Leon Lewinskiy.

It seemed to happen in slow motion. I saw the sudden

tensing of his muscles, the momentary catch of his breath as he recognised me; the tray falling from his fingers, falling as if with some strange delay.

The glasses crashed to the floor, shockingly loud as they shattered, sound echoing over me as he turned and ran.

And I was running after him.

Glass crunched beneath my feet; I saw the shocked faces of the other waiters as I sprinted past them. I reached the door just moments after Lewinskiy, barged through it. "Hey, you can't –" someone yelled. But I was already past them, past bottles of wine, a table of canapés, boxes of supplies, cutlery, napkins. And through the far door, still rattling on its hinges from Lewinskiy's passing; into a darkened room where footsteps echoed all around.

"Stop him," Lewinskiy yelled from another doorway.

"Security! Stop!" I cried almost at the same moment. Still I was running – into a stairwell this time. I caught a glimpse of Lewinskiy's back as he rushed upstairs. I followed, taking the steps three at a time. My breath came heavy and hard, but it seemed as if my muscles had been aching for the chase. My doubts fled. I was a policeman chasing a suspect (suspect of what? Involvement in a bar-fight and attending a protest. What was I *doing*?). That was all I needed.

Upwards Lewinskiy ran, past doorways onto new levels – upwards, always upwards. The stairwell was clearly little used; lights came on automatically as we ascended then extinguished after our passing. But then they didn't, and I realised that, over the syncopated reverberations of our footsteps, that someone – some others – were rushing upwards behind me.

Friend or foe?

I very much doubted they would be allies. I was chaser and chased.

But it didn't matter. I was running because my quarry

was fleeing. That's all I needed. Up, up, up; right up to ground level. No more stairs.

I felt a blast of frozen air envelop me as Lewinskiy burst into the vestibule. I grabbed the door before it could shut, threw myself inside.

Lewinskiy stood at bay by the exit. He glanced to the sides, at the racks of warmsuits just waiting to be taken. I advanced on him steadily. "Private Leon Lewinskiy," I gasped, "I'm arresting you for Breach of Contract, for going absent without leave." It was the first thing that came to me. I'd been too busy to think, too busy sucking oxygen into my lungs to plan ahead.

Lewinskiy's eyes were wild, heavy black beard trembling as he cast from side to side.

He grabbed a mask from the nearest rack and turned for the exit.

I leapt forwards. I grabbed him by the shoulder, felt the fabric of his uniform (such a soft sensation; and I was struck by the ridiculousness of putting such a rough man into a suit as fine as that the waiters wore)...

And then I was tackled from behind.

I fell hard, banging my knees painfully on the cold floor. I felt hands dragging me away, but I saw only Lewinskiy, lips drawn back in a triumphant snarl. He kicked away my hands then turned and hauled open the exterior door.

A blast of arctic wind howled into the vestibule. Someone swore behind me. The hands on me withdrew.

Lewinskiy dragged on his mask and disappeared into the darkness.

I struggled to my feet and went to hurl myself after him, to do battle with what felt like a tornado. But I was spun round by more hands on my back.

Two men. And though they were dressed, like Lewinskiy, in waiters' uniforms, it was clear to me that these were fighters. Something in the eyes, perhaps. Or the nose, broken and reset, of the man on the left. Or the twist of the lips, the balanced stances they were adopting...

I had my back to the exit. Wind-borne shards of ice shattered against me, the warm air of the vestibule inevitably losing the fight. But I had it better than my assailants; they had the wind in their faces, had to shield their eyes to see at all.

One swung a heavy fist at me. I ducked back hastily. They advanced, pushing me to the very edge of the storm.

Two men, both of whom were used to fighting, in close conditions.

"Security! Stop!" I yelled for a second time, this time over the roar of the wind.

"We know who you are," one grunted as he threw another punch at me. This one thumped into my shoulder as I twisted my head away. I staggered backwards – outside.

Immediately I lost my sense of hearing. All I was aware of was the roar of the wind that threatened to bowl me off my feet...

In winter, winds across Antarctica regularly reach hurricane strength...

And then, through barely-open slits of eyes, I saw the worst thing I'd ever seen in my life.

I saw the door I'd been knocked through start to close.

I saw the light that represented survival diminish, narrow, fade.

I threw myself forwards, tried to barge my way back inside. A hand smashed me in the face and I fell back.

The door closed.

* * *

The blood had already frozen on my face. Ice-spicules stuck

me like darts, but I was so numb that I felt only the pressure.

I struggled to my feet, the pathetic suit I wore already stiffening, becoming heavy as steel. I cast around urgently.

Lewinskiy had vanished. I couldn't even make out the wall that I knew was barely a few paces away. No way of knowing where he'd gone. I spared a second or two to ask myself why he'd been running, what he'd been afraid of – and why the hell I'd thought it appropriate to give chase.

The darkness was total.

No moon, no stars. Just the howling gale, roaring around me like a dragon, bombarding me with its breath of ice.

To stand around wondering was to die. I knew that. But which way to go?

I almost laughed. Here I stood, nearly a hundred thousand people within a two-mile radius, and I was going to die alone.

I reached forwards blindly and soon my numb fingers brushed against rough concrete. A moment or two later I felt the plas-steel of the door I'd been forced through. My chest ached, lungs struggling to process the freezing air of the Antarctic night.

There was no point trying to get in that way. My assailants had shut me out. It was impossible to think that they'd not sealed the door somehow.

I tried to call up my internal map of the city but my brain was sluggish, unresponsive. I just knew I had to move.

The door I'd fallen out of was one of four on the block, one at each cardinal point. I knew I had mere minutes before I succumbed to the conditions. I knew I didn't have time to circumvent the massive building whether I went north or south.

My only chance was to find the corresponding point on the neighbouring block.

I turned, placed my back on the door and took – tried to

take – a deep breath. I lined up my heels and strode forwards.

It's simple, I told myself. *The doors are all aligned. All you have to do is walk straight and you'll find an entrance. Fifty yards, no further.*

So simple.

Simple if you can see. Simple if you can orientate yourself against something. Simple if there isn't a tornado that staggers you every few paces, drops you to your knees every dozen, keeps hurling ice in your face.

I tried to jog, to run; anything to keep the blood flowing, to keep the heart pumping.

I couldn't feel my face. Couldn't feel my hands, or my feet. I kept slipping on the ice (why hadn't I worn my damn boots?), kept falling and kept fighting to get back to my feet. I was bent almost double in my attempt to force my way through the wind – and then, as if mocking me, there came a calm and I overbalanced.

I fell hard, heard the crack of bone as my arm broke on the unforgiving ground.

I barely noticed. I'd lost all sense of feeling.

Time had ceased to have a meaning. I could have been walking for three minutes or three hours when the wind suddenly dropped – and didn't pick up again. In my addled state I didn't realise what that meant until I walked into a concrete wall.

I reached out with my one good arm, all around, but I couldn't feel any door.

Left or right? North or south? The directions didn't mean anything. All that I could keep in my mind was the urgency of *finding a door*.

I could've been a yard from safety or I could have been half a mile.

Left or right? A toss of a coin. A choice of life or death.

I went right. Then I changed my mind and went left, brushing my good arm across the concrete, desperately hoping for a change in sensation beneath my brittle fingers.

Blindly I shuffled along the wall, as fast as my malfunctioning body would take me. Even without the buffeting of the wind, I kept stumbling. My feet were too numb to properly feel the ground beneath them.

Then I was sideswiped by a wind-borne avalanche of ice.

I picked myself up slowly, painfully, my left arm useless at my side. I'd reached the north corner of the wall and found no entry.

I'd chosen wrong.

I found the corner of the building and, head down once more, forced myself into the gale.

I was a mind without a body. All I was aware of was a constant ache; from my legs, my broken arm, my lungs... My thoughts stirred sluggishly. *Why not go back? Try for the door you knew must have been on that last flank? Why not take advantage of the lee the wall gave you?*

Should've tried to circumnavigate the original block. You've only made things worse for yourself.

I gave myself no answer. I had no answer to give.

Where was Lewinskiy? Why were you chasing him anyway? Wasn't it so out of character for you to be so gung-ho? You only chased him because of your frustrations at Mikhail and Ferraldi and Francis – and because he ran – and look at you now.

I had no answers.

My only anchor was the tips of my fingers against the concrete.

My strength was rapidly failing me now. Every step was pain. Every time I stumbled it became harder to regain my feet. Every breath hurt a little more than the last. I must have swallowed my own bodyweight in ice. My ridiculous dress-suit was a millstone. I'd have taken it off if I'd had the use of both arms.

I must go on.

I must go on.

I must go on.

I stopped. Had there…? Was that...? No, it can't have been – my mind playing tricks.

I turned and sidled back a few paces, placing my hand on the wall.

A door. *The* door. My mind had become so warped that I'd barely recognised the change in texture.

Now, one-handed and blind, all I had to do was open it.

I'd have cried had my eyes not already been frozen shut. To be at the door – to have reached salvation, and safety, and yet be unable to get inside.

Frantically I scrabbled my right hand all around the plas-steel frame, desperately hunting for the release. I was dimly aware that something was wrong with my fingers, something beyond the numbness. I couldn't work out what it was – but then, oh glorious *then* – I felt the control panel, raised harshly from the ice-slick surface. I desperately, blindly, ran my hand over it. I couldn't feel the buttons, couldn't find the tiny bio-scanner or the emergency access button.

A fit of manic anger swept me away. I hammered the panel, threw my hand into it again and again and again. Pain reared through the fog of my mind, but it was a tiny, tiny thing – a flea biting at a statue.

I've no idea how long I was standing there flailing before there was a clunk and the door unlatched.

I threw my good shoulder into it. For a moment it didn't move, ice sealing it closed. I barged it again. And again. The third time did it: I fell inside. Gasping, panting, crying, I dragged myself forwards before twisting to kick the door

shut behind me.
    I was alive.
    And life brings pain.

Eleven

I slept for a night and a day. I barely needed the drugs they gave me. Didn't hear the discussions, wasn't aware of the surgery. And then, when I awoke, it was all I could do to give my account.

Francis paced the room, his face never once releasing its scowl. He kept glaring at me, as if it was my fault I was in this situation.

"Tell me again why you chased this Lewinskiy."

"He keeps popping up where he shouldn't. He has questions to answer." I'd been through this. It was hard to keep the exhaustion out of my voice.

"You had bigger things to worry about that some rogue UN soldier," Francis snapped.

I said nothing, just closed my eyes momentarily.

"So what did you find out at this damn reception?"

I bit down my retort. "Nothing I haven't already told you."

He huffed. "So you're out of action and have nothing to show for it, that's what you're telling me."

I nearly died – was nearly murdered – and that's all you care about.

There was silence save for the sound of his footsteps on my bedroom carpet.

"Has Lewinskiy turned up yet?" I asked.

Francis shook his head. "We have bigger things to worry about," he said again.

"Like what?"

His neck snapped round and he fixed me with his piggy brown eyes. "Like working out what the hell Ferraldi's up to," he snapped, just a few decibels short of a yell.

"Ferraldi is doing exactly what he said he was," I growled back. My head was hurting. I just wished he'd go the hell away. "He's conducting a report. He's interviewing people. Evaluating Australis."

"Is there nothing else you can tell me?"

"If I think of anything I'll let you know."

After he'd left I let my head sink deeper into the pillow and groaned. I ached, despite all the drugs that had been pumped into me. My skin felt like it had been stuck with a thousand little skewers. My left arm was dead, numbed to nothing, sealed rigid inside a bone-knitting sac. I'd lost all the skin on the fingers of my right hand. The concrete wall had been rougher that I'd imagined. It too was sealed inside a wound-pack.

I was also bald, my hair frozen, snapped and finally shaved clean. My beard too was gone. When I looked in a mirror I saw a stranger, the circuit-board scar-brand on my forehead making me look like some refugee from an old science-fiction movie.

At least I'd never have to wear that damn smart suit again. The medics had cut that off me.

I'd had no visitors. Francis didn't count.

I realised I needed to piss. I put it out of my mind as best I could, but eventually I swung my legs off the bed and hobbled into the bathroom. Without hands the procedure was somewhat... awkward.

Whose side was I on?

Francis had told me to spy on Ferraldi. Ferraldi wanted me to spy on Francis. Right at that moment I didn't care much for any of them.

What the hell was Lewinskiy doing, working as a waiter?

I couldn't even pick up my datapad to make enquiries. Couldn't get hold of the control for the viewscreen for some entertainment. Couldn't sleep.

I was hugely grateful when Bartelli came to visit. Letting him in was a bit of a mission, mind.

He followed me patiently into the main room and sat, before getting up almost straight away to fix us both a coffee. This... this *helplessness*, I detested it.

I gritted my teeth and took it. We took seats facing each other, my broken arm set unbending at its awkward angle. I looked him over carefully; he looked absolutely drained. He'd always had a tendency to slouch, but now it seemed as if he was barely holding himself on the seat. The bags under his eyes seemed set to overbalance him.

"So how long have you been playing the violin?" I asked, first question that came to me.

He blushed; it was strange to see the way the tips of his moustache seemed to droop. Maybe that was my imagination.

"Since I was a kid," he mumbled. "Is a hobby, you know? Relaxing."

"And the quartet?"

If anything he got redder. "Jus'... We met through the servers. Eight months ago. We practice ev'ry fortnight."

"Get many gigs?"

"The other night was our second."

"You're very good." I was embarrassed at the way he perked up at that; I'd barely have noticed it every single note he'd played had been wrong. I'd have just assumed they were playing some modernist composition.

"So what's been going on whilst I've been... out of action?"

He sighed deeply. "We been busy. Lots of trouble – no,

don' worry, it's been little things. Bar fights. Arguments. Vandalism; that great mural outside the administration centre – you know, the one that's supposed to signify all nations working in harmony – was daubed with anti-Exec Committee slogans."

"No CCTV?"

Bartelli shrugged. "The perpetrators wore warmsuits and came in through an exterior door. No way to trace them back."

People learned quickly.

"None of the incidents are anything to worry about in themselves," he went on, "there's just a lot of them. An' of course people are still very unhappy about the massacre – the video that surfaced. We've been rushed off our feet."

No wonder Francis had been angry at me. "I'd no idea. I'm sorry."

He shrugged again and smiled weakly. "Not your fault. You couldn't have helped. Unless we propped you up in a bar with a sign saying 'Big Brother is watching you'."

I laughed, though the joke was weak. I hadn't had enough absurdity in my life recently. "Look, Bartelli, I'm going mad sitting here on my own all day. Think you could help me?"

"What is it you want?"

"Well, for a start, could you help me with my coffee?"

He looked puzzled for a moment, then realised I couldn't grasp my mug. He fed me a few sips – oddly intimate, the gesture. But I trusted Bartelli. And God knew he'd seen me weak often enough.

"Next," I said when he'd set the mug back down and retaken his seat, "can you call up the CCTV footage of Ferraldi's reception?"

"Of course."

He pulled out his datapad and tapped at it for a few

seconds. "What are you looking for?"

"The waiters."

He shot me a glance from under heavy brows. It was enough to let me know that he understood.

"Here," he said.

He came to sit beside me and showed me the screen.

"How many can we ID?" I asked.

"Will take a little time…"

This time his tapping went on for several otherwise silent minutes. I had to wait; to stop myself from interrupting his work, from giving needless comments and instructions. He knew his business.

He was frowning.

"Most… Most easily accountable," said slowly. "Ferraldi – him or your friend Petrovic –" he pronounced the *vic* harshly, missing off the unwritten *h* – "seem to have hired a team from Garcia-Lomax's office."

"Most? Not all?"

He shook his head slowly. "There are some… two men, one woman…"

"Let me see."

He held the datapad so I could examine the faces.

I shook my head. "I can't… can't be sure…"

"What?"

"Maybe the one on the left… No, I can't be sure." I grimaced. "Damn." I looked up and saw that Bartelli was looking at me, patiently awaiting an explanation. "The people who threw me out of that damn vestibule. I was hoping… but I can't sure."

"You think it might be the waiters?"

I looked at the three faces again. "Well, they were both men, so that rules her out…" *A nose, broken and reset.* "It could've been the others, but… Who are they, anyway?"

"That's the point. I can't find matches for them."

"Have you tried the guest list?"

"You are, in other words, expecting them to be part of Gísladóttir's UN team."

"Lewinskiy is. Why not these others?"

"Let's check shall we? A moment…" He swiped and tapped at the pad. "Ah. Possible matches. Not enough for the system to be sure."

I looked up at him. "How is that possible?"

He gave me one of his big expressive shrugs. "None of them looked at the cameras. Or, to put it another way, cameras in the wrong place. A bit of time and I could grab enough shots to build a composite – that should increase the probability…"

I stared absently at my encased hand. "Did you…"

"Sir?"

"Tell me, did you look anywhere but the main reception room for these images?"

"I did not."

"The service rooms behind – can you get a look in there? Or on the stairwell?"

Silently he took back the back and spent a few more minutes tapping and muttering to himself. And then a steam of quiet Italian invective that I took for swearing.

"No," he said eventually. "Feed's been wiped."

Silence. A long silence.

"I don't know why we even bother with surveillance cameras," I said, surprising even myself with the calm in my voice. "They've proved to be one disappointment after another."

"Everyone knows they're being watched." Bartelli matched my tone. "A smart criminal always takes that into account."

"So what now?" I said to myself.

Bartelli tapped his teeth ruminatively. "Well, I should go.

Is there anything else I can do for you?" he added as he dragged himself to his feet.

He stood looking at me as I thought.

"Yes, actually. Yes there is. Can you find out where Agnetha Gísladóttir's lodging?"

* * *

There was nothing wrong with my legs.

You wouldn't believe how many times I had to tell myself that next morning – how many times I had to force myself to stop hobbling, to stop wishing I had a cane – before I got to the outskirts of the city. The newest, only just completed, sections. The sections that were empty, undecorated, quiet and cold and smelled of industrial solvents.

This block was the closest Australis had to a hotel.

I flexed my fingers, testing the new skin on my right hand. My left was still dead, still buried under accelerated-healing pads.

I couldn't convince myself that my legs didn't ache. I settled for shifting from one foot to the other as I rode upwards in the elevator.

If I'd had a cane I could've rapped the handle on the apartment door. Give me a little personality.

Gísladóttir answered within seconds. She threw the door open wide and stood there, tall and strong. She surveyed me coolly. "Sergeant Nordvelt," she said.

"Captain Gísladóttir."

She said nothing more for the moment, continued her evaluation: my sealed arm, rigid at my side; my bald scalp; the scar that was once half-hidden now proud on my brow.

She took them all in, unsmiling. Then, abruptly, she turned and strode into the main room.

I followed her through the vestibule, closing the door behind me.

I found her waiting perfectly still in the centre of the room. She was wearing a simple grey vest darkened by a wide V of sweat that pointed from chest to belly. I felt terribly self-conscious in the full force of her gaze. An exercise bench and set of weights had been installed in the corner.

"To what do I owe this pleasure?" she asked without warmth.

"Do you know what happened to me?"

Her gaze flicked once more to my arm. "I saw nothing on the servers."

"I ran into Private Lewinskiy."

"He did that to you?" A note of surprise, but any emotion was quickly smothered.

"Not him. But two nights ago someone tried to kill me."

"Why are you telling me this?"

I got out my datapad and, without asking permission, I moved past Gísladóttir and sat on the settee. It seemed unused. She was obviously not one to make a space her own.

She stood watching me as I set my pad on the low table before me and, one-handed, manipulated the screen.

"I'd like you to look at some of these pictures and tell me who you recognise."

"Are you asking me as a policeman, Sergeant Nordvelt? Or do you just want me to do you a favour?"

I looked up at her. "Would it make a difference? I'm asking because I need answers."

I turned the pad so it was facing the seat opposite and raised an eyebrow at Gísladóttir. She took the hint and, sighing, sat across from me and took up the screen.

"It is a party," she said. "You want me to identify everyone here? Surely you have people who can do that better than I? Or is everyone in Australis blind?"

"The waiting staff," I said patiently. "Look at them."

She frowned at me, then returned her attention to the pad. Her frown deepened into a scowl as she studied the image I'd called up for her. It was taken from one of the surveillance cameras; too blurry, too shadowed for the automatic facial recognition software – time to see if a human could do better.

She examined the image for a long time before passing the pad back to me. Her expression hadn't changed much. But I thought I heard a slight note of resignation in her voice when she next spoke; a trace of tiredness too, a speck of pain quickly wiped from her eyes.

"I see."

"I take it you recognise him?"

"You clearly know all the answers," she snapped. "Why bother me if you already know what you're looking for?"

I didn't. I'd only had a hunch. But Gísladóttir was not the sort of person to admit that to. "Tell me, how many of the waiters do you recognise?" I passed her more queued-up images.

Again she took her time and studied them carefully before responding. "Aside from Lewinskiy? Three. I think I could put names to three."

"And those names are?"

"Corporal Akineev and Privates Fisher and Okur."

"I'll need you to send me their records."

"It is not a crime to pick up casual work whilst off duty."

"But attempted murder is," I shot back.

She was silent.

"Tell me, where are these people now?"

She didn't reply; she stood, uncertain for a moment, before stepping away to the exercise bench. She lay back and reached up for the barbell racked over her chest.

"I don't know," she said quietly before hoisting the bar; she held it above her for a moment, muscles prominent on her bare arms.

"You don't know?"

Bar down to her chest; up again smooth and steady. Down once more. A fine mist of sweat pricked her brow. "I don't know."

"You're their commanding officer. How can you not know?"

"Because this is such a damn stupid place, a stupid, stupid city," she hissed, hoisting once more.

I said nothing.

"I don't know," she said again, her voice softening. Her exertions barely affected her speech. "Something has gone wrong."

"What has?"

"Something has gone wrong with my command." She was still measuring the weight perfectly but her voice was starting to catch a little.

"Can you be more specific?"

Rise, fall; rise, fall. She controlled her breath carefully, inhaling and exhaling in time. I watched her chest move, a purple corner of her sports-bra just peeking out from beneath her vest.

She set the barbell back in its cradle but didn't move to get up.

"I think I have lost them," she said.

"Who?"

"I try to keep them disciplined, but they're off duty. Here is this black world, this underground… this tomb. It's enough to drive you mad. What should I do? Should I keep them drilling every day? They were promised they would be home by now. All I can do is keep an eye on them, threaten them with punishments. Look the other way when I can."

She lay there, staring straight up at the ceiling.

"What's been going on, Gísladóttir?"

"I am losing control," she said.

"How so?"

"I do not know where my troop is. I came here with thirty soldiers. I organised them, trained them, imposed myself upon them. When we found we had to stay here, in… in *Australis*, I found them rooms, made sure they were comfortable and safe. Tried to get them something productive to do with their time." She sat up abruptly, not needing to use her arms, just the taught muscles of her stomach and a flick of the head to avoid hitting the barbell as she rose. She looked at me for the first time in minutes and, although her blue-grey eyes were as fierce, as defiant, as ever, for the first time I saw fear in them.

"You don't like to be out of control," I said.

She did not consider that worthy of an answer.

"What's happened? Specifically?"

She shrugged, a gesture that struck me as uncharacteristically weak. "People – my men – they are getting harder to trace. Lewinskiy's vanished. Fisher, Okur and Akineev – they've not been seen for a week or so. I make sure to gather my squad together every few days, just to keep some sort of coalescence – it's so *hard* in this environment, when they're supposed to be at leisure. People are either not turning up at all or have black eyes and bruises and *won't tell me where they got them*."

"What do you think's happening?"

"Bar fights. Jealousies – you don't have enough women in this damn city, you know that? I've even had privates making passes at me, can you imagine? I tell them I made that mistake once before, now I don't piss in my own nest. You don't have enough whores, that's the problem."

"And the people who've disappeared?"

"Only Lewinskiy has disappeared," Gísladóttir snapped. "It's far too soon to say that of the others."

I didn't think it worth arguing. "Have you looked for them at all?"

She shrugged again, swinging a leg over the bench so that she was facing me properly. "I am asking my men to keep an eye out for them. To listen out for word."

"Do you want our help?"

Her face crumpled into a scowl and it looked like it took an effort of will to bite back her immediate reaction. "Why are you so interested in my command?"

"Because two of them tried to kill me. And because they're an unknown."

"Only to you."

"It seems like you don't have much idea about them either."

Her eyes flashed. A bead of sweat dripped on to her chest.

I got to my feet. "I should go. Sorry to have intruded."

I was at the door before she called me back. "Nordvelt."

"Yes?"

"I'll call a muster. I'll let you know how many people don't attend."

"And who?"

"And who."

I smiled at her. She didn't smile back.

Twelve

I did not trust Gísladóttir. She gave me information, it's true, but I had no way of assessing its worth. For all I knew, Privates Fisher and Okur and Corporal Akinfeev were operating on her express instructions. For all I knew Gísladóttir was working hand-in-glove with Ferraldi. For all I knew...

The UN soldiers would have the incendiary devices needed to burn up the medical facility. They'd have the explosives needed to kill Guder. Trust? No, I had no reason to trust anyone.

I chased up the investigation into Guder's death but there was nothing new. Francis didn't seem to have anything but forensic reports that told only what we already knew. No fingerprints, no useful CCTV, no suspects.

I felt useless and so, so frustrated. It already felt like a cold-case. Guder – and Jackson, and their families – deserved better.

But I had my orders, and though I was technically still signed off work I couldn't sit around doing nothing. In something of a daze I wandered down to stores and signed out a handful of listening devices. Then I went home and paced my living room. All the time my cast held one side of me rigid, unbalanced.

Well, this was an unbalanced situation.

I looked at the bugs I'd obediently fetched. Barely the size of a thumbnail and not much thicker, they adhered to just about any surface and, once activated, would broadcast any sound within twenty yards to a secure police server.

I was not happy about this. I'd read too much about the Gestapo, about the KGB, the Stasi — hell, I'd read too many spy novels — to be comfortable about this level of intrusion. Not on mere suspicion.

My scalp itched. I hoped that was my hair growing back.

Someone rang the doorbell.

I hurried through to the vestibule and threw the door open.

Benitez Ferraldi stood there, head bowed, a faint smile on his lips.

"Mr Nordvelt," he said. "I thought it might be an idea to talk. May I come in?"

I stood uncomprehending for a moment. I felt something harden inside. "Of course."

I violated the rules of hospitality by showing him my back and leading the way inside. I made sure he didn't have a chance to see the bugs before I could sweep them out of sight. When I looked round he was standing just inside the living room, closed door to the vestibule behind him.

"Take a seat," I said. Inside my mind was working fast. "What did you want to talk about."

He sat on the settee, bending knees and waist together almost like he was a collapsible chair. He really did seem to have some kind of bird in his ancestry. "First of all, I... I should have said at the reception, but I forgot." He angled his head in apology. "I heard about Officer Guder. Mikhail and I would like to extend our condolences."

I nodded, my face stiff. "Of course."

"You should know that the actions of madmen won't play a part in my report. I'd be remiss if I didn't track the course of the investigation, though. How... Francis handles things *is* relevant."

Why did he hesitate before saying Francis' name? He accompanied the pause with a little smile that was almost like a wink. What was he trying to say? That he had no faith in my boss? That he knew I'd be handling the search?

"I can promise you that everyone will do their utmost to... find out what happened." I'd almost said 'to find the killer'.

"Of course you will," Ferraldi said smoothly, just that little croak to deepen his tenor. "I have every faith in you."

Did he mean me personally, or the whole security team?

What did I want to hear?

"You've seen many changes in Australis since you first came here, haven't you, Anders? – you don't mind me calling you Anders, do you? You've been here almost since the start, after all."

I shrugged. "I've seen the city grow."

"But you've seen – like no-one else, I suspect – the changes that have been sweeping over the world. Maybe you've not seen the effects yet – maybe no-one has – but you've been intimately involved in the shaping of the world. Oh, you've not thought it in that way? Well, look around you. Who could have dreamed even twenty years ago we'd have a city in Antarctica? We're solving the problems of the world, Anders! New farming techniques, as pioneered by our friend Professor Ling. Rare earth minerals so new they don't even have names. A city powered primarily by the sun. And, perhaps most importantly, this is *virgin land*. There are too many people in the world, Anders – any chance to spread us out a bit has got to be good."

"Only if the people who come want to be here," I growled. "Anyway, I know all this. Why are you telling me again?"

"Because that's only part of it. That's the good part. There are... other factors. Changes to the very fabric of the

Company." His face was serious now. He cleared his throat and leaned forwards. "The old Gods are dying, Anders. Going the way of the dinosaurs of capitalism, democracy, communism – all those ridiculous 'isms'. The Psych test that assigned us our futures, that dictated where we were assigned to and what work we did, had become an article of faith – you know that as well as I do. And then suddenly it's proved to be… unreliable. The UN is withering, a mere shadow now so many states are controlled by the Company. And… I'm not sure I should be saying this, but… the Company's in trouble, Anders."

He held me with his eyes. Trapped there I was unable to argue, to shake my head, even.

"You've seen the video. The massacre. I'm trying to find out where that happened. Trying to get to the bottom of it. But there are clearly problems. Corruption. We thought we had it beaten, but still human nature can rear the ugliest of heads. Corruption and misappropriation and the mechanisms that were put in place to see to its end – Oversight – are as dangerous as the disease itself."

"Why are you telling me this?"

"Because I want you on our side, Anders."

"To do what? To help dismantle the organisation that's supported me my whole life and's proven to work when all those governments have failed? Have you forgotten the war criminals in our jail?"

Ferraldi winced. He leaned back and sighed. "No. I've not forgotten. And I'm a Company man, just like you. The Company's the best chance humanity has. This city's the evidence of that. But *things must change*. Things have to get better. That's why I'm here. I'm not here to get at Baurus, but – well, there are… questions. Questions of his superiors."

"You're playing politics."

"Yes."

"So what... you say you want me to join you. *What do you want me to do?*"

"Nobody knows Australis better than you, Anders. Not Baurus, not Francis, certainly not Unity or the UN. You've seen that Professor Ling – Maggie, your friend – agrees with me. And Mr Ferguson. And Mr Keegan. These people–"

"I know who they are, thank you."

He inclined his head. "I just want you to be open with me, like they are. You're cautious, I can see that. I know you've been used. No, don't worry, I'm not going to go digging in your past – where would that get either of us? But if you can see the way clear to being open with me I'm sure it'd add a great deal to my report. Tell me what you *really* think of Baurus and Francis. What do you owe of them anyway?"

I could see my own reflection in his eyes.

He stood, unfolding to tower down on me. "Well, I'll be going. You must be exhausted."

I got up but didn't follow him to the door. I said nothing.

Half-way into the vestibule he paused and looked back at me. "The old Gods are dead, Anders," he said. "The old Gods served us well, but now they're done. It's time to build some new ones, Anders, and we're the ones who can shape them – in our own image, perhaps, or... or maybe not."

He nodded at me and left.

* * *

Ferraldi wanted me to spy on Francis. Francis wanted me to spy on Ferraldi. I cursed them both.

I lay on my bed, sleepless in the dark. I stared at the

blackness that was the ceiling, wished I could see stars.

There were too many words in my head. Too much had happened, too much had been said, for me to process in a rational fashion. And each time I closed my eyes I saw Jackson, lying in the debris of the explosion. I must have drifted off because I could see Guder's half-headed corpse standing over me in the night.

It occurred to me that I didn't know much about either of them. I knew Guder had been in a relationship, but Jackson? Did they have children? What of their friends?

Who'd be crying for them tonight? I should find out.

I couldn't feel emotion, not then. I was numb.

I got up and paced naked into the kitchen. Got myself a coffee and sat at the table, idly toying with the bugs Francis had made me take.

Francis or Ferraldi?

Ferraldi or Francis?

Eventually I dressed and grabbed three of the little transceivers. I went out into the early hours, where, despite the artificial light and the perfectly controlled temperatures and the sunshine murals, the city had never felt more shrouded in winter.

It took me the best part of two hours to plant the bugs. Walking from block to block, descending, climbing stairs, not meeting more than two people of my journey.

The actual task of setting the devices was simple. My security overrides got me through all doors. All of my targets were absent or asleep. I just ghosted in, left my mark and walked out. I didn't try to hide from the surveillance cameras I passed; they'd never check as long as they had no reason. My broken arm was no hindrance.

Easy.

Ferraldi's office. Francis' office. Mithu's front room.

They want to use me? Fine. I'll do their dirty work, all of

them. They want me to spy? Fine. I'll spy on them all.

    And I can choose whether I report to anyone but myself.

Thirteen

Bartelli tried to smile as I slid the mug across the table to him, but the bags under his eyes gave lie to the gesture.

Australis was quiet this morning – as if the citizens knew that some heavy-duty politicking was going on and were waiting for the right moment to raise their voices. The bars were empty, the coffee-shops only had a couple of customers. It was as if the whole city was holding its breath.

I looked out of the window, into the atrium. One of Francis' teams were patrolling – Ramswani and Finch. 'High-visiblity policing'. To reassure the public that the security service was still in control.

Personally, I felt the constant presence of police in the corridors spoke of repression. But maybe that was just me.

When the patrol had moved on I looked back to Bartelli. "So how's the murder investigation going?" I asked.

His moustache twitched as he grimaced. He shrugged. "Nothing so far. The message – the warning sent to you – it came from a public terminal. The account was created using a false identity. Dead end."

"How is that possible? I thought all accounts had to be backed up with biometric data and linked to a name – not necessarily displayed, but a name in the records nevertheless."

"You're forgetting the guest accounts."

"The ones for the UN soldiers–"

"And similar outsiders, yes."

I sighed. "So someone got access via a guest password?"

"Neatly bypassing the necessity for a biometric scan. That's right."

"This is so frustrating."

"You want to be on the case yourself," Bartelli said.

"I know you're every bit as competent as me—"

"But not being there, hands on, when it matters so much. I understand, *signore*."

"You know you don't have to call me 'sir'. We're both sergeants."

He gave one on his big, almost theatrical, shrugs. "Habit. What can I say? It amuses me. Anyway, I'm as pissed off as you about the warehouse." He shook his head, jowls settling a microsecond after the rest had finished moving. "Fire and flood destroyed lot of evidence. Initial reports suggest a small compact explosive device was used – we found what we think was a trip-wire."

"Anything on the explosive?"

"Forensics thinks it produced a lot of explosive power for its size – assuming they're right about that small size. They're not using the word, but I can't help but think we're looking at a land-mine, or possibly a grenade."

"Where the hell did anyone get their hands on either of those things?"

He shook his head again, opened his mouth to speak before hesitating.

"What?"

"Well… is nothing, no."

"Come on, Bartelli, it's me you're talking to here."

He sighed, took a drink of coffee. A few drips lingered on his top lip. "Explosives in the city… engineering have a supply, but after… after the problem with biometric markers being copied by the biothieves, they are tightly controlled, yes?"

I nodded.

"There is one other group who may – *may* – have brought explosives here with them."

"The UN soldiers."

"The UN soldiers. Wassername – Gisla…"

"Gísladóttir's men. Lewinskiy…" I rested my chin on my hand, thinking hard.

"People who also have been given guest accounts for the forums."

"Have you spoken to her?"

"Not yet. But I will. The question is – will she tell me the truth?"

That was a question. "I'd have said yes…"

"But?"

But what did I really know? I only had her word that Lewinskiy was AWOL. For all I knew, Gísladóttir had been giving him his orders all along.

"I will ask her anyway," Bartelli was saying. "It has to be done. Maybe the way she answers will tell me something."

"Any suggestion of a motive?"

He shrugged again. "Well, that depends, yes? The warning – the trap – it was sent to you. Who was the target? We got to speak to Guder's family, of course. His partner. And the same for Jackson. We've got to do all that. But if the killer was after you…?"

I glanced out of the window again, as if I might see a murderer lurking in the shadows. If there'd been any shadows.

"I don't know why anyone would want to kill me," I said half to myself.

"What about Shakil Mithu?"

I jerked my head back to Bartelli. "Why do you say that?"

"After he went for you in Francis' office… after the death of his wife… And after his campaign to get him and his fellows home? Do you think him not capable?"

I shook my head slowly. "I don't know. I just don't know anymore."

"At the moment I'd say Francis is just about ready to swing for you," Bartelli said dryly, his moustache showing his weak smile.

"Have I pissed him off that much?"

"I dun' know. Not really. You know what he's like; all bluster and bark. Might be best if you kept away from the office for a day or two, that's all."

"No problem with that. He's given me orders that'll keep me away for a while anyway."

"Why aren't you leading the investigation anyway? Not that I'm unhappy at it falling to me, but…"

"You know, I'm not exactly sure." And in that moment I really wasn't. Why was Francis so afraid of Ferraldi? Was he becoming obsessed? Surely Guder's murder was the priority for the unit.

I absently touched my scar, ran my hand over my scalp.

Bartelli finished his coffee. "I should go. Got a lot to do."

"Thanks for keeping me in the loop, sergeant."

"No problem, *signore*." He gave me a mock salute and left.

I tapped the app for another drink and went back to staring out of the window. Wondered what on earth I was supposed to be doing now. Investigating Ferraldi, I supposed. How had I ended up in this limbo state? I felt like I was at once out on the margins, pushed out of my true job, and right in the centre of things. Uncomfortable.

The waitress slid a mug in front of me and I gave her a smile. She was young, maybe seventeen; too young to know that smiling back at me was just an invitation. I watched her walk away and wondered how she saw me? How did I see myself? Was I a bitter old veteran or some green, callow youth? My beard was slowly growing back. I was branded by my scar. I was bald and stiff-armed.

The mug was warm in my hands. I blew gently and watched the steam spiral away.

I felt no guilt about planting the bugs. I felt guilty about feeling no guilt. This city had made me as cold as the wastes outside.

I slipped my datapad onto the table before me and jacked in the headphones. One after another I listened to the pickup from the bugs. The software automatically removed the long sections of silence, left me only the conversations. I heard Francis, as belligerent with my colleagues as he was with me. I heard him on the phone to someone high-up, presumably Baurus. I heard him instructing Bartelli to take the lead in the murder investigation. I heard him caution my friend that he wasn't to keep me informed. That I wasn't to be trusted. That Ferraldi might have 'turned' me.

Bartelli had mentioned nothing of this. I felt a moment of gut-twisting discomfort. Did that mean I couldn't rely on my one friend in the office? Or did it mean that he'd already decided to ignore Francis?

From the bug in the Mithu's apartment I picked up little more than an argument between father and son. I ran it through a translation program and found that, apparently, Kaiser had been playing truant. So much for Mithu's 'he is a good boy' mantra.

I got nothing from Ferraldi's office at all. Francis had better keep on hoping that I'd find some dirt.

Whose side was I on? I felt my resolve harden. I was on the side of the truth. I was on the side that found Guder's killer. I was on the side of the people who needed my help. I was on the side of doing the right thing.

Fuck them all.

I was on a side of one.

* * *

That night found me sitting in the Comms Building, the miners' bar. I cradled one of their God-awful beers and settled into the darkest, dingiest corner I could find. There'd been changes since I was last here; they'd added insulation and powerful outside lighting in preparation for the winter.

Maxine Oluweyu, friend, former lover and genius with a welding torch, had made the statue – the great android pugilist – that stood at the door. It was a constant in a place that seemed to have changed every time I visited. The bar had expanded to take up almost twice the space as it had on my first visit nearly half a year ago. The quality of the beer had improved too. Could almost get a decent drink now. Almost.

It had been a message from Weng that had sent me up here. It'd come that afternoon, whilst I'd been having my cast removed. *Comms Building, 8pm tonight*. That was all.

I picked up my pint and sipped cautiously. Molasses-thick and bitter as hell, I grimaced with every mouthful. My arm was stiff, slow to respond, but there was no pain. No consequences. I set the tankard back down and scanned the room again, wondered for the thousandth time what Weng had wanted me to see. There were only a dozen or so customers and I recognised none of them. Could see nothing suspicious, just the sort of rough, battle-scarred faces that would come straight from a hard day's digging to sit in a half-legal house like this and drink rot-gut in an Antarctic winter.

I stared at faces, my back to the wall. There was a

commonality in the emotions; they were almost caricatures, parodies, of feelings. Where there was passion there was white-hot, oil-fire passion. Where there were jokes they were told as if they were the last joke that ever be told. Where there was anger it was the type that overwhelmed reason and consumed flesh.

As I said, the types of people that'd end up in a miserable shack half-way up a frozen mountain on the arse of the world.

The vestibule door opened and two people walked in, still in their warmsuits. They walked right past the statue with barely a glance. They didn't see me – or at least saw no more than a lone drinker – in my corner, and stood by a table on the other side of the room. They took their masks off, and I smiled to myself.

Lewinskiy. Big-bearded and broad. How did Weng know he'd be here tonight?

I was so taken with bringing Lewinskiy in that it took me a moment to really notice the other man. There was something in the way he moved; something almost liquid, slippery. Collins. Ferraldi's bodyguard. He walked like a dancer, loose-limbed and light. He made Lewinskiy look like a mountain.

Collins sat and Lewinskiy bought drinks. They talked quietly – I couldn't have hoped to hear them from where I was. I watched them carefully. Collins checked his datapad. Lewinskiy spoke, and then grinned. Collins tapped long, slender fingers on the tabletop.

The door opened again. This arrival was taken aback by the android but no-one laughed. Collins and Lewinskiy had gone quiet, watching. The background chatter resumed but eyes remained on the stranger as he came further into the bar.

He looked to Collins and Lewinskiy and strode over to

them, long legs crossing the rough floor quickly. He stood facing him and pulled off his mask.

Shakil Mithu.

And the door opened a third time. This person took of their mask as soon as they entered.

Maxine Oluweyu.

Despite myself my mouth fell open.

Fourteen

Max had once been my lover; briefly and dangerously entwined. We were friends now, though perhaps time had opened up the differences that should have been apparent from the start. The best engineer I'd ever met. A friend of Maggie's, too, and the rest of the original crew who'd turned against Baurus and the Committee.

I was angry at myself for not thinking to bring any listening devices, no way to amplify conversation. But body language can tell you a great deal.

Max, for example. She sat stiff in her seat for the whole half-hour meeting. She repeatedly shot dark glances at both Lewinskiy and Mithu, but when she spoke she leant forwards, elbow on the table, sharp gestures underlining her points.

As for Mithu, his eyes kept flicking between Lewinskiy and Collins, looking down on them through his plastic-framed glasses. For the most part he stayed back in his chair. His words too carried intensity, passion.

What were they talking about? It was clear that this was not a meeting of friends. This was business; and judging from the way they stared holes in each other, this was cut-throat dirty-dealing.

Lewinskiy didn't say much, just the odd interjection. Mostly he leaned back and let the animosity roll over him. Collins did most of the talking for him.

The meeting ended with handshakes and nods. An

arrangement.

Mithu stood and left the table. He paused a few paces away and turned back. "I expect you to keep your side of the bargain," he said, loud enough for the whole room to hear.

Lewinskiy raised a hand. Mithu strapped on his mask and left.

Max left next, silent and straight-backed, at ease in her skin. But unsmiling.

The last two took their time, finished their drinks, exchanged some quiet words. Lewinskiy laughed at some comment of Collins'.

And then, less than an hour after they'd arrived, they got up and headed for the exit together.

Hastily I threw on my mask and, when the pair had closed the vestibule door behind them, I got up to follow.

I almost walked into them outside the building. They were idling on the pack-ice, in the full glare of the halogen lights mounted above the entrance. I mumbled an apology and staggered, playing the part of the clumsy drunk and grateful to the anonymity given to me by my warmsuit.

I ambled away, ignoring them until I was out of the halo of light. Almost immediately I was blind. Not just because of the contrast between the illuminated are and out here in the darkness, but because there was nothing to see. The moon, the stars, they were still obscured by heavy cloud. I fumbled with my mask and dialled up the night-vision setting.

Now I could make out a little of my surroundings, highlighted with a tinge of bilious green; could see the rough road, the rutting ice-cut path up to the mine. I headed for this and then, when I guessed that I was obscured by the corner of the bar, turned back and pressed myself against the cold concrete.

"Come on," Lewinskiy was moaning, "how long does it

take to get transport out here?"

"Be patient," Collins said. "It'll come soon enough." His voice reminded me of my old boss, de Villiers, who'd been the first to die in Antarctica – in this new world project, at least. De Villiers had been South African and I finally twigged that Collins was from southern Africa too.

"God, this bloody city drives me crazy. Don't know how they do it, live underground all the bloody time. Drive me nuts."

Collins said nothing. I heard feet moving lightly on the ice.

"So, what d'you think? Reckon they'll do their part?"

"They'll do it. They both want something they think we can give them. And they don't see the price we're asking as too high. And it's true – it's not a big deal for them. Baurus out – they want it already."

"Don't trust that bloody Mithu though," Lewinskiy said. "D'you see the way he was looking at me? Like he wanted to knock me bloody block off."

"Won't be the first time, hey?"

"Hey –"

"I think that's our ride."

I looked around. I'd been so caught up in the conversation that I'd pushed the sound of the engine to the back of my mind. Now I saw headlights coming down the road from the city; one of the over-engineered four-by-fours that served as general-purpose transport vehicles. I drew back, out of the line-of-fire of the headlights.

The vehicle slewed to a halt before the bar. I shuffled back to the corner and peeked round in time to see Collins and Lewinskiy getting in.

The barcode on the vehicle was facing me. I quickly fumbled with my datapad and, just as the four-by-four was moving off again, managed to snap the ID.

And then the vehicle was racing away, climbing easily through the frozen night, up the hill and out of sight.

I leaned back against the concrete, stared up at the infinite blackness.

* * *

I walked the half-kilometre up to the mine, up the ice-cut stairway, past anonymous figures in their warmsuits. We could have been different species for all the notice we paid to each other – just a raise of a hand in passing, one lizard-creature passing another in silence.

I could have emulated Collins and Lewinskiy and ordered up a car to take me home – there were plenty of off-duty drivers looking for a few extra credits – and charged the expense to whoever I ended up reporting to. But instead I rode one of the free transports that carried miners from their shift to the city. Mine was pretty much empty. It was cold inside and its suspension had seen better days.

I didn't go straight home. It was, after all, barely nine-thirty and I was way too wired to sleep. And I had to get the taste of that damn beer out of my mouth. So I went to the Company bar in town to have a proper pint, and to sit, and to think, and to try and pull some of the pieces together.

I sighed as I tasted my beer, as I slumped into a proper, upholstered seat. Hadn't realised how tired I was, how stressed. I took another pull at the drink, felt the froth on my lip. Tossed my mask on the table and got out my datapad.

Message from Jawad: forensics have finished their investigation into the fire at the medical centre. Cause: slow-fuse chemical incendiary.

I blinked. The words meant little to me so I scrolled through the tech report for details.

Most of this was indecipherable: yield ratios, formulae, numbers, numbers, numbers. But there were a few pictures, a few notes in plain English. The illustrations showed shards, tiny fragments of metal and glass that had been recovered from the scene. And then a reconstruction of what the evidence-analysts thought they'd have looked like in their original form.

Almost like an egg. An ovoid object that could fit in one large hand. In two halves, one aluminium, one clear.

And below a list of all known devices that resemble such an object.

Basically, as Bartelli had indicated, I was looking at an incendiary grenade.

My thoughts immediately went to Lewinskiy.

My drink had all but disappeared. I got another, noticing for the first time how busy the place was. Busy – not full, but busy. But it was so *quiet*. As if everyone was waiting for something to happen.

I went back to my seat, took up my datapad. The car that had picked up Collins (was that a first- or a surname? How could I find out?) and Lewinskiy. Easy to trace, given I had its ID. A quick canter through the security networks and I had it. As expected: it was licensed to the Transport Department. I put a call through to the dispatcher. Took me a few minutes to establish my credentials, to be shuttled through to a supervisor. Finally I got the driver's name and contact details.

I checked the time. Should I call straight away? Might she still be driving Lewinskiy around? Worth the risk.

"Sandestrom here." A bored looking women, mid-forties, lined face, appeared on my screen. "Where d'you want to go?"

"Eleanor Sandestrom?"

Her features sharpened as she stared at her screen with more interest. "Who is this?"

"Sergeant Nordvelt, Security." I held my ID up for her to see.

"Right," she said with a frown. "Right. What d'you want, then?"

"You just picked up two men from the Comms Building, right?"

"I've picked up lots of people from there."

"It'd have been about quarter to nine."

"Yeah?" She sounded uncertain, not sure if she wanted to co-operate. "Yeah, I picked up two guys around then."

"I just want to know where you took them."

"I'm not in any sorta trouble, am I? Hey, I just drive where I'm told to go, I'm not involved in –"

"I just want to know where you took them. Which block. Nothing to do with you."

She was still frowning, twisting her bottom lip with her fingers. "Look, I don't want any trouble –"

"All I want to know is where you dropped those gentlemen off. Just tell me which block."

"Didn't take them to any block."

"Where, then?"

"Hell, it's a big one, getting paid double for this. I still got 'em in back –"

"Can they hear you?" I interrupted urgently.

She shook her head. "Cab's sealed."

"So where are you taking them?"

"Hey, have they broken the law? Am I in danger here?"

"No, no, you'll be fine." She would be fine, surely. Lewinskiy was just a murder suspect, an AWOL soldier, and with him was a professional bodyguard. Just exceptionally dangerous people.

"Well, don't ask me to lock the doors and bring 'em home to you," Sandestrom said with a glance behind. "I ain't damn stupid, not worth my neck for."

"No, it's okay, it's okay. Just tell me where you're taking them and I'll not interfere, I promise."

She glanced behind again and I cursed the anxiety in her face. If she gave them any indication...

"Taking them to the jail," she said shortly, almost hissing the words.

"The jail?"

"The jail. You deaf or something?"

"Thank you. Get them there safely and get home."

That could have gone better. But I'd got what I wanted. I'd found where Lewinskiy was hiding.

The jail. A massive building, currently empty save for fifteen prisoners and a skeleton staff to see to their needs.

What better place to hide?

Fifteen

I was just getting myself ready to leave, taking my glass back to the bar, when I saw Gísladóttir. And when I saw her I stopped still and stared.

Never had her cheekbones seemed so perfect, the low lighting and gentle make-up accentuating her natural structure. Her pale hair seemed almost white. She'd rouged her lips, her customary frown becoming almost a pout.

But my surprise was more at what she was wearing. I'd only ever seen her in uniform or in simple work-out gear that did nothing for the figure. Now she was wearing a delicate navy-coloured dress. Nothing lacy; just simple, plain, and – on her – incredibly attractive. She had a handbag slung over one shoulder.

She saw me and raised a hand in bored greeting. I quickly raised my eyes from her lean body and crossed to her.

"Agnetha Gísladóttir."

"That's 'Captain Gísladóttir', Sergeant Nordvelt."

"In that case, it's 'senior sergeant'."

She raised an eyebrow then turned her back on me to speak to the barman. I leant against the bar next to her.

"Vodka. Double. No ice," she said. "Nordvelt?"

I hadn't realised she was going to get me a drink. I hid my surprise and got another beer.

Once the barman had gone she turned and leaned back against the wood. I also turned to stare out over the sullen tables.

We stood in silence. I wasn't sure whether it was awkward or not. When the barman returned with our order she thumbed his credit-pad without looking, then cradled her glass in front of her chest.

She took a sip at the clear liquid. "You might as well call me Agnetha," she said abruptly.

"In that case, it's Anders."

"Okay."

"The bald look – well, I won't say it suits you, but it's not so bad, you know."

I shrugged, uncertain how to take that. "Thanks. I think."

"You look younger without the beard."

"Is that a good thing?"

"It's just a thing. What's the scar?"

I self-consciously ran a finger across my brow. "Warmsuit burn. A bit of the circuitry overheated whilst I was wearing it." On the night that Mikhail broke his back.

Gísladóttir looked at me, nodding slowly. "Perhaps you are more interesting than you first appeared, Mr Nordvelt."

I shifted on my feet. "So what brings you out here tonight?"

She shrugged, her chest rising and falling. Her skin was cool and clear.

"Sick of being cooped up in my room. I'm off duty. See if there's anything to do in this place. Any one." She took another drink.

I couldn't think of anything to say.

"What about you?" she asked. "You got a fuck lined up for tonight? Or will you take matters into your own hands?"

I searched her eyes for any sign that she was joking, but I couldn't see anything.

"Well? You have a girl at home? Or a boy?"

"No-one."

She raised an eyebrow at me, sipped at her vodka. I felt she was looking for me to say more, but I didn't want to. Not then. Not to her. She shifted against the bar. "How come there are no decent men in this damned place?"

"This is still the first generation. Most people came here already with families. Most of the others are specialists, experts – not a status that's easily achieved in youth."

She gave me another sidelong glance, appraising with those cold blue eyes.

But before she could say anything else I set my drink on the bar behind me and pulled out my pad. "Here, you can do me a favour."

"Oh? And what do I get in return?"

"Take a look at this. What does it put you in mind of?"

She took the pad and gave it a glance, looking at the schematic I'd pulled up with a sigh. With a disinterested thumb she flipped the screen quickly back and forth. "It looks like a Mark III Weston-Suzuki incendiary grenade, although whoever drew this obviously has never seen one in real life."

"Did you bring any with you to Antarctica?" I said as I took the pad back.

"I think there were a couple in our arsenal." She was speaking slowly now, almost warily, and I could see calculation in her eyes. "Why do you want to know? What is that report?"

She reached to take the pad back but I jerked it out of reach. Her arm came to rest on my chest; it lingered there for a moment, then she drew back. Now, finally, she turned to face me fully, setting her drink on the bar next to mine. Her stare was intense, but I held it.

"I can't tell you that, I'm sorry," I said quietly.

She held my gaze for a long, long, moment. Then a slow smile spread across her lips. "Always the policeman, hey, sergeant?"

I smiled back. "*Senior* sergeant."

She took up her drink. Downed it in one. Waved to the barman.

Odd to think that one chance meeting with a murder suspect could save your life.

* * *

I hadn't known what I was doing. Hadn't decided whether I could go through with it. I'd like to think I'd have given Agnetha my bed and slept on the sofa, but... but I might be lying.

She'd been unsteady on her feet when we left the bar. This elegant, hard-as-ice woman, professional to the core, was now clinging to my arm and giggling to herself. I should've called her a car or walked her back to her apartment, but she wanted...

She said she wanted to see my place, get a feel for how the residents lived. Wanted to talk.

That's what she said. I was a little drunk too. I let myself believe her, and – who knows – it might even have been true.

I steered her slowly down into the elevator, along the corridors, helping her with a hand on her back, unable to decide whether her laugh was metallic and alien or if it was the cold echoes that took a pretty thing and made it harsh.

Emergency sirens in the distance, coming closer – coming damn close! I pressed Agnetha to the wall, allowing a team of paramedics in their odd little tuktuk-cart to race past.

The sirens faded but didn't disappear into silence. And I

heard a shout ahead.

I pulled Agnetha onwards, faster. She seemed to think it was some sort of a game; she hurried ahead, dragging me and still laughing, until we were both running.

Together we hurtled round the last corner – and I stumbled to a halt. Agnetha half-fell against my flank. I put an arm back around her, holding her awkwardly, but I wasn't paying attention.

Something bad had gone down here. Right outside my door.

I couldn't take it all in. Not then. Not all at once.

The paramedics who'd overtaken us: their cart in the foreground, the three team-members huddled round… something slumped against the wall.

Policemen: Ramswami, pale, shaking, talking urgently into her radio; Finch with one of the paramedics. And through a haze of smoke I thought I could see Bartelli, his back to me, escorting away people some part of me recognised as neighbours.

The floor was wet. The sprinklers had been on.

The door to my apartment was open.

My apartment was the epicentre.

I almost lifted Gísladóttir, half-carried her forwards. She wasn't laughing now. She was turning her head almost like in a cartoon, as if she could only see directly forwards. Her hair tickled my scalp, my forehead. Her handbag slapped against my thigh.

The walls of the corridor were scorched and distorted.

Gísladóttir was scrambling for purchase in her soft shoes. She sent a sheen of water rising ahead of us.

The paramedics scrambled aside. One of them grabbed a stretcher from the cart, the others prepped a figure for removal.

The door to my apartment wasn't just open. It had been

blown off its hinges.

The figure was rolled, lifted, set on the cart. The paramedics scrambled up and the agile little vehicle turned fluidly and hared back towards us. Once more I pressed Gísladóttir into the wall.

The man on the stretcher was Rampaul. The front of his uniform was covered with blood.

"Sir!"

It was Finch. He gaped at me, open-mouthed, took in Gísladóttir still clutched to my side. His face was white. His mouth flapped open and closed. He stumbled a few paces towards me.

"Sir," he said again. "You... you..."

"What the hell's happened here, Officer? What the hell–"

"Sir, there's been... There's been an incident. Rampaul's hurt–"

"I can see that! *What the hell's happened here?*"

He cleared his throat. Gísladóttir shifted her weight and, distracted as I was, she slipped free. With a squeak of annoyance she slumped to the damp floor, cursing me amiably. Finch cleared his throat again.

I ignored Gísladóttir. "Officer Finch, will you please tell me what has happened here?"

"An explosion, sir. A bomb. Attached to your front door."

Sixteen

I let myself fall against a wall and slide to the floor, my arse quickly soaked. I didn't care. After a second Gísladóttir slumped down beside me. Her dress darkened as if she'd wet herself.

Someone had blown up my house. Someone had tried to kill me. Rampaul had taken the brunt of... of whatever it was. *Lewinskiy has an alibi*, I thought. *And so does Collins. Wait, is that right? They were in the Comms Bar until around 20:30, then they got Sandestrom to drive them to the jail. They'd have had time to come straight back here. Anyhow, I've no idea when the bomb was planted*. No alibis, then. No immediate answers.

Finch had wandered down the corridor. I could hear voices all around but they didn't mean anything to me.

Gísladóttir pawed at my arm. "Handbag," she said.

"What?"

"M' handbag. Where is it?"

"On your shoulder."

"Right. Right... shit, can you help me?"

I bit back a scowl. I... needed to be alone in my despair, my self-pity, not dealing with a drunk; not even an attractive one like Gísladóttir. Not one I didn't trust.

I took her bag and unzipped it. "What do you want?"

"Need my injection. Should be a... like a pen... 'ringe."

I fished in her bag, spilling her datapad to the wet floor. "Is this it?" I pulled out something that looked a little like a stylus but with a top like an old-fashioned pen. It felt like cheap plastic.

"That's it. Remove the cap, that's good. Now put it – here…" She took my hand and guided it over her neck, the hollow point just below her ear. "Now – press."

I pushed the trigger and she gasped, then sighed. "Okay, give me a minute…"

"Sir."

I looked round. Bartelli was standing over me, looking – if possible – even shabbier than usual.

"We should talk, sir," he said, glancing down the corridor.

I looked at Gísladóttir. She seemed happy enough, rolling her head on her shoulders and mumbling to herself in some language I didn't recognise. Icelandic, probably.

"I'll be back in a moment," I muttered to her, and used the wall to help me to my feet. Water seeped down my thighs.

"Let's go in here," Bartelli said, leading me into my own apartment.

The damage wasn't as bad as I'd imagined. The door had been blasted back into the vestibule and was clearly never to be used again. The walls of this small space were cracked and bowed and they too would have to be replaced, as would the spare pairs of shoes and the warmsuit I kept in there. But as Bartelli led me, damp arse and all, through into the main room, the only damage I could see was a few mugs which I'd left lying about which now lay cracked and chipped on the floor. Oh, and my spare datapad – the one upon which I had my novels cued up – had a shattered screen.

A sudden sadness welled up in me. I'm not sure why. Maybe I saw some symbolism in that.

Bartelli gestured for me to come away from the entrance, where various security- and medical-staff still buzzed. He sat in one of my chairs and rubbed at his face.

"What happened here?" I asked quietly.

"Someone booby-trapped your front door," he said.

"One of my neighbours reported something and Rampaul came to check it out?"

Bartelli looked at the floor. "Something like that."

I suddenly felt terribly, terribly exhausted. I sighed and limped round the sofa to sit facing my old partner. "Guder, Jackson, Rampaul... is it all because of me?"

"What you mean?"

"My door, the message sending Guder and Jackson into that trap... sent to me. Is someone all out to kill me?"

"Or the police in general?"

"Is Rampaul...?"

Bartelli shrugged. "He wasn't dead when they took him away." His shoulders were slumped; he looked small, old.

"Can you tell me anything else?"

"*Non*. No. Nothing. The explosion happened fifteen minutes ago. Automatic emergency sensors picked up the... I don't know, how do the damn things work? The fire, the shock, the damage, I don't know. Then your neighbours started phoning. We got down here just before..."

We sat in silence for a moment.

"You're saying that Rampaul was here before the explosion went off? The neighbours saw nothing?" I asked.

Bartelli swore under his breath. "Yes."

"Why was he here?"

"Francis told him to bug your room."

Again, silence.

"I see."

"I protested, s*ignore*," he said with a wave of an arm. "I said, 'Nordvelt is one of us, why are we spying on him?' but Mr Francis was sure. Adamant, yes? He gave it to Rampaul to do."

I almost laughed. "So Francis saved my life." That, and

meeting Gísladóttir in the bar. If it hadn't been for those extra drinks it would've been me. I was empty, drained. An almost hysterical laughter rose up in me. I struggled to keep a straight face.

"You should go, sir," Bartelli said gently. "The clean-up crew will be here soon. Maybe Francis himself will come. Forensics –"

"I can't even stay in my own house, is that right?" I snapped.

He waved a negation. "No, no, it's just – you should get some sleep. We can't do anything here, not 'til the evidence-scanners have been round. Go and do something useful. Get some sleep."

"And where am I going to sleep, huh?"

He looked taken aback. "Well, sir, I'm sorry – I thought, since you were here with that woman... Or we can sort you a room, just a call..."

I'd forgotten about Gísladóttir. Too much to think about, always too much in my brain. I felt, put upon, used; I sighed, long and deep. Bartelli was right. Sleep.

I got up and went to the vestibule door. I'd speak to the captain and then get a room somewhere.

"Ah, there you are, Senior Sergeant." Gísladóttir was directly on the other side. She was crouched down, one knee on the floor, her dress pulled up to show her well-toned calf. She was examining the outer door, the one that had been blown off by the explosion.

Her eyes were clear. Her body language was professional, smart. She held her muscles under perfect control.

I gaped at her.

Finch was hovering nervously behind her. He looked at Bartelli and, obviously receiving some message in his face, bobbed gratefully away. I stepped aside to let my sergeant into the conversation.

"Small yield explosive," Gísladóttir said, rising to her feet. A drop of water dripped from her hem. "Placed in the centre of the door. See the way it's blackened there – all the cracks radiate out from that? Not sure it ignited fully. Amateur job."

"How you know all that?" Bartelli asked.

She gave him a superior look. "I'm a soldier. Now, how it was triggered – there'd be more debris if it was timed. We're looking at pressure-detonation. Pressure-release, I mean. Like a letter-bomb."

"Attached to the centre of the door?"

"Mm. Little odd, but that's how it looks." She wiped her hand on her dress.

"Um." I wasn't sure what to say. "We should…"

Gísladóttir stared at me, measuring. "You don't want me here?"

"No, no – it's just…"

"Nordvelt should not be here either," Bartelli said. "Go and get some sleep, both of you. Best not be here when Francis arrives."

"You'll let me know how Rampaul is?" I asked.

He nodded. Gísladóttir watched us for a moment, then turned to exit my – now very public – private quarters.

Bartelli leaned closer to me. "I'll see you get a copy of the forensic reports as well, sir."

I nodded, my eyes still on the damp behind of Gísladóttir's dress.

Sleep. And please, please, no dreams.

Seventeen

Gísladóttir offered me her bed but I turned her down. Too much in my head. Too much I'd stored up in the attic of my brain, too much threatening to smash through the floor and drown me in panic.

Gísladóttir was a problem. How much could I trust her? How much did I like her?

Could her appearance in the bar really have been coincidence?

Why would anyone want to kill me?

Why *would* anyone want to kill me?

I got dispatch to find a vacant apartment and check it out to me for a night or two. Not a problem here in Australis. No need for hotels – not yet, at least.

I lay on the unfamiliar bed and stared up at the unfamiliar ceiling. I made sure that nobody save the dispatcher knew where I was staying – although of course Francis could hunt me down if he wanted.

Why would Francis try and bug me? Did he have so little faith in me?

A little bitterness twisted in my chest.

Could it be called paranoia when someone had just tried to blow me up?

Okay, one thing at a time. Gísladóttir, with her magic elixir that could sober her up in a matter of minutes. A UN tool for off-duty soldiers, she'd told me, to make sure they could be combat-ready in short order.

I wondered again how much I could trust her. I had clear evidence that the UN were up to their necks in whatever was going on here. We had Lewinskiy, a UN soldier, turning up in places he shouldn't. We had the use – alright, probable use – of a UN incendiary to start the fire in the medical unit. I wouldn't have been at all surprised if it were proved that the explosion that'd killed Guder had been caused by explosives from Gísladóttir's arsenal. UN soldiers had shoved me out into the Antarctic winter and shut the door behind me.

Was I to believe that Gísladóttir knew none of this? Could a commanding officer lose track of her troops so completely?

Had she really been drunk? Had she been playing me the whole time? That injection just seemed a little science-fiction for me.

And then there was Ferraldi. Ferraldi, with his bodyguard and Mikhail at his side; Ferraldi who said he was impartial and yet seemed to be doing his best to undermine Baurus.

Did he have a point? Baurus had promoted Francis over me, and now Francis was pushing me into Ferraldi's arms.

I felt a twinge of guilt about the bugs I'd planted. Okay, Francis had the right to use them – the right in what law there was – but on suspicion alone? I didn't like it. And yet I'd been the one to set them up.

Did Francis have reason to mistrust me? I had to admit it was possible he did. I'd argued with him, disagreed with him so many times. Of course he'd suspect me of crossing over to Ferraldi.

Poor Rampaul. Innocent victim of a mad bomber and an over-suspicious boss.

I'd have to talk to him. I should see Jackson as well. If they pulled through.

I fought down an image of Guder's mangled corpse,

blood making the water around him pink, the tang of wet static in the air.

It was no good. I wasn't going to sleep. I got up, irritably throwing the duvet aside. I strode naked into the living room, cold without the debris of my existence. I wished I had someone to talk to (*not* Gísladóttir); Unity would have fit the bill, even Bartelli.

But it was late – past three in the morning – and no-one wanted to talk to me right then. Maybe it was best this way. Alone I could cause no pain.

I paced up and down, still air cold on my flesh. I went into the kitchen but there were no coffee sachets or caffeine tabs. I settled for water, splashing my chest as the jet came on too strong. I started to shiver.

Why was Mithu meeting with Lewinskiy and Collins? Why was Max there too? Okay, I knew Mithu was on Ferraldi's side; he'd do almost anything to get himself and his people home.

(I snorted to myself. 'Get his people home'. As if he were some sort of prophet.)

But what was the link with Lewinskiy? Was he there on Gísladóttir's orders? Assume that Collins was representing Ferraldi. Lewinskiy representing Gísladóttir. Mithu the Exiles. Max...?

What were they discussing?

Was Max there on behalf of Maggie? That might explain how Weng came to hear of it. It'd also make everyone at that clandestine meeting an opponent of Baurus. Had my old colleagues thrown in so wholeheartedly with Ferraldi?

I shivered again. I felt like I was hiding. Felt like I was hunted, haunted. Felt horribly like this strange room was my cell.

I wondered if I should go and break in to another vacant apartment; go somewhere random, far away, make sure nobody could find me.

I was on a side of one. I was alone. I was afraid.

I went back to the bedroom, tried to stop myself from trembling.

With all this politicking, all these games, was anybody really concerned with finding Guder's killer? I was so far out of the loop, now. If I walked in the morning to my desk in the security centre, would I walk out again, or would I find myself locked up?

I wasn't afraid. Not like I should've been. I was too tired for that.

I got back into bed and waited for the trembling to stop.

* * *

"God, Anders, is that you? For a moment I thought you were Ferraldi – you know, the baldness and all..."

I had to keep moving as Max didn't stop, kept moving deeper into the storeroom for the parts she needed. She consulted her datapad, checking items off as she went.

"We need to talk, Max," I said as she bustled on.

"Yeah? Well, I'm busy right now, kid. Want to swing by after work?"

"Max –" I stepped back against a rack of shelves as she suddenly turned back, loading another section of wire into the little cart she was using. "Max, I saw you last night."

She muttered something under her breath, her attention back on her pad.

"Max, I saw you in the Comms Bar. With Mithu and Collins and–"

"What the hell were you doing there?" Now I had her attention. She looked at me, unsmiling, through angry brown eyes.

"Having a drink," I said.

"Yeah? You just happened to be up in the Comms Bar the one night —" She cut herself short. "Weng. I bet it was bloody Weng, wasn't it? Stupid girl," she said with a shake of the head. "Knew it was a bad idea to talk to Maggie in front of her. Look, Anders, what do you *want*? Has Francis sent you here? 'Cause we weren't doing anything wrong, you know."

"I just want to know what you were talking about."

She sighed again. "Fine. One second."

She pushed the half-loaded cart into a corner and made sure the door was properly closed before standing arms crossed in front of me. "Well?"

"So why were you meeting?"

"We weren't doing anything wrong. It was just… to discuss Australis, you know?"

"It didn't look like a casual chat to me."

She scowled at me. "Look, Anders, I don't have to explain myself… you know how things are going. You know how unhappy we are —"

"Do I?"

"You see how we're put into the shittiest job, huh? You see how they've got Maggie and Fergie and Dmitri buried at the bottom of the pile? I mean look at me — I spend all my time clearing up other people's messes."

"You were happy to do that in the old base."

"That was different! That was — that was trying to make a difference… to improve the situation for all of us, to make our lives better and to come up with solutions to problems! Here…" She gestured dismissively.

"Here?"

"Here I just *fix* things. You see what they've got me doing now? Replacing a burnt-out circuit. You sure as hell don't need to be a professional engineer with thirteen years' experience to do that."

"So you were explaining this to Collins, and Lewinksiy – and to Mithu."

She shifted her weight, glanced down. "Well, I'm not too sure about Mithu. I think the others were just saving time by having us meet at the same time." She wiped an invisible speck off her cheek. "All I know about him is that he wants to get out of here. He was very clear about that. Wants a better life for himself and his son – and you can't blame him for that."

No. But things are never that straightforward, are they? "So what did Collins and Lewinskiy say to you?"

Max sighed and leaned back against a shelf. "I don't know how much Weng's told you. Things are… not great around here."

"Round where?"

"With the working classes. With the miners, and the scientists. Mithu… well, whatever else he is, he seems to have a lot of sway with the miners. A lot of friends, his Exiles, down there. They're threatening to go on strike. And…"

"What?"

She looked through me. "We're thinking the same."

"You… you're…?"

"We're threatening a walk-out," she snapped. "It's not just me and Maggie, you know. A lot of people think Holloway's mishandling us. He's not up to the job, you can see that, can't you, Anders?"

"I remember him being an irritating son of a bitch, but not incompetent." I didn't mention his role in Oversight. I didn't think he was likely to order the assassination of hundreds of striking scientists. Like Francis had said, he was a busted flush.

"Well," she sniffed, "you don't work under Holloway."

"So you met up, the four of you in the Comms Building, to plan a 'day of action'?"

She glowered at me. "Actually, Lewinskiy was trying to dissuade us."

"What? Really?"

"Somehow he and Collins had got wind of our plans. They were trying to tell us that it wasn't going to get us anywhere, just cause needless disruption."

"Why Lewinskiy? Why was he there?"

"Well, he's the UN representative, right? Below Unity, I mean."

"Wait, what? Lewinskiy's the UN rep?"

"Well, yeah. Of course. Isn't he?"

"I thought he was just a soldier. Under Gísladóttir."

"That's not how he was introduced to us. He said he was acting for the UN. Wanted a stable Australis. I presumed…"

"That he was acting for his superiors."

There was a moment of silence.

"Is that all, Anders? I really need to get on."

"One more thing. How did the meeting end?"

Max sighed and glanced to the door. "We – Mithu and I – we agreed to hold off on taking any action. For now."

"That's something, at least," I murmured.

"*For now*," she repeated. "The problems ain't gone away, boy. It'll only take one more thing… there's a lot of angry people out there, you know. Only take one more thing, and then…"

Eighteen

I went to visit Jackson and Rampaul. It was hard to persuade myself that I could walk openly and wasn't a suspect in any crimes; that I was still a serving security officer and didn't have to hide. And that someone was trying to kill me.

My officers were both mending; they were going to live. Rampaul couldn't tell me anything more than Gísladóttir had; he'd gone to my apartment, seen an envelope pinned to my door with my name on it. He'd ignored it and opened the door with a security code given to him by Francis. And that was all.

I stayed with him, uncomfortably standing over his bed, knowing nothing about him and nothing about what to say. I wanted to accuse him of being Francis' agent, of spying against his own — but he knew that. It wouldn't help either of us. Instead I mumbled platitudes and apologies and wished I knew how to be a human being.

I think Rampaul was relieved when I left.

Jackson was so heavily wired up to medical instruments that it was difficult to know where she ended and they began. Her missing arm was horribly revealed by the flatness in the bedclothes.

I did my best not to stare at it. I smiled at her, and she smiled back through her mask of wires.

"Jackson," I said softly.

"Sir."

"How are you?"

She tried to shrug. "I'll... I'll be fine. Don't think I'll make it in for work tomorrow, though."

I laughed. "I suppose you've an adequate excuse."

She smiled again, but a tear crawled down her cheek. "Sir, I just... I just want..."

"What is it, Jackson?"

"I just want to... to say sorry."

"Sorry? What've you got to be sorry about?"

"If... if I'd just taken a little more care... If I'd been a little more alert –"

"Jackson, this wasn't your fault."

"...If I'd gone first I might, I might have seen the wire..."

"You couldn't have done anything, Jackson. None of this was your fault. Whoever set the trap, it was down to them. *They* killed Guder, not you."

"I know I'm not the best officer. I know I'm not that bright – no, don't say anything. I've seen the way you look at me sometimes. I just want you to know I'm sorry. I'm really, really sorry."

I had to leave after that. Couldn't take here misplaced guilt. Couldn't take her blaming herself when really it was all my fault. I should've gone into that warehouse, not farmed the job out.

Guilt, anger, grief – yes, I should've gone into that warehouse. Nobody would've grieved for me like they were for Guder. If I'd lost my arm, or my head, then Rampaul wouldn't be in hospital. Everything would be so much simpler. I wouldn't be alone.

Who wanted me dead? Who hated me that much?

Francis? Baurus? I might not have many friends, but I didn't think I had many enemies either.

Lewinskiy – a UN rep? By whose authority? Had he been working on Gísladóttir's orders all along? I should speak to Unity.

According to that driver, Sandestrom, Lewinskiy and Collins were hiding out at the jail. But if either – or both – of them trying to kill me then the last thing I wanted was to go up there on my own.

A side of one. That's what I was.

And now I realised that my legs were taking me to the home of another enemy. On my own.

At least this was an enemy I felt I could trust.

* * *

I stood outside a familiar door and scratched at my scalp. I rang the bell and pulled myself into a better posture, put my public face on.

Kaiser opened the door. He stood, not inviting me, not saying a word. Just staring at me expressionlessly, his Bangladeshi skin paled by the inside life that was Australis. No longer the skinny little boy he'd been when I'd first met him, Australis was at least helping him fill out his frame. Mithu may hate Australis and the circumstances of his arrival, but the food certainly seemed to be to his son's liking. He was blooming, nearly as tall as me already.

He stared at me, I stared at him. He had Mithu's fierce eyes.

"Is your father home?" I asked.

For a moment he did nothing, just kept looking through me as if he didn't understand. Then, without warning, he stepped back and walked away, deeper into the apartment.

Taking this as an invitation I followed him through the vestibule, shutting the front door behind me, then hesitated at the open inner door. There were voices beyond; Kaiser and his dad speaking in Bengali. The boy's voice wavered, as

I should have expected from someone going through puberty; the father's — Shakil's — quiet but somehow powerful.

I cleared my throat deliberately and walked in.

The boy was standing in front of his father, who was sitting in an armchair near the kitchen door. Shakil Mithu looked at me and smiled grimly. He adjusted the ridiculous glasses he wore then turned back to his son.

Another word in Bengali. His son tried to respond but was cut off. One last look at me — a look that could hardly be called friendly — and Kaiser stamped out of the living room into what I knew to be his bedroom.

The first time I'd been in this apartment had been to find Shakil's wife murdered, Kaiser's mother stabbed through the chest. Mithu had been the chief suspect, going as far as to confess to the killing. He'd been exonerated but, months later, the atmosphere was still that of a mourning house.

I took in the little table by Shakil's chair. It was covered in tiny shreds of paper, torn and rolled into pellets, then discarded. Empty cups, unwashed, sat on top and amongst these, sitting crooked-based on other papers, some of which had writing on, some obscured and warped by careless spills of tea or coffee. The chair Shakil occupied was creased and dirty, stained and torn.

Mithu may have been a leader amongst the Exiles but this wasn't a place of planning. It was a place of silence, of tears, a place where it felt like a wall had been ripped out and the building tottered on the verge of collapse.

Without Lata Mithu the order, the love, seemed to have been drawn from the apartment.

I suddenly found myself unwilling to actually get to the point. "How's Kaiser getting on?" I asked.

"He is a good boy," Mithu said, his voice slow and heavy. "He is clever. He got his mother's brain, thank God. He... he gets into trouble..." He shook his head. "Kaiser gets into trouble. But he is very clever. He learns. He is already smarter than me. Better at mathematics, electronics, computers... he has a lot of hobbies. Sits in his room all day and thinks... Kaiser is a good boy," Shakil repeated, a strangely formal little mantra. "He is all I have now."

That comment had teeth, a little bite in it. 'Don't get between me and my son," it said, "or you'll suffer". I thought of how I'd heard – through the bug – that Kaiser had been playing truant. "Mr Mithu," I said, "I need to talk to you... Do you mind if I sit?"

Another wave of a hand, eyes elsewhere. I sat.

"Mr Mithu – Shakil –" I hesitated. Last time I'd tried to call him by his first name he'd bitten me off. Now... now he just sighed and looked down, dragged a relatively clean sheet of paper from under his collection of empty mugs and started to toy with it.

...fold back, corner to corner – had he taken up origami?

"Perhaps, Mr Policeman Nordvelt, you might get to the point? Why are you here? To what do we owe the pleasure this time?"

"I'd like to know your connection to Collins and Lewinskiy."

He smiled bitterly. He almost laughed. "Of course, of course. It was you in that filthy bar. It was, wasn't it? I saw you, sitting alone in the back. At first I'd thought it was Ferraldi, watching over his men for some reason. But it was you. We weren't doing anything wrong. Just talking." He tore his paper – once, then twice. Smaller and smaller...

"What about?"

"None of your business."

I sighed. "I'm trying to find a murderer, Mithu. That may not interest you –"

"There were no murderers at that table!"

"You're sure of that?"

Mithu leaned forwards. "Look, Mr Policeman Nordvelt, I admit that I was not heartbroken to hear of the explosion that killed your colleague. I am hardly the best friend of the likes of you. But I mourn his death as I would any stranger. I had nothing to do with that explosion."

"I never said you did."

"Who, then? Not your friend Maxine Oluweyu," he said. "Collins is a representative of the Company – surely you don't suspect your own? Lewinskiy? UN representative? I don't think so."

"Who told you Lewinskiy was a UN representative?"

He waved a hand. "Everyone knows that. He came with the soldiers, right? He says he has orders–"

"Orders to do what, Mithu?" I asked into the sudden silence.

Shakil shifted in his seat. Rolled his paper into a tight little pellet and started on another. "He said he had orders to make sure... to make sure that Collins and Ferraldi weren't stirring up trouble against Baurus. He said he was there as a neutral party."

"You were planning to lead a walkout, weren't you?"

"What? I don't know what you're saying."

"The miners. You were going to lead a strike."

He drew his lips back over his teeth in mockery of a smile. "Things can't go on as they are, Nordvelt." Neither confirmation nor denial.

I sighed. I suddenly felt terribly old, tired. "Maybe you're right. Maybe you're right, but I'm looking for a murderer. I don't care for these games, this... for all this politics. I just want to see my colleague's killer found."

"In that, I'm afraid I can't help you."

I stared at him for a long moment. He met my eyes evenly. I fought I heard a 'click' behind me, from the boy's room, but I didn't look round.

Old and foolish. My chin itched.

And in that moment I had a kind of... a kind of revelation. I wasn't a policeman any more. I was alone. My old friends – Maggie, Max, Mikhail – they weren't on my side any more. Bartelli wasn't my man, he was Francis'. I had no friends, no confidantes in the security team.

I wasn't a policeman any more. I was a non-person. On the lam. I was using my uniform illicitly, taking advantage of the ignorance of others.

But not bound by the rules.

"Mr Mithu, I think you should know..."

"Yes?"

"I bugged your room."

"*What?*" He straightened, knocking some papers to the floor. But he didn't take his eyes off me.

"A few nights ago I broke in to your apartment and planted a bug," I said calmly. "I'm sorry. Francis' orders. But I shouldn't have done it."

"Where?" Mithu was dangerously quiet.

I knelt before his side-table and slipped a hand under the frame. The plastic front felt warm under my skin. I detached the bug and held it up to Mithu. He was standing now, fists clenched.

"I didn't listen," I said. "Just the once – when you were arguing about Kaiser playing truant."

He glanced to the door of his son's room, then back to me. "Why tell me? Why are you telling me this?"

I stood. We faced each other, a couple of paces apart. Something – incense, or maybe aftershave – tickled my nose. "Because Francis went too far. He had no good reason for bugging you."

"But you said you planted it, not your boss."

"Yes. I shouldn't have."

He held out his hand to me. I placed the bug on his palm. He took it and studied the tiny thing carefully.

He opened his mouth to speak, but before his words came out someone rang the doorbell. Mithu glared at me, then silently crossed to the vestibule.

Voices: alarm, anger from Mithu, and in reply...

"We have a warrant for the arrest of –"

"What are you talking about?" Mithu snapped. "Arrest me? Why? What am I supposed to have done."

"Can we come in, Mr Mithu?"

I went cold. It was Francis.

What the hell was he doing here?

I had no time to speculate. He burst through into the living room, his large frame filling the doorway. He clocked me immediately; his eyes opened wide in surprise and he paused, only moving further inside as first Bartelli and then Mithu edged into the room at his back.

Bartelli was doing his best to hide his feelings, his face composed into its usual lugubriousness. Mithu looked furious – a fury that was once again directed at me.

"Nordvelt," Francis snapped as soon as he'd recovered from his surprise. "What the hell are you doing here?"

I stood stiffly, decidedly not to attention. "My job. Sir."

"Wanna explain a little further?"

"You asked me to look into Ferraldi."

"And what the hell's that got to do with this guy?" He jerked a fat thumb at Mithu.

"I demand to know what you're all doing in my house!" Shakil said.

"Shut up," Francis barked. "Sergeant, restrain him."

Initially I thought the order was intended for me to carry out. I opened my mouth to protest before I realised that he'd been talking to Bartelli. Then I thought the Italian was being told to restrain me, but it was Mithu that Bartelli moved towards.

"What am I being accused of?" Mithu demanded. "What in God's name are you doing here? What's the charge against me?"

Francis gave him a scornful look. "Where's the boy, Mithu?"

"What?"

"The boy. Where's the boy?"

"You want Kaiser?"

There was a sudden explosion of movement behind me. All my attention had been on the scene before me; I spun round just in time to see Mithu's son hurtle past me, rushing for the door.

But Francis was quicker than I'd given him credit for. He slammed his gut back just in time to catch Kaiser in the chest. The big man staggered back, for sure, but Kaiser was knocked right off his feet by the impact. He missed the door by a yard and slammed hard into the wall.

Mithu gave a bellow of rage and tried to surge forwards. But Bartelli was no fool. As Mithu moved, the sergeant simply grabbed an arm and twisted. In an instant the big Bangladeshi was on his knees, cursing loudly.

Francis ignored him. He took a pace over Kaiser's stunned form and nudged him with his foot. "Kaiser Mithu," he said with a satisfied smile. "We need to talk to you. The small matter of attempted murder."

I gaped, unable to move, as Francis hauled the boy upright. Kaiser had a smear of blood on his forehead and his eyes wouldn't focus properly. It looked as if he was trying not to cry. He kept muttering in Bengali, and all the while his father was roundly and loudly cursing us all.

"We'll want to talk to you shortly, Mr Mithu," Francis said. "And you, Nordvelt. I'll be very interested to hear your story. Bartelli, let him go. Let's get out of this dump."

My boss and my former partner dragged Kaiser out between them. Bartelli wouldn't meet my eyes.

Mithu got to his feet, cradling his twisted arm. He glowered at me. "Get out," he hissed. "Get out of my house, Nordvelt. If I never see you again it'll be too soon. Get out!"

I went. What else could I do?

Nineteen

Mystery one: why would they arrest Kaiser? What had led them to him?

I wandered from Mithu's apartment with no clear idea of where I was going. Eventually my feet took me to a block near the edge of the city. There were a lot of people around. A lot of people just standing, talking quietly. There's always less to do in winter; a lot of jobs that just couldn't be done. But was it just my imagination that they went quiet when I passed, gave me suspicious looks till I was out of sight?

I wound up in an anonymous coffee-shop. No effort had been made to make it distinct from any of the others that existed in the city. It even smelled the same: a false freshness overlaid with the artificial aromas of heavy caffeine.

I got a double espresso. Found a table in the corner where I could be alone. Watched the people pass by for a minute. Drank my coffee and got an Americano. Hot and bitter. I sat and watched the rising steam.

At least my hair was starting to grow back.

Gísladóttir says she has no idea where Lewinskiy is, and yet he's claiming to be acting on her authority.

UN explosives were used in the fire at the medical unit and again – probably – to kill Guder.

Was Lewinskiy working alone, or on his Captain's instructions? Surely Unity hadn't given any such orders. She'd never do such a thing.

I should talk to her.

I didn't trust Francis. I didn't trust Ferraldi. The old crew had moved on, had made their choices. Only Weng and I remained on the fence. Did that mean we were automatically on Baurus' side?

I took a sip of coffee, blowing gently across its surface. I took up my datapad.

The forums were still ablaze. A whole new chatroom entitled 'Baurus Out' had arisen. The anger at the Company massacre was still palpable. And yes, there were calls for protests, for walkouts.

If Mithu and Maggie were serious about striking, they'd have a lot of public support.

I didn't know what to do.

I could have just done nothing, I supposed. I could have just sat back and let events play out; let Francis run his own investigations, let Ferraldi complete his report, let Baurus fall. I could've hidden away through the winter, requested a transfer and been out on the first train come springtime. I don't think I'd have thought much less of myself if I'd done that. God damn I was angry – all of a sudden and with a bitterness that I imagined Mithu carried always on his shoulders. What had I done to deserve this? Why? Why had all my friends, my colleagues, turned away from me?

But Guder deserved some justice. Or at least the effort – even if I failed ultimately, I owed it to him to try. Owed him and Jackson and Rampaul.

I was interrupted by a call. It was Jawad. I was instructed to return to the station and see Francis.

I didn't go. My career was already over. I didn't need Francis telling me that officially.

Besides, I still had work to do.

* * *

People can be stupid sometimes. Really stupid.

If Francis had wanted me out of the investigation, wanted me arrested, even, or at least just shoved into some mindless Sisyphean task, he should really have rescinded my security access codes.

So I was able to watch his interview with Kaiser remotely, from my hiding place in full view of the public. Headphones jacked in, sitting in a corner, unnoticed, undisturbed.

"...so are you going to deny that's you?"

Live feed: should I replay from the beginning or watch from here?

The boy shook his head. I couldn't see his eyes – the camera wasn't placed right. But I could see the arms crossed over his chest, the belligerent scowl on his brow. He sat, a scale-model of his father, and said nothing.

Across from him sat Francis, his sheer bulk acting as an intimidation. Bartelli was on the side of the room, leaning against the wall, watching.

"Look, boy," Francis said, "we showed you the security footage. You've seen what we've seen. There you are, envelope in hand, trotting along to Nordvelt's flat. We've seen you fix it to his door, seen you trit-trot away. You've seen it. What've you got to say about it?"

Kaiser fixed that bomb to my door? My mouth dropped. *Kaiser*? He was what, fifteen?

"I don't have to tell you anything," Kaiser said. He spoke clearly and firmly, his anxiety only betrayed by the slight tremor under the last word. "Let me speak to my father."

Francis smiled nastily and leaned back, chair creaking beneath him. "Now, boy, let's just make clear what's gonna happen here. You know what was in that envelope, huh?"

Kaiser, pouting, shook his head.

"Well it was a bomb. We're damn lucky nobody was killed. We're damn lucky *you* weren't killed. As it is I have an officer in hospital – might never work again. You know what that means, boy?"

"No."

"In the old days it would have been attempted murder. Plus GBH and whatever else we want to throw at you. Now it's all Breach of Contract. Everyone here, even the minors, are covered by Company law. You wanna speak to your father? Best get used to being alone, boy, 'cause you might not see him for a long old time."

"You can't bully me, you…" He swallowed down the word. "I don't recognise you! I don't recognise your authority."

Francis laughed. "You don't recognise my authority? Big words – I believe N'Gepi said that at his war crimes trial, right, Bartelli?"

Bartelli shrugged and nodded.

Kaiser flushed. "I am nothing like that monster!"

"Yeah? Well, no need to worry about them, Kaiser. They can't hurt you. Security's top rate there. All the cells are wired with nerve gas – seconds mean unconsciousness, keep it on and they die," Francis said smugly. "Don't let them bother your pretty little head. But maybe you'll end up in a cell alongside them.

"Now tell me, Kaiser, whose idea was it to blow up Nordvelt? Was it Papa? Did your father tell you to put that envelope on the door?"

"My father is a good man," he said automatically.

"Yeah, right, a good man with an arrest-record as long as my arm. Fourteen times held for Breach of Contract. Assault and breach of the peace, mostly. A good man indeed."

I had to give Kaiser credit for not rising to the

provocation. He just sat there, arms so tight across his chest that he looked as if he might break himself in half.

"You can speak to this paragon of virtue," Francis went on, "when you answer some questions, got that? Where did you get the envelope?"

Kaiser looked away and for a moment I thought he wasn't going to answer. "I was given it."

"By your father?"

"No." Cold as ice.

"By who?"

"Just someone."

"Come on, Kaiser. You can do better than that. You think we're gonna stop there? 'Oh, the boy was given a murder-weapon by someone. Guess that's all we're gonna get, we'll let him go now.' Bartelli, put out an all-points bulletin for 'just someone', okay? No. Don't think so. Who was this man, then?"

"…He wasn't anyone I've met before."

"So it was a man? Well, that's a start, right?" Francis grinned. "So tell me, boy – this man was a total stranger?"

"Yes."

"So a total stranger comes up to you and gives you an envelope, says 'take this to this apartment and pin it on his door' and you just go do it? I don't think so."

"He paid me."

The waitress came over and took my empty mug. She looked at me suspiciously as I angled my datapad away from her.

"…twenty credits," Kaiser was saying.

"Did you even bother asking what was in the envelope?"

"He said it was a present. I figured him for some faggot."

Francis laughed – big, belly-shaking fake laughs. He wiped a finger under an eye. "A faggot, huh? Very good. Okay, Kaiser, we'll leave that for a moment. Tell me, what did this man look like?"

The boy shrugged and looked away.

"Look, you want to be out of here, right? At the moment I'm prepared to believe you. Prepared to believe that you were just running a little errand – yes, I'll even believe it was a total stranger who approached you. But you're not blind, kid. I wanna know what this man looked like. Was he black, white? Tall? Clean-shaven? Tell me this and we can move on."

Kaiser took a deep breath. "He was white. Big."

"Does 'big' mean tall or fat?"

Kaiser shifted in his seat. "Both. Not fat but... big."

"Big," Francis repeated. "Okay. What else?"

"He had a beard."

"How old?"

"I didn't ask the age of his beard." The boy smiled with bitter triumph, satisfied at getting one over his interrogator. "He was old. A man."

"How old?"

"I don't know. Just old."

"Old like me or Bartelli? Older? Younger?"

"About... a little younger than my father."

"God, you must think I'm fu- I'm fricking ancient," Francis muttered. "Hair?"

"Black. Crew-cut. Or it had been."

Lewinskiy, I thought, was big, had a soldier's haircut and a beard. And no need to worry about alibis if he'd left Kaiser to plant the bomb.

"Good. Good," Francis was saying. "Anything else you remember about him?"

"I didn't stare at him! I didn't write down a description! He was offering me money for a simple job! I took his damn credits and took his damn envelope and left. We only spoke for, like, two minutes!"

"Did he have an accent?"

"I don't know! I'm telling you I don't know!"

"Okay, Kaiser, calm down, calm down. Anything else you want to tell us?"

"No."

"Anything you think you *should* tell us?"

"No," the boy hissed.

Francis stared at him for a long time. "Very well. We'll get you to reconstruct the face and then…"

I switched off the playback. Leaned back in my vinyl chair.

How truthful had the boy been? I couldn't see his eyes, couldn't gauge his body-language as well as Francis or Bartelli, but…

I considered his story. Nothing inherently implausible about it. Just… for someone determined not to tell the security team anything at all, he'd actually given a pretty good description.

Of someone who'd tried to kill me once. Or at least, I thought, striving at least in the privacy of my own head to be as scrupulous as possible, had been involved with people who had tried to kill me.

Francis was right – Mithu, his father, was the obvious candidate. The man hated me. I thought back to when he'd charged into the security centre – after the video of the Company massacre had come to light. He'd gone straight for me. For him I *was* the police. I was the Company.

So Mithu had the motive.

But I wanted it to be Lewinskiy. That man… just in too many odd places at too many odd times. He was a loose end, a scab I couldn't help but pick at. I wanted to see whether it was blood or pus beneath.

Did Lewinskiy have a motive? God, I just *didn't know*. He was up to something. He was up to something, and I just didn't know what, or with whom. Was he acting for Gísladóttir? Why would she want me dead?

I checked my messages. Far too many of them. Orders from Francis, insisting that I return to the office. I ignored them. A note from Bartelli. One from somebody called Michael Nguyen asking for a meeting. Max, Maggie, Ferraldi, Weng – they'd all been in touch, all wanted something from me.

I felt heart-sick, cold. Everybody wanted something from me. I felt... I felt, just for a moment, a dislocation, a sociopathy.

Just for a moment, I could feel what my father must have felt. A disdain, a hatred for the rest of the world.

I shivered.

It was time to move on.

* * *

I spent two days hiding. Two days wandering the blocks aimlessly, sleeping each night in a different room. Simple for me, with my security access and training, to find an unoccupied apartment and override the locks. I'd walk into a bare room and walk out next morning, the stubble on my scalp the only indication of progress.

I didn't know what to do.

I'd spoken to everyone I could think of, didn't have any evidence to look at. I needed to go to the jail, but I wasn't the man to brave it on my own – not when a suspected arsonist and murderer was holed up in there.

When thinking got too much for me I'd retreat into the forums and watch an uneasy peace spread. Baurus' critics had taken to sniping with words rather than bullets. Maybe

– maybe – a little more time and the winter would lift and all this would be forgotten.

Until Ferraldi submitted his report. But I'd be well out of the city by then.

When had I decided to leave?

When the two sides had developed. When they'd demanded I join one camp or the other. Sick of them both, I was. I just wanted out.

And then the equilibrium was shattered.

Twenty

I was back in the Company bar, drinking coffee, keeping low, keeping dark. I was counting the days until winter ended. Wondering what sort of career I'd end up with after this failure went on my record.

I was staring absently across the floor, seeing but not seeing. It was quiet, early afternoon. An early drinker – judging by his grimy brow and leaden movements a shift-worker – was leaning heavily on the bar. A few quiet couples sat at tables. No-one spoke – or at least I could hear no voices. It was a dead kind of day, the doldrums of the city.

My datapad cheeped with a new message but I ignored it. I'd been ignoring a lot over the last few days.

Then the viewscreen above the bar, the one that usually played sports feeds from distant continents, snapped into life. I got a front-row seat.

The elements were there immediately. The sombre, dull room with two rows of chairs. A central raised dais set before a large rendering of the Company logo; another on the lectern before it. A woman stood there. She wore a dark suit – serious, professional. Lines creased her forehead as she frowned down at a man stood before her. He was painfully thin, dressed in little more than rags. He kept casting around him as if he wasn't quite sure where he was.

The image blurred and swam momentarily. I wondered who was filming this.

"Pedros Viella Gonzales," a man said. He was standing

next to the thin man. "Habitual criminal, fifteen counts of Breach of Contract – mostly theft, some criminal damage, one recorded instance of reckless endangerment."

"I – I only –" the man before the lectern stammered, "I only try to survive, to –"

"And what brings him before us today?" The woman's voice wasn't unfriendly; the vowels were cultured, educated. But there was dispassion there. Any warmth was towards the man reading the charges, not the accused.

"Arrested –"

"I just trying to feed my fam'ly!"

"– in a raid on a seditious meeting lead by separatist rebels."

"Please, we're just talking! Just talk, yes? Just talk!"

"Psych report?"

"It'd probably take twenty years' training to get him up to a decent grade."

"A candidate for reconditioning?"

"It's what I'd do." The official smiled at his superior.

"Please!" Gonzales wept, "please, I jus' want my –"

"Send him down, then," the woman said, tapping at her datapad. "Bring in the ne-"

Gonzales gave an anguished cry; the camera shook again as he leapt forwards, away from restraint, and ran for a door in the side of the room.

Then he screamed; a noise that began as agony before rising almost above human hearing and finally descending into a long, slow keening as he fell twitching onto the plush carpet.

The camera panned back to the officials. The woman looked more bored than upset. She beckoned for an attendant to drag the man out. Her aide held some sort of weapon lightly at his side. It looked like a baton with its hard, matte-plastic exterior and long black haft. The man wore a satisfied smile. He holstered the device easily and turned away, bringing up his datapad as another tattered man was shoved into position before the podium –

– jump cut. Now you're walking along a gantry in an industrial unit, almost like something from the Soviet era. The camera's held awkwardly at thigh-height. You're following a group; two men dressed as medics pushing a gurney – and on it the still form of Gonzales. His face lolls around as the trolley grates over the rough metal. The camera's even more unstable than it'd been in the previous scene. Something small and hand-held? A secret recording?

There's an official walking next to you. He's saying – it's hard to make out over the surrounding noise, but it sounds as if he's saying something about... about it being safe. Harmless, that's a word you can pick out. Proven. They speak in English, of course. Everybody does.

The gurney crashes onto a lift. You step on alongside. You're facing the person you were talking to. Mostly you can see his crotch. He dresses to the left. His buttons are well-worn brass.

The lift descends. Gonzales mutters something in his sleep. Bad trip, man.

The ground floor is more like a medical facility that a factory, but in truth there isn't that much to distinguish them. Big engines – computers, maybe, or scanners – are regimented along the floor. Dials, buttons, readouts – the way the camera's turning it's impossible to gain any sort of understanding.

Gonzales is moved efficiently along the side of the hall. You pass other technicians and doctors on the way. No-one gives you a second glance.

The man at your side gestures to one of the machines. It's your destination.

There is a pause as the medics hook their way into

Gonzales' skin. Small, delicate cuts carried out with the precision of men who've done this too many times before. Gonzales twitches, moans, but remains unconscious. Finally his head is roughly shaved and a skull-cap eased on. The two medics lift him bodily onto a padded bench. One stays by him whilst the other crosses to a control-panel. He presses a few buttons and the bench slowly withdraws into the large machine. Gonzales goes with it, carried unresisting into the heart of the device.

There is a pause. The medics relax. The technician —

— jump cut. A room, empty, functional; just a simple table with three people sitting behind. It seems as if the camera has been stuck to the wall. You look down at the backs of the officials, see them playing with their pads as they wait.

An interview panel. Like the one that sent you to Australis in the first place.

A door opens and a man is escorted inside. He walks confidently, relaxed. His eyes are alert. His bald scalp shines beneath the lights.

It's Gonzales.

"Well," the man in the middle of the panel says. "Your name?"

"Pedros Viella Gonzales." He stands smartly before the table.

"Tell me, Mr Gonzales, why do you think you're here?"

He frowns. "I'm interviewing for a job. At the maize plant in Falcón?"

"Good, good." He makes a little note on his pad. "Well, this is just a little prelim. Nothing to worry about."

"Tell me," says the woman at the far end of the table, "how do you feel about the Company?"

Gonzales is still puzzled. "The Company? Well... the Company is everything, isn't it? It gives us..." He gestured vaguely, flapping an arm in a roughly circular motion.

"Yes?"

"It gives us everything, right? I mean, without it we'd... I can't imagine a world without it, to be honest."

"So," the man closest to you puts in, "would you say that the Company has been good for the world? Or bad? Indifferent, maybe?"

"Oh, it's been good. No doubt. Without the Company..." he shakes his head.

The man in the middle looks to the woman, then to the other man. His eyebrow is raised. He gets slight nods from both. "Very well, Mr Gonzales. That's all. Please proceed through the door at the end — yes, that's it — for your interview."

Gonzales gives one last confused look then heads in the direction indicated.

The video ends. The screen goes black.

* * *

The music that provided a constant background in this place had never seemed so intrusive, so... wrong.

I came back to myself by degrees; objects slowly became real, solid. I saw things in series: the viewscreen I was facing; the dark grain of the fake-wood table before me; my pad still in my hand; the empty cup with a dun stain just inside the rim.

And then the bar. The *artificial*. The fake carpets, fake metal, fake music, fake glass. Fake culture.

My mind was still holding the meaning of what I'd seen from me. It was there, I knew it, I could feel it... but I didn't want it.

Someone coughed. Apart from that, apart from the ridiculous music, there was silence.

I exhaled. Slowly.

Everybody needs somebody, crooned the singer, sultry, indeterminate sex, *and I need to be with you tonight*.

I didn't know the truth of what I'd seen. I didn't know... I didn't know what I'd seen, not for sure.

My datapad cheeped, and cheeped again.

Someone got up and walked out of the bar. Their footsteps were almost imperceptible on the soft floor.

The shift-worker left a few moments later.

I knew what they'd be saying. Not now, not straightaway, but soon. When they were alone. When they were with friends. On the servers and the forums.

Didn't know what I'd seen, but I knew what it looked like.

I picked up my datapad, glanced at the screen, then set it back down. I got up, the scraping of my chair the loudest thing I'd heard for years. I went to the bar. If the establishment had been nearly empty before then it was dead now.

The barman saw me and came over. He wouldn't meet my eye.

"Brandy," I said. "The good stuff."

He turned and fumbled with a bottle. It was as if his wrists wouldn't work properly, as if his skeleton was slowly melting. He tried to pour once, twice, then gave up and stuck a glass and the bottle in front of me. "It's Nordvelt, isn't it? From Security? Here, you can serve yourself," he said. "I don't care anymore." He oozed away.

Heavy gold invaded my nostrils. I watched the barman's back for a moment, then sloshed a healthy measure into the glass.

I should have downed it, like a cowboy, or like some Scotch Laird, rich in his power. Instead I took a sip, sweet acid etching my throat. I stood for a moment longer, then took the bottle back to my table.

Twenty-One

I became invisible.

All my messages were about the video. I scanned subject lines but didn't read them.

I drank slowly, yearning for the oblivion of drunkenness and yet desperately needing to keep alert. For an hour or so I sat in an empty bar. Then the doors swung open and a party of around twenty came in. They wore the same simple clothes of the miner who'd been in earlier, carried themselves as if their muscles were steel.

They were uneasily quiet. Barely said a word between them as they scuffed to the bar. When no-one came to serve them they helped themselves; stood around or stumbled to tables, groups fragmenting.

There wasn't any anger, not then.

I found their presence comforting. I wasn't alone in the shock, the numbness. They gave me the strength to take up my pad and skim the forums.

Throughout Australis people had simply left their jobs and gone home. They'd done as I had, as these miners with their small conversations were doing. They tried to understand.

The Company was the great plank on which we all stood. It had been there all our lives. It had fed us, clothed us, entertained us, used us, buried us. No-one Company-born could imagine life without it. It was our father, our mother, our God.

What was it Ferraldi had said? It was time for new Gods.

Baurus had acted quickly – unusually so, by his standards – and released a statement. "People of Australis – I, like you, have seen the video that was released onto the forums today. Like you, I am shocked and alarmed by the implications of what I saw. Please rest assured that my team and I are doing all in our power to trace the source of this recording. Like you, we are seeking the veracity of what was shown. I ask you, in the name of all we're trying to achieve here, to remain calm. Continue to do your jobs. We will get to the bottom of this.

"Thank you for your co-operation."

I wondered if he really thought that would help.

Time passed. Steadily the anger bubbled up, rising to the surface like the kraken, reaching out its tentacles to drag down the fishers of hope.

Soon the question was asked: how many?

How many people here have gone through the process that had transformed Gonzales?

Mithu, with his anti-Company diatribes, had never appeared so credible.

People had been trickling into the bar, arriving in small groups; the type of people who needed others in order to see themselves. They mingled freely, although eyes weren't met. Conversation was gentle, muttered.

Gradually the room filled – nearly half capacity, now. I saw people making note of the drinks they were taking so as to repay later; honest folk, even under the most trying of circumstances. Or maybe they were just afraid of repercussions.

I topped up my glass. I'd got through nearly half the bottle. The liquid no longer burnt but kissed as it slid down. I thought, guiltily, that I too should be recording how much I owed the bar. But then I shrugged and carried on. I could afford to make good, if there was any good to be made.

In these strange circumstances I suppose a fight was inevitable.

The miners – I don't blame them, but they'd been here longest and the drink gone furthest. They were first to anger.

The people here were barely talking but they had been interacting in cyberspace. A group stood at the bar, each individual frowning at their datapad. A man turned to his neighbour; he spoke, then jabbed at his screen. Curious, I tried to find something new, something inflammatory, on my own datapad but there was too much chatter on the forums. Impossible to pick out an unnamed individual.

Now the noise, the temperature, was building. Sides became to coalesce. At almost every table faces drew bitter and pleas were ignored. I couldn't hear properly, the background music – as if things were normal – the welter of voices, the cotton in my brain... I couldn't hear, but my eyes were working fine. The snarls on lips, the pointing fingers...

Finally the undercurrents began to take physical shape. Arguments became heated and groups splintered; the minority view, whichever that was, would leave and drift until they found others of their own kind – a sort of covalent bonding, alchemical magic.

I saw that the impassioned ones were winning. The ones that seemed more governed by reason, were more cautious, were outnumbered nearly two to one. Supporters of the wait-and-see, the status quo. Baurus' supporters by default.

The angry ones? They supported no-one but themselves and their sense of betrayal.

The punches weren't long in following.

The set-up was almost comical. I couldn't help of *West Side Story* – two gangs posturing pathetically before me. I knew I should intervene, should call Jawad or Bartelli and bring in the security services. Should act as intermediary, try and calm the two sides down. But I was invisible. Ethereal. I didn't feel like I was there at all.

I did nothing. Didn't move a muscle, save to raise the glass to my lips, again and again and again.

The fight was lacklustre, almost an afterthought, a duty. Punches, kicks, tables overturned and glasses broken. There was blood, and there was yelling. And it lasted a long time, as these things are reckoned; most fights are just one, maybe two blows. This went on for minutes and at times resembled more a game of kabaddi than a real scrap.

The bar was almost empty again when Bartelli arrived with a small team – Alexandros, scanning the room nervously, and a couple of the new guys whose names I hadn't got down yet. The few people remaining in conflict were quickly separated; Bartelli, looking as tired as I'd ever seen the man, took names and sent them on their way.

I was invisible. No-one so much as glanced at me.

My hand found the neck of the bottle and refilled my glass.

The bar was empty, now, save for my old colleagues. Bartelli gestured to his men and they went to seal off the bar, close all exits, make sure no-one else could help themselves to booze. From some twenty yards away I watched the shabby little man roll his head around his shoulders and lean on the bar. His moustache seemed to be weighing him down.

Alexandros reappeared. All was clear, the building secure and empty. Bartelli waved him out, then shuffled round to the staff-side of the counter. He disappeared behind the bar, and then the lights started to go out. The music stopped: its abrupt disappearance shocked me. As if I'd thought I was deaf only to realise I'd been wearing ear-plugs the whole time.

In seconds the only light left on was by the main entrance. I heard Bartelli shambling across the carpet, a little cough and the sound of him blowing his nose. Then his bent figure entered the pool of light.

Alexandros had a quiet word with him, and Bartelli waved his team out of the building. He stayed where he was and took a long look around the smashed interior of the bar.

He seemed to be looking right at me. He raised his right arm and gave a lazy salute. Then he turned and left.

He was no fool, Bartelli.

* * *

I slept in the bar. I let myself slump onto one of the padded benches, gave my body some time. I wasn't hungover when I woke, which was a relief, but my neck ached from the unnatural posture. I was chilled. It was dark, still only the one light glowing.

I stumbled to the toilets, then took a juice from the bar. Drank it down greedily, took another. I wiped the drips away from my stubble. Wiped the sleep from my eyes.

Today... I'd had enough hiding. Whatever holes had been left in me had been patched with chainmail. I was ready to go to battle.

And I was doing it for myself. For myself and for Jackson, for Guder, for Rampaul. I was going to find this bomber. I was going to do it. Or I would break myself in the process.

But I didn't rush out. I took my time, breakfasted on stolen crisps and nuts. I didn't feel guilt at the theft. Part of me wondered if I should.

Time to review the evidence. I skimmed through the forums, trying to take the pulse of the city. The anger was currently being kept down by confusion – the 'wait-and-see'-ers bolstered by sleep. I wondered how many of the people still calling for action had been up all night.

Still, it seemed as if nobody was going in to work today. Maggie had her strike after all – but not for the reasons she's wanted.

There was nothing from Mithu, or the Exiles. That seemed odd.

Whilst I read, a plan came slowly to mind. Two calls. Two calls, and then out into the wilderness.

It was time to go and get Lewinskiy.

Twenty-Two

Bartelli came first. I was waiting for him at the garage – I'd got him to arrange the vehicle. It seemed easier, given my uncertain status, to have a definite serving policeman make the request.

Even in his green-scaled warmsuit and all-encompassing mask, it was clearly Bartelli. No-one else could slouch like that.

"Sir," Bartelli said as he approached the four-by-four. "So what's the plan?"

I gave him a sort of mock-salute, trying to dispel some of the tension I was feeling. "We've one other person to wait for. Then we go and get Lewinskiy."

"You said. 'Go to the jail and get Lewinskiy.' Fine." He sighed, turned his head away. "If you don't want to tell me…"

"How are things at work?" I asked into the resulting silence.

He looked back sharply, then returned his attention to the floor. "Tiring. Francis, he has us… there is no leave, just overtime, overtime, overtime. Work and sleep is all there is."

"How were you able to sneak out for this?"

"I'm not asleep, am I?"

I was pierced suddenly with guilt. I hadn't thought…

But the anger seemed to have drained away as quick as it'd come. "We patrol all the time," Bartelli said. "We break up fights – can't arrest anyone 'cause we've no spare cells. Names, we collect names, we move people on, we tell them to get on with their work... We're already seven men short..."

"Guder, Jackson, Rampaul...?"

"Ramswani's left," Bartelli said, his voice barely audible in the great empty space of the garage. "And Sweeten – did you know him? – and Finch. Say they can't carry out Company orders at the moment. Francis – Mr Francis, he was... not happy at all."

"And the seventh?"

"You."

Ah. "I've not left, you know, not really... I'm still trying to find out who killed Guder. Just obeying my orders–"

"Not the orders you should be obeying."

"You think it's important to spy on Ferraldi whilst Guder's murderer is out there?"

"You're hiding while your colleagues are pulled apart!"

"What?"

Bartelli held up a hand, an apology, a peace. "Things are... not good right now. Kaiser Mithu's been sent home, by the way. Can't trace the man he described, not yet."

"You know that describes–"

"Lewinskiy. I'm not an idiot – of course I know! But where's your proof? Still, it's why I'm here."

A door thumped shut behind me. I spun round as sharp footsteps rolled towards us across the concrete. A confident figure, suited like us, was striding towards us. They wore a heavy-looking rucksack, looped easily across one shoulder.

"Gísladóttir?" I called.

"Nordvelt. Who's your friend?"

"Captain Gísladóttir, Sergeant Bartelli. Come on, let's get going."

We clambered in. I let Bartelli drive, made Gísladóttir

stay in back. Once the interior of the vehicle had warmed up a little I unclasped and drew off my mask with a sigh of relief. The others followed suit.

As Bartelli manoeuvred the four-by-four out of the building I sneaked a look back at Gísladóttir. Her blue eyes were as sharp and cold as the black city we were driving through. She made Bartelli look like a tired old teddy-bear, patched and sewn and missing half his stuffing.

We drove in silence until we were on the deserted ice-road that took us all the way to the prison. The windows showed only a few stars, pinpricks in the great expanse of nothing. Bartelli relied on the inboard computers to keep us true.

"How can Lewinskiy be at the prison?" Gísladóttir asked eventually. "Haven't you people there? What about your governor, what was his name…?"

"Augustin. I don't know. I called him before the two of you. I was just told he was busy, unavailable."

"So there is a staff there?"

"There should be people working there. I think there's a team of a dozen, plus a couple of medics for N'Gepi, that split the shifts."

"You didn't give any clue that we were coming? Or why you were calling?"

"No."

"Good."

"So what," Bartelli asked, "are we expecting to find? You say Ferraldi's bodyguard was with Lewinskiy when you saw them in the Comms Building? Might be they just be meeting someone at the jail? Doing a check on the prisoners?"

"Late at night, after a clandestine meeting?"

He shrugged before taking one hand off the controls to gesticulate. "Ferraldi is investigating the city, yes? Why not check this unlicensed bar? Why not send someone out to check the prison? Need to see the night shift does their jobs properly too." His moustache flexed.

"It's possible," I said reluctantly.

Gísladóttir sniffed. Silence fell again.

"So what are we going to do when we get there?" she said about twenty minutes later. "Are we going to just roll up to the front door and ask for my man?"

"Do you have a better idea?"

"Is there another way in?"

"It's a prison. No, there is no other way in."

"You say you have evidence to link Lewinskiy with Guder's death?" she asked.

I shifted in my seat. "He has questions to answer. There've been too many coincidences involving him."

"And that's why Captain Gísladóttir is here with us?" Bartelli said. "Because he is under her command?"

"Yes." *And because, sadly, I'm not sure I can trust either of you fully.*

Bartelli was nodding slowly. "And say you're right, sir. If Lewinskiy is the killer. What's to stop him killing all of us – just shoot us as soon as we get out of the car?"

"I'm hoping that the three of us will be able to subdue one man."

"You're hoping?" He smiled humourlessly. "What if it's not just one man? What if there's a whole squadron of UN soldiers there just waiting for us?" He glanced back at Gísladóttir.

"There's no way they could hope to keep our deaths quiet," I said before she could snap back. "They don't know who else knows where we're going. They won't dare harm us."

The rest of the journey was spent in silence.

* * *

We rolled up to the front gates. They opened for us soundlessly. A few miles back we'd got a call from the prison, demanding to know who we were and why we were coming. I'd told the truth as to our identity – no way they'd have let us in without proving ourselves – but all I'd say beyond that was that we needed to see Augustin urgently.

The passageway through the walls was wide and high, but there was only blackness beyond, like we were entering the mouth of a great dragon. I was immediately thrown back to the age of the castle, as if we were riding our white steeds into some recalcitrant baron's demesne. And then the courtyard lights snapped out and we were blind.

Gradually the lights dimmed – that or I just accustomed quickly. And the image of the castle reappeared as I realised we'd entered a courtyard. High walls towered over us, whilst the main buildings of the prison lay scowling before us.

Bartelli eased the four-by-four along, parking beside a dark staff-bus. Silently, a last glance passing between us, we got out. We cast long shadows in every direction as we crossed to reception. Gísladóttir's rucksack made her look like a hunchback.

A smartly-dressed young woman greeted us just inside. She tried to smile. "S-Sergeant Nordvelt? I was told to come meet you…"

I took off my mask. At each shoulder I was dimly aware of my companions doing the same.

"Unfortunately Mr Augustin is busy right now. I'm sorry you've had a wasted trip –"

"Busy doing what?" I asked.

"He-he's not on base, he's…"

I smiled at her. She wasn't capable of playing this game

and we both knew it.

"...I-I think – let me just go and check–"

She turned and all but ran through a door in the corner.

"Do we follow her, you think?" I asked.

"I think we do," Bartelli said.

We strolled after her. We were in no rush.

God, this felt good. Nothing like a little bullying and intimidation to dispel the doubts.

I am a horribly cynical man.

The door led us into a corridor. The sound of footsteps guided us along to the end. We walked it as if we owned the place. We saw nobody. The doors we passed were heavy, yes, but this looked more like an office than a prison.

But of course, the main business of the site was carried out underground. I spared a thought for the fifteen war-criminals below our feet – the only long-term residents at present.

We reached another door. It swung open easily and, in a large cold room with a large set of doors at the far end that I guessed led back into the wastes. A third door was to our right. And in the middle of this space, obviously the start of the real business-end of the prison, the young lady we'd been talking to was having an anxious conversation with Augustin.

The warden was a short man, faintly ridiculous with a wispy beard and gut that looked like they should belong to a committed pipe-smoker. He spun round to face me, mouth slightly open as if about to kiss. I smiled warmly at him.

"Warden Augustin. A pleasure to see you again."

"Sorry, have we...?" he stammered. "What – Officer Gísladóttir–"

He recognised her from a mere glance a week or so ago.

"Where is Private Lewinskiy?" Gísladóttir asked.

Credit Augustin for trying to gain some control. He didn't

reply immediately, took a moment to draw breath, straighten his shoulders and turn to fully face us. "I'm sorry?"

"We know Lewinskiy's here," I said. "Or do you want us to search every room in the complex? You're welcome to accompany us. You can explain anything unusual that we might... happen upon."

"You... you have no right!" Augustin said. "You can't just come in here, and – and–"

"Whether or not he can do it, he is here now." The new voice sent me spinning round. There was Ferraldi, smiling his smile of ages, just inside the door that we'd come through. Collins, the African with the sinuous walk, was at his shoulder.

Instinctively I took a step back. But Ferraldi's head was slightly bowed; he seemed apologetic rather than angry.

"Warden Augustin," he said, "please will you show Captain Gísladóttir and Sergeant Bartelli where they can find Private Lewinskiy. Yes, he is here. I'll be curious to know how you traced him, but we can talk about that later. I think it might be an idea if myself and Senior Sergeant Nordvelt had a little talk, mm?"

"We should stay together," Gísladóttir hissed.

I didn't take my eyes off Ferraldi. I hadn't expected – but I *should* have been expecting him to be here, shouldn't I? Where else would Collins go but back to his master? And what did that mean for Lewinskiy's part in all this?

I watched the tall man's benevolent brown eyes. I couldn't... I couldn't see why he'd get me away from the others just to attack me. They had access to the entire security network of the prison: nerve gas, graded to knock-out and to kill, electrified doors and floors and God knew what else. And then there was Collins, the bodyguard. I shifted my gaze to his. He grinned.

If they wanted us dead we already would be.

But what if they did to me – or to Bartelli, or Gísladóttir – what had been done to Gonzales?

"No," I said. "It's fine. Bartelli, get Lewinskiy. Charge with murder and attempted murder."

"Military law takes precedence," Gísladóttir contradicted, but she allowed herself to be led off without further protest. I had to trust that they'd bring Lewinskiy in under one jurisdiction or the other.

I'd started to look away; I nearly missed the change in expression on Ferraldi's face. The smile had gone. The mouth had fallen open just slightly – but then it was gone, his Adam's apple bobbing as he swallowed.

"Very well," he said. "Augustin, show them down. Mr Nordvelt – if you'd accompany me? Best put your mask back on, I think."

I nodded to Bartelli and Gísladóttir, then followed Ferraldi and Collins back the way we'd come.

* * *

We left the admin building and crossed the courtyard to the Warden's house. Not a word was said as we went. I knew to put my mask on. I knew how to wait.

Collins strode ahead to get the door and held it open for us. I couldn't shake the idea that he was grinning at me behind his mask.

Collins and Ferraldi stripped off their warmsuits in the vestibule inside. I kept mine on. They led me downstairs into a needlessly rustic interpretation of a house. A fake log fire burned endlessly, the flames never really touching the charred timbers. The lights hung low over replicas of solid-wood furniture. Ferraldi's taste, or Augustin's? At least this wasn't the laboratory, the factory, I'd secretly feared.

I took the offered armchair with its ridiculous patterned fabric. Ferraldi took the seat opposite, facing me across the fire. Collins remained standing.

"A drink, Sergeant?" Ferraldi said pleasantly.

"Thank you, no."

He nodded to Collins, who carefully shut the door behind him as he left. His absence reassured me – I wasn't comfortable with that silent little man around. Not that I was under any illusions that he'd gone far. That I wasn't being watched.

"So," Ferraldi said, "you found where I was hiding Lewinskiy. Satisfy my curiosity – how did you know that?"

"Why are you here? I thought you had an office in the city."

He shrugged, head seeming to bob down between his bony shoulders. "I do. Mikhail runs it – you can check our staff lists if you like. It's our point of contact for the citizens. You know why we're in Australis, after all."

"Do I?"

He smiled. I felt like a stubborn child.

"As for why I'm here," he went on, "I thought it best if I have a base of operations... a little out of the way. In case..."

"Yes?"

"I'm not too sure how long it'll be before Baurus – or perhaps your good friend Mr Francis – decides I'm a problem that can be removed."

"Baurus would never do that."

He raised an eyebrow. "No? Maybe not. You know him better than me. Can you say the same for Francis? In any case, I've seen too much, been in too many... uncomfortable situations, not to take precautions."

"What's your connection with Lewinskiy?"

Ferraldi steepled his hands in front of his mouth and looked at his fingers reflectively. "He's my agent."

"What?"

"He's my agent. I was looking for someone to... do a job for me."

"Like plant a bomb?"

"No, no, nothing like that! I..." He sighed. Looked at me earnestly. "You're talking about the... incident that resulted in Officer Guder's death, aren't you?"

"And in the maiming of Officer Jackson. And my attempted murder – an attempt that left another of my officers in hospital." The bitterness flowed off my tongue, but Ferraldi merely looked sad. The dancing flames reflected in one deep eye, the other invisible in shadow.

"I was sorry to hear about that," he said quietly. "I promise you, I knew nothing – if Lewinskiy is a suspect – I had no idea."

"So you didn't order him to remove me?"

"No, Sergeant Nordvelt, I – I would never–"

"Then you'd better tell me why, how and when he came to be acting as your 'agent'. And what he was doing on your behalf."

Ferraldi nodded and wound his long fingers together. "Where to begin... I travel with a skeleton crew. Just Collins and Mikhail. It's nothing out of the ordinary, I've done this many times before. I have a brief. I have to give a full account of the workings of Australis. I am the oversight – small 'o'."

"I know all–"

"But I cannot complete this task alone. As soon as I arrive I have to hire new staff. This is all standard procedure; it is expected and accounted for. You can see my records."

"Lewinskiy?"

"This time... the situation is unique. I arrive on the last

train in – no-one enters or leaves the city until the summer. Suddenly here are a group of bored United Nations soldiers looking for something to do. So I hired one or two of them."

"'One or two'. To do what?"

"To be waiters," he said with a tight smile. "To be dogsbodies. To move furniture. Little jobs like that. A few credits for them, a job done for me."

"But…"

He held up a hand. "But Lewinskiy. The fact is that I was after… a bit more. And he struck me as the kind of intelligent, motivated man who –"

"Who didn't mind a bit of moonlighting?"

Ferraldi smiled again. "Indeed. A certain… self-interest."

"So what did you have him do?"

"You have to understand what I'm here for, Mr Nordvelt. I work for the Company. I want the best for the Company – and for humankind. And I want to be fair – yes, I want to be fair to Baurus. As I said, questions have been raised. But my report is not yet written.

"People come to me all the time. To me, or to Mikhail in the city. A lot of people want to tell me what's going on–"

"You mean you have your sources of information."

He bowed his head to me. "I have my sources. They've made me aware of certain bodies that–"

"Please, Mr Ferraldi, stop talking around the subject. What are you trying to say?"

"I knew of the strike that your friend Maggie was planning. I wanted it stopped. I sent out Collins to talk for me. I sent out Lewinskiy to speak as a UN representative."

"Is he anything of the sort?"

Ferraldi smiled tightly. "What do you think?"

"Why did you want the strike stopped?"

"You're still under the impression that I'm here to force Baurus out. I'm not. I'm here to see to the good running of the city. And to make Australis work better. A strike is in nobody's interests."

"So Gísladóttir knew nothing?"

"Gísladóttir?"

"She didn't send Lewinskiy to you?"

"Are you saying that Lewinskiy might have been reporting to her? I must say, I'd not considered the possibility…" He frowned, deep brows drawing together.

"And that's it? That's all you've got to tell me?"

"What more did you want to know?"

"What do you know of the videos that have been released on the servers?"

"No more than you. It's shocking, shocking… I don't know what to say."

"Is the Company responsible for massacres?" I felt hard, cold despite the fire and my warmsuit.

He shook his head helplessly, shadows ebbing and flowing across his face. "How can I answer that? Before I saw – yes, I've seen the videos and I'm as horrified as anyone. Before I saw them I'd have dismissed the idea as preposterous. But how can I doubt the evidence of my own eyes? There must be an inquiry. But I can't see what's happening on the other side of the world. I'm just one man – a small cog in a great machine. Like you, Mr Nordvelt, I am only a pawn."

I frowned. No man liked to be called a pawn, no matter how true it may be. "I see you more as a bishop," I said.

He smiled at that.

"And the – the second video?"

He shook his head again. "That is… that is even more disturbing. That process… the… the *conditioning* of civilians? It shakes your whole world-view, doesn't it?"

"You've never been aware of it going on?"

"If I ever was it's been purged from my memory."

Another humourless smile.

"What do you plan to do about it?"

"Ask a lot of questions when I get back to Brasilia. But we both know I'm stuck here until the equinox. I'm sure Baurus has reported it. Hopefully an investigation is already underway."

Silence fell between us. The fire crackled. Behind him Ferraldi's shadow seemed to be pecking at something as he nodded his head slowly.

My datapad cheeped. Bartelli and Gísladóttir were waiting.

Collins was back in the room before I'd fully stood. He waited at the door, a ghost's smile in the gloom. Ferraldi presented me with an open, attentive expression.

"It is good we got to talk again, Mr Nordvelt. I hope I was able to put your mind at some sort of ease."

I hesitated. There were so many more questions to ask... but I couldn't marshal them at that moment. "I may need to talk to you again, Mr Ferraldi."

"Of course. You know how to find me."

I was at the door with Collins waiting to lead me out before I turned back again. "What precisely is your relationship with Warden Augustin, Mr Ferraldi?"

"Well, I told you I needed a place—"

"You could have gone through channels and we'd have ordered him to put you up. But you didn't do that."

"No. You're right. I paid him to keep quiet."

I mused on this as Collins led me back upstairs. Another man on the take. I'd thought that the Company had ended corruption, the hideous self-interest of the last days of the nation states. The Resource Wars that had brought the fifteen prisoners, eventually, to this very place.

God, I was so naïve.

And would I have done any differently? If a Company

man – a superior – had asked me for a quiet place to work in secrecy... If I agreed with his aims, would I have refused a few extra credits to cover my time and inconvenience?

The Company wasn't the problem. Humankind was.

I thought again of the factory in the video, of Gonzales' transformation.

I pulled on my mask and walked back out into the night.

Twenty-Three

Lewinskiy was in the back seat of the four-by-four. Gísladóttir was standing next to the vehicle, mask off, exhaling great clouds of air into the floodlit courtyard. Bartelli was leaning against the vehicle.

"Any trouble?" I asked as I strode up to them.

"No..." Gísladóttir hesitated. "No trouble. But I did find another three of my men in there with Lewinskiy. Akineev, Okur and Fisher."

I grunted. The pair who'd pushed me out of the vestibule, naked against the night? Plus one other. I bit back a surge of anger. There was no room in this vehicle to bring them all into custody. One thing at a time. "Has Lewinskiy said anything?"

Gísladóttir shook her head. "Once Bartelli charged him – though I still say he should be under military jurisdiction, at least until I've seen the evidence – he said nothing but to ask for a lawyer. Can we get the hell out of this place now? We should be back in the city."

I sat next to Lewinskiy in the rear. He spent the entire journey staring straight forwards like – well, like the soldier he was. I studied his face carefully, or at least the side I could see. He spared me the odd glance; he was listening, obviously. But his jaw stayed shut, heavy black beard still.

The miles rolled by. Bartelli took a nap, leaving Gísladóttir to drive us home. I watched her neat precise hands, the set of her eyes. The light of the dashboard made her look pensive.

"Why did you try to kill me, Lewinskiy?" I asked at one point.

He flicked me an impassive look. "I'm not saying anything without a lawyer."

"You've no right to a lawyer," Gísladóttir snapped back. "You're serving in the United Nations army. Subject to military discipline."

The big man looked to her and then back to me. "So who's arresting me? The police of this ridiculous Goddamn village, or my commanding officer?"

"I am," I said firmly.

"Then I won't speak until I see my lawyer."

We spent the rest of the journey in silence.

* * *

Nothing in this world is ever simple.

Back in the garage: it would have been about midday but it's disconcerting, being out in the black. Makes you feel tired even though you should be wide awake. Bartelli, who'd been working all hours anyway, almost fell out of the four-by-four.

We left Lewinskiy in the vehicle for a moment and sorted out what was to be done. The suspect had to be taken in to the security centre, but that was the last place I wanted to be. What was Francis to be told?

We agreed that Gísladóttir would accompany them; she would say she was the one who found Lewinskiy. And she, as his superior officer, would represent him – would be his defence.

I was a little uneasy at that. Too many opportunities for

conspiracy. I frowned at her – pointless, as we were both masked – but couldn't think of a way to prevent it. She was his commanding officer. She did have the right.

She and Bartelli escorted the cuffed prisoner to the nearest vestibule and disappeared. I was left staring after them. The adrenaline had gone. My arm ached, a curt reminder of the break that was in its final stages of healing.

Even in the warmsuit I felt cold in this dark, empty garage. I hurried to the vestibule and got changed.

* * *

No-one was at their work. There were too many ghosts in the machine – little acts of sabotage or obstruction – not so much, I thought, to cause damage as to register discontent. *I am not going to let the situation pass. I will accidentally erase a day's work from the computer logs. I will forget to take the office datapad off the incinerator chute. I will set the drilling machine off at slightly the wrong angle.* From the petty to the less petty. Hundreds of little protests snowballing into days-worth of lost effort. All deniable. All of which would have to be investigated and accounted for and corrected.

The corridors were crowded with people doing nothing, just muttering sullenly amongst themselves. They gathered most thickly in the atria that centred every block. I walked deliberately, avoiding their gazes. The air was tense. I witnessed loud arguments that were paused as soon as a stranger passed, only to resume when they'd – I'd – gone by. There was an expectation in the echoes, an… an *anticipation*. People were waiting to be told what to do. Or to be told what not to do so they could disobey. It was haunting. It was frightening. I couldn't help but crane my neck around, to make sure no-one had recognised me, no-one was following me.

The crowd was thickest in the admin building. I caught a glimpse of Fergie there, talking with a group I vaguely recognised but couldn't name. Miners. Was Maggie in there? Would've been surprised if she wasn't.

I didn't want to be seen. Didn't want to be caught up, didn't want to be drawn into politics. Wanted to be invisible, anonymous, a nobody. But I had to go to the front of the crowd to get to my destination.

The door to the offices – Baurus' offices – was locked. I felt the pressure of the crowd at my back, watching me, muttering, speculating, judging.

"Nordvelt!" someone called. I ignored them, pressed the button for attention.

No-one answered. I glanced round, saw the faces all staring at me, felt a chill down my spine.

I turned back to the door and, quick as I could, entered my security override.

"Hey, Nordvelt, whose side you on?"

The door clicked open. I shouldered my way through.

"He's going in, come on –"

The sounds silenced immediately as the door closed on them. I heard the door latch once more – just before I felt the faux-wood shudder. I leaned back against it and felt the blows reverberate through me.

I straightened, wiping a hand across my brow. I was trembling. The ache in my arm was getting worse.

But I had something to do. I needed to speak to Unity.

Her secretary was a handsome young man; the sort of person who seemed born to be competent. I knew him enough to nod affably as I entered her working suite. "Is she free?" I asked with a gesture to the inner door.

The secretary smiled coolly. "I'll see if the United Nations representative is available." He pressed a button on his desk. "Miss Unity – Sergeant Nordvelt is here to see you," he said crisply.

He paused, listening to a reply that only he could hear. He pressed a finger to the clip on his ear.

He nodded, and to me he said, "She'll see you shortly. If you'd like to take a seat?"

She kept me waiting.

Ten minutes – I'd thought I'd be in and out by now. Fifteen. I shifted uncomfortably on my seat. It was the sort of chair you only ever seemed to find in receptions and waiting rooms. In front of me the secretary carried out his duties as if I weren't there. He tapped away at his viewscreen, made discrete phone-calls: the model of the modern hyperefficient adjutant.

I was really starting to hate him.

Twenty minutes.

Why was I even here? I had a lot better things to be doing with my time (did I? why couldn't I think of them?). Yeah, I had to watch Lewinskiy's interrogation. I should call Maggie, or Weng. Get the inside scoop, get the pulse of the city. Like the old *noir* detectives. I should be helping my colleagues keep order. Or I should be out there protesting. One or the other. God, I didn't even know whose side I was on anymore.

Half an hour. Forty minutes. Was she deliberately making me wait? Was this a message? So what the hell was she actually trying to say? Why, why, why was I so bad at this?

The secretary sent me in. I checked the clock. Forty-nine minutes. I couldn't quite bring myself to thank the smug, supercilious asshole.

Unity's hair hadn't been brushed properly. It flicked up

at the ends in a way I'd never seen before. She was sitting at her desk poring over some papers, barely gave me a glance as I shut the door behind me. The bonsai tree on her desk needed a trim.

"Unity," I said, unsure whether to sit or not.

"Senior Sergeant Nordvelt," she said coolly. She tapped her papers together and set them aside. "What can I do for you?"

"I..." What *did* I want? A smile would be nice. "I need information." But not, perhaps, as much as I needed a friend.

"And how is Captain Agnetha Gísladóttir?"

"That–" *as if you haven't guessed* – "is who I need information on."

"You've been getting close to her."

"We've been working together."

"That's not what I meant."

I stared at Unity. She stared back, inscrutable – except not as quite as inscrutable as normal. Little cracks; the imperfection in the hair; lipstick slightly askew; fingers tapping against her papers. "Are you okay?" I asked.

She took a breath. "I am fine," she said with perfect control. And just like that the little signs of weakness didn't seem to matter. "I've been busy. You've seen the videos. You think they wouldn't interest the United Nations? Of which, in case you have forgotten, I am representative here." She stood and turned to her bonsai tree, examining it with a frown.

I didn't know what to say.

"I have been trying to chase the source of that damn video. *Working!*" She held up a twig and severed it neatly with her knife. "What do you want to know?"

"If you trust her."

"You're sure this isn't personal?"

"There is nothing between me and Gísladóttir."

"I heard she was drunk and clinging to you the night of the bomb in your apartment."

How had she heard about that? Did she have a network of informers – like Ferraldi, like Francis – that reported to her every move in the city? "Look, Natsuko," I said, using her real name, "one of her men's been trying to kill me. I need to know if she's likely to have given him the order, or if he was acting alone."

She raised an eyebrow at me before returning to her horticulture. Another twig severed. "Agnetha Gísladóttir," she said. "Thirty-four years old. Captain in the United Nation Peacekeeping taskforce. Icelandic. In the army since she was eighteen. Reprimanded twice – once for being drunk on duty, the other for fraternising with a member of her command. Both infractions when she was a sergeant. High IQ. High potential. Impatient. Passed training programmes in leadership, light infantry tactics and battlefield medicine."

"That's all from her report?"

Unity nodded, removed another leaf.

"You can remember all that? You don't even have to check?"

She didn't deem that worthy of a reply.

"Have you met her?"

"She came to see me after she arrived. She is technically under my command whilst she's in the city."

"What are your personal impressions?"

She smiled bitterly. "That is definitely a question you can answer better."

"Natsuko, please."

She sighed and finally straightened. The light caught the blade of the knife as she toyed with it. She stared straight through me.

"Natsuko, do you think Gísladóttir is the kind of person

who might be on the take?"

"On the take?"

"Could be bribed."

"I'm not sure she has the imagination."

It was my turn to raise an eyebrow, but she said no more.

"Would you trust her?"

She took a long time in replying, staring at me with eyes that said nothing. "Yes."

I sighed. I'm not sure what I wanted her to say. I almost wished she'd said no – and from the look on her face it seemed that she did too. "Okay," I said. "Thank you."

"Was there anything else?"

"Lewinskiy."

"Private Leon Lewinskiy. Yes. Currently in your holding cells."

"He's claimed to be acting as UN representative–"

"Not under any authority I'm aware of."

"Good. I didn't think so. But good. Thank you." I opened my mouth, then closed it again. "You said you'd been looking into the video that started all the anti-Baurus sentiment–"

"It didn't start it. A lot of people have been unhappy with Baurus' orders for a long time."

"Stirred it up, then. Have you found anything?"

She frowned. "I have... made enquiries. I have talked to my superiors. They are yet to get back to me."

"So you have nothing?"

She flashed me a scowl. "I have also made enquiries... locally."

"And?"

"I'd advise you to talk with Michael Nguyen."

The name rang a bell with me, but I couldn't think where I'd heard it before. "And what would he tell me?"

"I don't know. That's why I advise you to see him."

Fine. "Where do you stand on Baurus and Ferraldi?" I asked.

"What is this — is this an interrogation?"

"I'm trying to find a killer," I snapped.

"You're just trying to prove yourself useful. To prove you are not your father's son."

I physically recoiled, looked at her in amazement. She did not back down, just stared right back.

"Baurus — Ferraldi — they are both Company men. As long as the United Nations has a presence here, their squabbles are irrelevant to me."

"You're not that naïve."

Again, the look she gave me was blank. I was going to change the subject, but then she spoke. Slowly.

"I would prefer... to put my trust in the devil I know."

I examined her carefully. Those little signs of strain I'd noticed when I'd come in — I saw them again. The wild hair. The ruck in her blouse. The way the papers were strewn over her desk. It wasn't like her. And it wasn't like her to say something like that — to be so clear. So unguarded. I desperately searched her for a sign of what she *really* meant, for I struggled to imagine her actually saying what she really meant.

I really, really wished I was better at this.

Her intercom chimed. "Miss Unity," her secretary's voice came. "Your three-thirty is here."

Natsuko drew herself straight. "That is all," she said. "I have work to do."

I stared at her for a long moment before I turned away.

* * *

I almost ran straight into Francis on my way out. He'd just passed Unity's office, deep in conversation with Baurus – the Mayor, the man himself. I hesitated for a moment, then followed.

Baurus wasn't an impressive man, not physically. Francis, tall and broad and heavy-set, dominated his superior. Francis' immaculately-pressed clothes made the Mayor look shabby in comparison. Even Baurus' walk looked dejected.

And Francis was dominating the conversation as well. He spoke earnestly, too soft for me to hear anything but that he *was* speaking. Each word was accompanied by a short chopping gesture, one pudgy hand slapping against the other. The Mayor's replies, when he could get them in, were completely inaudible, addressed to the floor more often than they were to his subordinate.

They didn't go far. To Baurus' office, his suite in the centre of the building. Francis reached over the Mayor to push open the door. They went inside, allowing me just a glimpse of the replica-rainforest that Baurus was growing. Another seeking peace in nature.

The door swung shut. I stood there for a moment, then turned and tried to remember if there was a rear exit. I didn't want to have to force my way back through the crowds.

Twenty-Four

I managed to escape the admin offices quietly and was looking for a quiet place to watch Lewinskiy's interrogation – part of the arrangement with Bartelli and Gísladóttir was that they'd stream me the interview footage – when my datapad cheeped. It was a message from Weng.

Science Block H, 16:30. An invited speaker is talking. You should be there.

It was just after four now. I summoned my mental map of the city. I could make it –

But should I? I had so many things to do, and part of me knew that what I needed more than anything else I needed a little time to just sit and think – or even just to not-think – for a while.

But it was Weng. I'd only ever turned her down once. And... I felt like she needed me. Like she was a kid sister.

She'd given me good advice so far. We all need our informers.

I turned towards the scientific section and picked up my pace.

The cold corridors – the murals painted on some sections somehow feeling like festering war-wounds rather then something to lift the spirit – were busy, but it wasn't the sort of busyness that I'd been used to. Before – before whatever it was that was happening here – the activity had been professional, businesslike. People would always be carrying things; pads, charts, goods. Now they were empty-handed. Back where I'd come from, there'd been all sorts of people lounging around, hands in pockets. Here, though, in the science department, there was more movement. There was a general drift of the crowd. All in the same direction I was going in.

I checked the time: no problem. I slowed. Gave myself more time to appraise –

"Anders, my friend," a voice said in my ear.

I glanced round to see Dmitri, the big Ukrainian miner, had come to my shoulder. He looked ahead as we walked together for the moment.

"You're coming to see the address?" he asked. He sounded serious, almost sombre.

I nodded. "And you?"

"Yes."

"Do you know who's speaking?"

He shook his head. "Max organised it. She said we should come – all of us."

"She didn't let me know."

In my peripheral vision I saw him frown down at me, then quickly smooth the expression away. "I am sorry," he said quietly. "I'm afraid that... some of them aren't sure what side you're on."

"Them?"

He shrugged.

"I'm on the side of finding whoever killed my colleague. And has been trying to kill me." Did I sound bitter? Dmitri didn't give any sign.

"Of course, of course," he said. "But... beyond that..."

"I'm on the side of doing my damn job, keeping some sort of order whilst maintaining free expression" – and now I did snap – "the same as I've always been. How about you?"

He lowered his head. "I should... I'll see you later, Anders. Enjoy the meeting." He slipped away into the crowd.

And it was a crowd now. Gradually more and more people had been coming together in this corridor, all heading in the same direction. Some of them I vaguely recognised. All looked serious, intent. Even grim.

I was just a man amongst many. If anyone else recognised me they said nothing, barely even looked at me. Slowly we funnelled into the auditorium; I kept in the scrum so I wasn't greeted by the sharp-suited women who were smiling everyone in. They felt like guards.

The back rows were full. I found a seat at the far side of the room, near the emergency exit. I waited.

After a few minutes Maggie walked to the lectern at the room's focus and the buzz of conversation died quickly. She smiled warmly up at us, her wrinkled face still managing to find that spark of mischief even in these difficult times.

"Friends," she said, her voice amplified to a comfortable level. "Welcome again to our series of afternoon seminars." She paused and let a ripple of laughter die away. Obviously some sort of in-joke.

"As you know," she went on, "we usually spend this time listening to one of us – a scientist sharing the latest on his research. This time, however… With all that's been going on in the city recently, we thought it might be interesting to hear from someone who's been an outspoken critic of the Company in the past. Some of you may have heard of him; may have read his news-sheet or seen his videos. Some of you might see him as a troublemaker. Whatever your preconceptions, I ask you to listen with the even-handedness of a scientist and judge him on his words and not what has been said about him. Ladies and gentlemen – Shakil Mithu."

I should have expected it. After that introduction, who else could Maggie be describing? I felt extraordinarily stupid as he walked out from the wings purposefully, acknowledging the crowd with a wave and a smile.

Someone had made an effort with him. Or maybe this was just the real Mithu – the man he'd been when he first came to Australis, before the death of his wife had aged him, thinned him, reduced him to the man I'd seen rolling pellets in his room just a few days ago.

He was impeccable. In his suit and those silly glasses he walked like a Bangladeshi Malcolm X. His smile was intent but encompassing, beard and hair immaculately trimmed. Behind him, almost invisible in the shadow of his father, came Kaiser, and then Bhinde. Mikhail Petrovic – I smiled grimly. Should I have been surprised to see him here?

Was Guder's killer on the stage before me, or was he already in the security centre cells?

Mithu's entourage took their seats behind him as he approached the lectern. Kaiser watched his father with big eyes and a tight-set mouth. He sat stock still in his chair.

"Friends," Mithu began, "thank you very much for inviting me here to speak today. As you can imagine, this has been a busy time for me – for all of us. And thank you especially to Professor Ling for putting in the effort to organise this meeting."

He cleared his throat and glanced down at the lectern.

"I'm sure most of you know all about me and my history. I don't want to dwell on that too much tonight – I want us to focus on the future, not the past. I don't want to dwell on the fact that my family and I were sent here as exiles, not as volunteers. I don't even want to talk about the murder of my wife –" He paused and raised a hand to his cheek, just touched himself gently and then dropped the arm again. "I've gone over that enough times. And it still hurts.

"Today I want to talk about the future. I want to talk about Australis. I want to talk about the Company."

A low murmur rose above the crowd, but I couldn't tell if

in disapproval at Mithu or resentment against the Company.

"I've spoken many times," Mithu went on, "about the way some of us were sent here against our will. I have come here to ask you the question: *how do you know you weren't too*? We've seen what the Company's capable of. We've all seen the videos – how much do we *really* remember about why we're here?

"But I will get to that later. I'd like to start with an announcement. After long discussions with my friends – and my family," he added with a little look back at Kaiser, "we in the Exiles have decided to give up the possibility of returning home."

The audience was silent.

"We have tried to talk with Baurus. We got nowhere. We have tried to talk with the United Nations. We got nowhere. Finally, we spoke with Mr Ferraldi. It was he who finally convinced us that, whilst we may be able to leave this prison, there is nothing of our old lives to go back to.

"Like it or not, we are here. And now we have to decide – what kind of a city to we want to live in?

"You all know that this city is a blank slate. The Company broke fresh ground when it founded this settlement. It is up to us, the first wave of colonists, to decide its future. To ensure that our children can prosper here or can go out into the wider world with the skills they need to survive this life – this world with its overcrowding, with its paucity of resources.

"We need this debate. We need a proper forum where you, the citizens can decide what sort of future we're going to have. I don't think anyone could disagree with this.

"Except, possibly, our Mayor."

Another low muttering swept across the audience.

"We need this discussion. We *must* have this discussion. But how can we? How can we have a proper, fair discussion when we are imprisoned by the Company? An organisation that treats us as mere resources, as employees, as *servants* towards its own ends.

"And this is where we must look to the videos that were anonymously posted on the forums. Videos that have highlighted the cruel practices of an organisation that's raised us, used us, consumed us all. A massacre in a slum: how many other massacres have occurred that we know nothing about? The 'conditioning' of the people: how many people have been 'refined' into model citizens?

"How many of *you* might have been through this process? How many of your neighbours?" His voice trembled with suppressed anger. He had a politician's skill with gestures, underlining his emphases with chopping motions with his hands, delivering his lines with an open chest, with power. He barely needed the amplification that Maggie had relied upon, but as it was his voice echoed back from the speakers around the hall, Mithu's own voice providing the counterpoint.

"Before we can shape this city we must have a full account of the past!"

So much for wanting to focus on the future. I scowled to myself, but the crowd was clapping, a short burst of applause. Was I the only one who –

Or was I just thinking this because I too had been conditioned? Had my corporate loyalty been subtly boosted? Lord knew I was suggestible, could be influenced subconsciously...

"Here is what I propose," Mithu went on. "I say... No work without answers!

"No work without a full accounting!

"No work without an open, honest enquiry!

"The Company can't intervene for six months – no troops, no employees, no strike-breakers can come before summer. The Company thought it was imprisoning us in Antarctica, but in winter *we* have the power. We have the power! What're Baurus or the fascist Francis going to do? There're only a few dozen policemen in the city – *they cannot control us*!

"This city is ours.

"I say that we demand access to our full, unexpurgated employee files. We demand representation – I say no work without representation!"

"What about Baurus?" someone yelled from the rear of the auditorium. "How can we work under him now?"

Murmurs of agreement came from all over the hall.

Mithu took a moment to let the noise subside. "I am not calling for a witch-hunt against any member of the existing government. No –" he raised a hand to forestall protests – "we cannot let ourselves become a mob. We don't know how deeply involved in the crimes that the Company has perpetrated Baurus is. He may genuinely know nothing."

Again he paused to let angry cries fade away.

"He may know nothing," he repeated, "but it is clear that he cannot continue in charge here. Tomorrow I will be leading a delegation to speak with the Mayor. And we will be demanding he hand authority of this city over to an interim council. Your complaints will be heard! Your voice will be heard! This city is yours!"

The applause was thunderous.

Mithu pushed his Malcolm X glasses further it his nose and smiled at the crowd. He spread his arms wide, as if trying to embrace us all.

"No work without answers!" he cried over the noise.

"Baurus out!" came an answering cry. "Baurus out! Baurus out…"

* * *

Maggie grabbed me before I could slip out. I wished I'd taken a seat nearer the exit – I had too many things to think about, too much still to do, just wanted to find some quiet corner.

But Maggie caught me as I was shuffling behind the mass of people all funnelling through the same set of doors.

"Anders," she said brightly, laying a hand on my shoulder.

I turned down to her, bracing against the flow of people. "Maggie," I said politely, "good to see you."

She smiled but her eyes lacked the spark of humour I usually saw there. "You too. Can I have a quick word?"

I let her lead me away from the scrum. Just ten yards was far enough; we took seats by the aisle, the hubbub from the crowd providing ample privacy.

She looked at me earnestly. "Anders, I must say I was surprised to hear you were attending today."

"I'm sorry, was it invitation only?"

"Oh no, nothing like that. It's just…"

"Yes?"

"Why are you here, Anders?"

How to answer that? I shrugged, made my words casual. "I was told it'd be worth coming, that's all. He's a good speaker, Mithu, isn't he?"

She waved that away. "Told by who? Francis? Baurus?"

"Maggie, what is this? We're friends, aren't we?"

"You've made it very clear that you're not on our side, Anders."

"Have I? How've I done that?" I could feel my temper fraying. The hall was just about empty now, just the last few stragglers left. Several had, like us, fallen into small discussion-groups.

"I didn't see you up there on the stage," Maggie said. "You – of all of us, you have the best access to Baurus and to Francis. Or are you going to tell me of all the work you've been doing behind the scenes?"

I smiled bitterly. "I'm sick of being used, Maggie. I don't have to tell you anything." I felt my heart break, then repair itself with iron almost instantly. Bitter, cynical, hard. Is that what I had to be now? Trustless, ruthless, friendless – was that the only way to survive?

She eyed me, the edge of a scowl on her lips. "No," she said quietly. "I suppose you don't. Just tell me this – did Francis send you here?"

"No-one sent me here."

We sat in silence for a moment, weighing each other up. Then Maggie stood, still hardly taller than me in my chair. "Well," she said. "I'm sure I'll see you again soon, Senior Sergeant."

"Professor." I nodded to her.

She left, confident, competent. I sat there for a moment longer, then headed for the exit.

Twenty-Five

I found my hole. Took a bit of time, a bit of wandering, but I found my hole; dug in to yet another empty suite. If you asked me now I couldn't quite explain why I didn't just go to my own apartment. It just... it didn't feel safe anymore. Surely the damage would have been repaired by then, but in my mind I could only see it with the door blown off. My imagination had drawn up a howling wind blowing through the corridors, rendering the walls in ice.

I lay back on my stolen bed and closed my eyes. Another friend lost. Oh, Maggie. Politics. It was stupid and I hated it. We had no reason to fight, to fall out: she was *right*. She was right and Mithu was right and Ferraldi was doing his job properly; so why couldn't I throw in with them?

I thought of the past. Of my life in Australis, and in the old mining base, and back... back to the blocks where I'd grown up...

I tried to remember my mother's face but I couldn't. She'd died when I was still too young. Every time I thought of her it was my father's face I saw. The pictures of him in court. When he was found guilty and taken away, out of my life forever.

Thank God.

But... but how did I know these memories were true?

How did I know if *anything* was true? I mean, the United Nations had controlled me once: my memories had been tampered with then. What else had been done to make me into a compliant... to *make* me?

But then again, if I'd been conditioned wouldn't they have done a better job of it?

I felt sorry for Baurus. I couldn't believe that he was complicit in any of this – I'd worked with him and whilst he wasn't an impressive man I couldn't imagine him as a slavemaster.

My stomach growled. When had I last eaten properly?

I rolled off the bed, landing neatly on hands and knees. The arm that had been broken gave me no complaint; the wound-packs had done their work. I went into the living room and checked the forums for a delivery company that was still open during this crisis. People still wanted to eat and drink. There was still money to be made.

When the food arrived I set up camp in the main room and wished I'd ordered a few beers whilst I was at it. I ate. And whilst I was doing so I pulled out my datapad. It was past time I checked in with Lewinskiy.

I accessed the feed, the recording Bartelli and Gísladóttir had set up for me, and skipped through the preliminaries.

"...I told you, I'm not saying anything without my lawyer present," Lewinskiy was growling, scowling at Bartelli.

"And I've told you, you are under my command and I am here to speak on your behalf," Gísladóttir snapped back. She was standing with an oddly formal stance that didn't match the impatience in her voice.

Bartelli stood facing the prisoner with his arms folded over his chest.

Lewinskiy bared his teeth at his commanding officer then swung his head back to Bartelli like a bear. "This is not a military investigation. You said it was murder – as if I'd kill like that!"

"Like how, Lewinskiy?" Gísladóttir asked.

He hesitated, blinked. "Well, I don't know... the

policeman, Guder, he was blown up, wasn't he?"

Bartelli cleared his throat. "You have a habit at turning up in odd places at odd times, Mr Lewinskiy," he said slowly.

"Oh? How so?"

"The fire in the medical centre, for example. How you come to be there?"

Lewinskiy had been in the medical centre? This was the first I'd heard of that.

Lewinskiy shook his head. "Was in a fight," he muttered. "Got a blow on the head."

"And it's just coincidence that the fire was started with a United Nations incendiary grenade?"

The suspect waved his arms helplessly. "Was it? I don't know, I s'pose it must be. Coincidence. Anyway, I said, I'm not gonna answer any questions."

Gísladóttir was scowling at Bartelli – embarrassed, perhaps by the reminder that UN equipment had been misappropriated – but on these last words she snapped back to Lewinskiy. "You're going to answer these questions, Private, because I order you to! Don't forget, Lewinskiy, that even if you had nothing to do with the crime, you still have me to answer to in the morning! You want a career? Do you want a career, huh? Believe me when I tell you I can kill it. Kill it stone cold dead. You got that, Private?"

Lewinskiy lowered his head but there was still fierce resistance in the set of his jaw. "Yes, sir," he muttered.

"I didn't hear that, Private."

"Yes sir."

If Lewinskiy had started the fire, under whose orders was he acting? The man was a follower, not a leader, that I felt I knew. Was he Ferraldi's man, or Gísladóttir's? Was this cross-examination all a charade?

"After the fire you disappeared. Why d'you do that, Mr Lewinskiy?" Bartelli asked.

"What're you talking about? I didn't disappear."

"You left your assigned room and didn't respond to Captain Gísladóttir's orders for you to return. Why was that?"

Lewinskiy shrugged lopsidedly. "I... I just – I was on leave! We were never s'posed to stay in this stupid little underground freak-show you call a city! You," he said to Gísladóttir, "you told us we were at our lee-sure until spring, you said –"

"I also said you were to stay in touch at all times," she snapped back, brittle as baked bone.

Lewinskiy subsided back into his sulk.

"So where did you go?" Bartelli asked mildly. "To the prison?"

He shrugged.

"When did you start to work for Mr Ferraldi?"

Lewinskiy shifted heavily in his seat. "Just after we got here."

"Was he paying you to cause trouble?"

"No! No, not at all – he just – just wanted bodies. To move things. To help with security – I worked with Collins–"

"Who gave you authority to speak for the United Nations?" Gísladóttir interrupted.

"What – what are you–"

"Your meeting with Shakil Mithu, Maxine Oluweyu and this Collins. Yes," she said with a laugh, "we know about that."

"How did you–"

"Who gave you the authority?" Her voice crackled.

"Well – well, no-one," Lewinskiy confessed with an attempt at a chuckle. He almost looked bashful. "But we – we were trying to stop trouble, right? A means to an end. I mean I don't know if you know – they were planning to strike. Mr Ferraldi asked me and Collins to try and put 'em off."

"A pretty responsible job for someone hired to move tables," Bartelli said.

"Yeah, well – he trusts me by then." Was he sweating? Couldn't be sure – the picture wasn't sharp enough.

"Was it Ferraldi who told you to plant the bomb in the engineering warehouse?"

"I didn't do that."

"Was it meant for Sergeant Nordvelt? Or did you not care who you killed?"

"I tell you, I didn't do that."

"Where did you meet Kaiser Mithu?"

"What?"

Bartelli smiled at him.

"Well... I don't know," Lewinskiy said. "He was... the man, Mithu, he was always around – with Ferraldi, you know? The boy'd always be on the edges, listening in, you know? Why do you–"

"Why did you hire him to plant the bomb on Nordvelt's door?"

"What?"

"Answer the question, Private," Gísladóttir snapped.

"I don't know what you're taking about – I never – what?"

There was silence. Lewinskiy stared in apparent bewilderment at the two interrogators. They stared straight back.

Eventually Bartelli sighed. "Let's get him back to a cell," he said to Gísladóttir. "We'll talk more later."

The playback ended.

* * *

I pushed what was left of the food aside. The room smelled of Indian, now; they'd have to air the place out before it could be brought into use. Well, anything to cause a little inconvenience; my personal act of rebellion. I tapped the edge of my pad gently on the table, then leaned back and stretched. Closed my eyes for a moment.

Lewinskiy... well, a liar is usually easy to spot. Easy to trap. But when a liar sprinkles his story with truth then... Of course, all liars use honesty first and foremost.

He wasn't telling the whole truth, of that I was sure. But his confusion when he was asked about Kaiser – that seemed genuine.

I wished I'd been in there. As good a view as I had, I wanted to be able to look him squarely in the eyes whilst he answered. Wanted to smell the air, to *feel* his reactions.

To be the one to ask the questions.

Where had this got me? What was I to do next?

The walls slowly slipped away and sleep took me. I dreamt of Bangladesh and of far-off Mandalay.

Twenty-Six

I awoke to a silence so deep that it seemed to be a physical presence in the room. It stared at me, holding me with alien eyes.

I struggled to my feet, feeling the crick in my neck, the chill in my bones. Checked the time – God, early. A shower restored me to something like operating temperature and, dressed, I flicked on the viewscreen to see if anything had happened overnight.

The forums were gone.

This was unprecedented. There was so much redundancy in the system, so many different data-hubs that it'd take conscious effort to bring them down. One or two, yes – discussions were constantly being taken down, their hosts going silent – but for the whole network to be unavailable? Unthinkable.

Was this Baurus' doing? Or Francis'?

I was gaping at a blank screen. I shut my mouth and played with menus. All the television channels, the sports feeds, the old movies – they were all there, all working properly. But I couldn't raise a single discussion-group. I double-checked on my pad. Nothing.

Displacement activity: I cleared up last night's dinner, erased the physical evidence of my presence. Then I stared around, wondering what to do.

The quiet was beginning to scare me. I fled my bolt-hole into a city still asleep; and the silence followed me through the corridors, hiding beneath my footsteps. I was almost panicking, although I'm not sure I could really tell you why. I tried to message Unity, to find out if she knew – or maybe just to hear another human voice – but the messaging system wasn't working either. With a mounting sense of urgency I rushed into the elevator–

– And where, precisely, was I going?

I needed to be in the security centre. I needed to be where there were orders and instructions and jobs could be assigned and we could find out what the hell was happening.

The lift stopped to admit a woman – on her way to work, I guessed from her uniform. She gave me a clinical nod and turned to face the doors.

Unable to pace around, I was forced to wander my own head. The security centre. That's where I should be, that's where I belong, it's where I can do some good. If I had any hope of repairing my career, that's where I should go.

Of course I didn't go there.

* * *

God, people were so stupid. So thoughtless, so careless. They placed so much faith in what'd worked yesterday they didn't even consider that circumstances change.

If I could just walk into Baurus' private quarters, so could anyone else – my security override notwithstanding. All it'd take is determination, a proper reason.

I'd barely seen anyone in the corridors, just a few cleaners. There was no guard, no controls at all. Sure, my every step was being recorded – but sooner or later there'd be someone willing to give up their future to get to the

Mayor.

It was before six. I knocked on his bedroom door. Loudly. And again.

"Who is it?" Baurus' voice was muffled, both impatient and sleepy.

"Nordvelt. We need to talk."

More muffled noises – couldn't tell if they were words or not. I took a step back and after a few seconds the door opened. Baurus stood there, blinking in the light I'd turned on when I came in. He wore a maroon dressing-gown tied with a clumsy bow. He needed a shave, still had sleep in his eyes.

"Nordvelt? What the hell are you doing in my private quar–"

"The forums are down."

"What?"

"Did you order they be taken down?"

"Nordvelt, I don't know what the hell you're talking about."

I drew back and pointed to the viewscreen – his viewscreen, almost hidden behind all the hanging fronds of his many plants. It was on, but showing only emptiness. "The forums," I said again, "are down. I need to know if you gave the order for them to be *taken* down."

Baurus blinked, took a few steps into his main room. "No," he said slowly. "No. Why are you here, Nordvelt? I thought – Francis said you were taking leave."

He did, did he? Well... he could've said worse things. "You didn't instruct anyone to stop debate?"

"No..." He frowned and I could see Baurus was beginning to grasp the situation. He took up his datapad and, as I'd done an hour or so earlier, began searching his viewscreen for life. "So it's not just here? The whole city?"

"As far as I can tell."

"Must be some fault... Why did you think I'd have ordered it?"

"Because that's what your enemies will say."

He frowned at me, maintaining a surprising amount of dignity for a man in a dressing-gown.

"They'll say," I went on, "they'll say that you want to stifle debate. That you're acting as a dictator, controlling the media. They'll call you a despot."

"But I–"

"It doesn't matter if it's true or not. That's what they'll say."

Baurus stared at the viewscreen for a moment longer, then flicked it off and threw the controller onto a chair. He glared at me. "And you woke me up to tell me this?"

"I woke you up to see if it was true."

"You could have warned me you were coming," he grumbled.

"Messaging service is down too." I wouldn't have used it anyway. I'd needed his uncontrolled reaction.

Baurus groaned and slumped into a seat. He looked up at me with a bleary scowl. "Since you're here, Nordvelt, since you've been so good as to wake me at – what time is it, anyway? – the least you can do is make me a coffee."

When I returned from his kitchen with two full mugs he looked considerably more awake. I set them down on his coffee table and sat opposite him. He drew his legs together self-consciously. He said nothing at first, just took a sip and scowled into the surface of his drink. "No sugar."

I just shrugged.

"What are we going to do, Nordvelt?"

"We?"

He gave me a long look.

"You need to speak to Francis, and to Garcia-Lomax. You need to let the people know that–"

"But if communications are down–"

"Find a way," I snapped. "You're supposed to be in charge of this city. Hire messengers, go out yourself. You're supposed to be an – what was your official title? – Operations Executive. Go and do your job."

"And you're supposed to be a damn policeman," he snapped back. "I don't see you out–"

"I'm trying to find who murdered Guder. And who's trying to kill me."

We stared at each other for a moment. Then he sighed and returned to his coffee. "What's the point? I never wanted to be here – you know that. I should just hand over to Ferraldi and let him sort out this damn mess."

I looked away.

"Is there anything else I should know?"

"Don't leave here without a bodyguard."

He grimaced. "You think someone'll try and kill me?" He laughed bitterly. "As if – as if I'm that important. As if I have any actual power."

"You represent the Company. The old Gods. You're a figurehead. It doesn't really matter if you have power or not."

He grunted. "I need to find Francis. And Garcia-Lomax. As you said. What exactly is happening with you anyway? Francis tells me you're on leave, I hear from others that you're with Ferraldi–"

"Who told you that?"

He waved away the question. "Where *do* you stand, Nordvelt? You walk into my quarters as if they're yours. You show no respect, no apology – and yet you give me a warning – or is it a threat...?"

"No threat. I told you, I needed to know if you gave the order to stop debate."

"I didn't."

"No. I can see that."

We both drank our coffees.

"So what will you do now?" he asked.

"I'm going to find a murderer."

"How?"

I just shook my head.

"You said I needed a bodyguard."

"I'd advise you not to travel alone, put it that way."

"Do you care for the job?"

"A minute ago you were asking whose side I was on. You don't trust me."

He shrugged and brushed his straggly hair back behind his ear. "I've no reason to trust you, do I? You've hardly been conspicuous in your support. But..."

"What?"

He shrugged again. "Nothing." He stared into the distance for a moment, then slung down his drink. "Right. Anything else I should know?"

I shook my head. "Not right now."

"Then I'd better get to work. Going to be another long, painful day, isn't it? And you –"

"Yes?"

He waved an irritated hand. "Does it even matter what I tell you? You're going to do your own damn thing whatever I say, aren't you? That was always your problem, Nordvelt. Could never take orders. No wonder Francis can't work with you. Okay, okay, just – just go. Do what you think needs to be done. Whatever you were going to do anyway, right?"

I stood, was at the door when he called me back. I turned and we stared at each other.

"Nordvelt," he began. "Nordvelt – I'd... I would like you on my side. I know we've never had what you'd call a close relationship, but..." He tailed off, looked up at me with his deep brown eyes.

I stared at him for a moment, then turned on my heel and walked out.

Twenty-Seven

The city was starting to come alive. It woke sullenly, as if hung-over. The cleaners were going home. The miners and oil-workers weren't going to work. No-one could make plans; no-one knew what was happening. The sudden isolation... what could you do?

The families stayed at home, inside. The heads of the household went out into the corridors and met their neighbours, began to understand how big the tech-failure was. And wondered what the hell to do. There were no instructions, no suggestions. No authority. No guidance. The Company had never felt more distant.

The shops I passed were still shut. Sometimes I'd see people hovering outside the locked doors, sometimes I saw people shuffling around behind Perspex, as if wondering whether it was worth opening.

No-one knew what was going on or what they were going to do about it.

"Sergeant! Sir!"

I span round. There was Finch – short, squat and permanently anxious Finch. He wore his security uniform tight around his barrel-chest. He hurried up to me.

"Sergeant Nordvelt! Have you heard?"

"About the forums? Yes. I've heard."

"Francis has sent me to talk to the Mayor. No communications, see?"

"I thought you'd left the team, Finch."

He reddened and looked at the floor. "Yeah, I did, yeah. But they're short-handed now – and with all the trouble that's... I had to go back, sir."

"So what are you going to tell Baurus?"

"Ask if he has instructions for Francis," he shrugged. "If not, I'm to go and round up everyone who's off duty."

"Knocking on doors?"

He smiled weakly. "Yeah. Knocking on doors. Francis knows what I'm good at, yeah?"

I smiled back. It was hard to dislike Finch, with his permanently apologetic aura. "Was there something you wanted of me?"

"No, not really – just thought I should let you know. Francis wants all hands in the office, that's the message."

"Message received and understood."

I watched him hurry off. So Francis knew what was going on (might *he* have ordered the forums cut off?). If I knew him, he'd have patrols going round the city as soon as he could get the personnel.

And that might give me the chance for a private chat with Lewinskiy.

* * *

It's a strange feature of modern life that we can have an intimate relationship with a person we've never actually met. That's what the forums give you. A chance to discover, love, argue passionately with someone on the other side of town, from another social circle, someone with whom you have nothing in common but a shared interest.

Now people were starting to talk with their neighbours for the first time. Wandering aimlessly into corridors, gradually coalescing into groups. Inviting people home for cups of tea, sharing uncertainties, confusion slowly blossoming into discontent, into anger.

It must have been the Mayor – who else would want to silence us...?

Genuine breakdown? I needed to talk to someone who knew. So I went in search of Max.

Before I found her I came across something I'd never seen before. It was a man, barely more than a kid, with a satchel slung across his shoulder. The top of the bag was open, and inside I saw many, many sheaves of paper.

He was walking from door to door, from group to group, giving away individual sheets. Curious, I went up to him. He smiled blankly at me and thrust a paper in my direction. I took it and he went on his way – I was too bewildered to stop him.

It was a news-sheet. Like the ones the Exiles occasionally threw out. But they'd never disseminated their propaganda like this.

Forums shut down across the city, it read.

No word from Baurus or the Committee. Citizens in the dark. Simple malfunction or Company plot?

Each sentence headed a brief column. I skimmed them quickly as I stepped up my pace.

On the rear was a picture of Mithu. The article below reported that *'...prominent citizen Shakil Mithu will be demanding answers of the Executive Committee this afternoon. He will be marching on the administration centre at two-thirty, the march commencing an hour earlier in the science block. All citizens are invited to join him and to show Baurus their anger. It is expected that Mr Benitez Ferraldi will also be present. Both men will give brief speeches and answer questions...*

There was revolution in the air. And Mithu was at the

heart of it.

This whole mess was working out pretty well for him. Malcolm X, Martin Luther King – a far cry from the grief-stricken man I'd known a few short days ago. I pictured him there, sitting in his chair and rolling his little paper pellets. He'd needed a crisis to come alive.

Or had he manufactured his own crisis?

I strode on down the corridors.

Twenty-Eight

I couldn't find Max. She wasn't at home, and without communications I'd no idea where she'd gone. I tried her work but she'd not been seen; barely anyone was in engineering, just a frightened looking receptionist. She said she'd come in because she'd no idea what else to do; was very helpful once she realised I was after nothing more than information.

I tried to find Max in the warehouses but they were empty. She could've been anywhere – up at the mine, in the Comms Building, even at the damn prison. God knew.

And time was moving on. Always the clock was ticking. Past ten, eleven – soon I'd have to make a decision.

Was I going to this damn march? And, if so, whose side was I going to take? Would I be a marcher, or would I join the thin line of security personnel trying to keep them and Baurus apart?

Francis, at least, was easy to predict. Order, order, order – that was all he cared about. He'd have every loyal employee in their riot gear and defend the admin building to the last man.

So I avoided the march. I waited until I was confident the speeches would be underway, I gave up on my search for Max and headed to the security centre.

As I'd expected, it was deserted. Locked up. No-one there but the ghosts of coffees and late-night pizza deliveries. I slipped inside easily and relocked the door behind me.

It felt eerie, that big space – that big, messy space filled with the echoes of my footsteps and the signs of suspended activity. Like the *Mary Celeste* of the policing world. For all our modern kit, our high-tech set-ups and the most advanced evidence-detection systems in the world there was something almost... mediaeval about the abandoned room. I checked the armoury: shields like those of ancient soldiers had been spilled on the floor; racks of batons had been pillaged.

Man the barricades. The enemy is on the move.

I hurried past, trying to walk quietly in case I disturbed some long-caged spectre. I almost jogged to the far end of the room and into Francis' office.

I searched for evidence, but, with no real idea of what I was looking for, I found nothing. Couldn't access his compscreen without his biometrics, and his papers all seemed to be routine.

There was a form in his in-tray. It had my name on it. It was a request for a formal disciplinary hearing. It was completed, all typed with my details. Under 'Reason for Request' he'd put 'Dereliction of duty; lack of co-operation; poor attitude'. He'd left plenty of space for other infractions.

It was unsigned.

I stared at it for a long moment, then left it where I'd found it.

Francis' filing cabinet was locked. I thought longingly of jemmying it open, of finding my full personnel file, but it wasn't worth the inevitable hassle. The room had its own security camera: best not give Francis a reason to check the footage.

I strode back down the hall and headed for the small room that led to our holding cells. It was *so easy*. It was so easy. People are idiots. How could they be so stupid as to abandon their headquarters? I had the advantage – I was technically still a security officer – but these doors wouldn't stand any sort of concerted effort to get in.

I was an idiot too, of course. I should've been slower, more cautious. Hell, I should've taken the transfer out of Antarctica when I'd had the chance.

I took a deep breath and entered Lewinskiy's cell.

He was lying on the single cot that took up nearly half the room. He was awake, and alert, and the look he gave me when I entered was... clever.

"Oh. It's you," he said as if it were the most natural thing in the world. He brought himself up to a sitting position as I locked the door behind me. "How're you going, Senior Sergeant Nordvelt?"

I said nothing for the moment, just watched him watching me.

"What's going on out there? Why hasn't anyone brought me breakfast? Or lunch?"

"You're a soldier. You can stand to miss a meal or two."

He laughed at that and patted his belly. "Aye, s'pose you're right. Might not be a soldier for long, though."

"Considering a career change?"

"Let's just say... I'd be open to offers." He grinned at me, a cynical hitch in his lips.

"Of course, as it stands you'll be going straight to prison."

He raised an eyebrow. "Reckon you can make these charges stick?"

Of course there was no evidence at all. Just circumstance.

He must have seen his answer in my face. He laughed again.

"Why don't we make a deal, you and I?" I asked.

"What can you possibly offer me?"

"Tell me the truth – the whole truth – and I'll make sure

you get the minimum possible sentence."

"Ha. Have to convict me first."

"You'll be in prison – in this very cell – until a competent board of enquiry is set up. That'll be a long time, I promise you. And in the meantime?" I took a pace towards him, forcing him to crane his neck back to see me properly. "In the meantime," I hissed, "I can make things a hell of a lot less comfortable for you."

He glared hard at me. "You don't have the balls," he snapped. "And you've got nothing on me. Why d'you think you'd get anything out of me? Your colleague, Bartoli or whatever he's called, he's already asked all these questions. And I'll tell you what I told him – I ain't saying nothin' without a lawyer."

"I heard. Managed to piss off your commanding officer in the process, didn't you? What d'you reckon your UN career's worth now?"

"Don't give a fuck about Agnetha. Got a better offer."

"From Ferraldi?"

He grinned again.

"Why d'you call her Agnetha? Why not Captain Gísladóttir?"

"Oh yes, the lovely Agnetha," he leered. "You got your teeth into her yet? We were having bets, me and the others – you banged her yet?"

"That's none of your business."

"A hundred credits says it is my business."

"You'll have to ask her yourself," I said tightly.

"That's a no, then." He leaned back against the wall, hands behind his head. "Heh, you don't know what you're missing, Nordvelt."

"You don't know what you're talking about."

"No? Don't believe me? Don't believe I've sampled that particular fruit?" His grin widened. "You should ask her, man. Mm, she was... tasty. Likes a bit of rough does our Agnetha. She got in trouble for it, I seem to remember... Mm-hmm."

Her record. Fraternising with a member of her command. But... Lewinskiy?

Maybe he was just trying to make me jealous. Make me angry, make me stupid. I tried to keep a straight face. "Why are you trying to kill me, Lewinskiy?"

He scowled. "You're determined to put that on me, aren't you? I'm just an odd-job man, doing a bit of work on the side... I've got nothing to do with your colleague's death, or anything to do with you. Why would I want to do that? I ain't got nothing against you, save that you're on the wrong side. And that ain't personal. You're just the wrong jerk in the wrong place –"

"So who gave the order to bomb my apartment?" I asked.

"I don't know anything 'bout no orders."

"Does Ferraldi want me dead?"

"If he don't he's about the only one," he said. The light of mischief was in his eye.

"Who got Kaiser Mithu to pin the bomb to my door?" I pressed.

"I told you, don't know nothing about that. Kaiser..."

"Yes?"

He shook his head. "He's just a kid, you know? Smart kid. Always by his father – hey, you want someone who hates you, go see Mithu. 'S what the boy says. Yeah, the lad and me, we talk while Mithu senior and Ferraldi and your 'friends' – the Chinese professor and the Scotsman and the black woman – were havin' their meetings."

"What did you talk about?"

He shrugged. "Life as a soldier. The UN. He was interested. As I said, smart kid."

"Let's cut the crap, Lewinskiy. You started the fire in the medical bay, didn't you?"

"Did I?"

"Ferraldi's been paying you to stir up trouble, hasn't he?"

"Has he? You'd have to ask him about that. I just do what I'm told."

"Including shoving me out of a fucking airlock," I yelled, my temper finally breaking.

"Hey, that weren't me, that weren't nothing to do with me! You were behind me, remember? I didn't know anything about that until I got safe back inside!"

"Your colleagues then," I said, hating the weakness in my own voice.

He shrugged. "An accident. Tried to grab you, ended up shoving you out instead. They got the door open as soon as they could, but you'd disappeared. It was *dark* out there, man. What could they do?"

I snarled at him, had to force myself to back down. If only because he was bigger than me, and combat-trained too. "This is all bullshit, Lewinskiy. You're lying. You're lying to me."

"Prove it."

Again I bared my teeth, but before I could say anything else the door behind me burst open with a sharp crack and I found myself stumbling forwards. I turned, alarmed, to see a masked person in the doorway: an old-style balaclava covering all but the eyes. God, I almost laughed. High drama or what? But I didn't. Partly because I was too stunned, partly because he had a gun in his hand, pointing straight at me. There were others behind him in the corridor.

The air smelled tight, bitter; an acrid hint of cordite. Slowly I straightened, raised my hands.

This is it. I'm going to die. I felt no fear, no panic. No regrets. The world would carry on perfectly acceptably without me.

"Well?" I asked impatiently.

"Come on," the man in the doorway said to Lewinskiy.

The big man was already on his feet and heading for the door. He slipped past his rescuer into the corridor.

"What about him?" the gunman said with a wave at me.

Lewinskiy stared at me other the gunman's shoulder. He grinned nastily. "You think I wanna kill you, huh? You think it's me that wants you dead? Here, give me that." He reached out of sight and grabbed something from one of the other masked figures. "Well, here's something to make sure you never forget about good ol' Private Lewinskiy." He raised his fist –

It felt like every part of my skin was on fire, fire ants, fibre-glass, all rubbing me raw, biting, burning… Burning, burning – I could hear my own screams; I was on the floor, not even aware of falling, my skin melting, slewing off in great sheets…

"Christ, what setting's that on?" someone asked.

And Lewinskiy: "give my love to Agnetha, Nordvelt. Tell her I'd be willing to give her–"

But then I passed out.

Twenty-Nine

I woke in a pool of my own piss. Jerked for a moment like a half-dissected frog. Scrambled to my knees, to one knee, before I could see. Couldn't stop my fingers twitching. Couldn't stop blinking.

I found a bed and fell onto it. By degrees I came to myself, realised I was still in Lewinskiy's cell. That I was still alive. That I was alone.

I lay and breathed – in, out, in, out, in… and slowly the twitching subsided and the pain was just a memory. Like it'd never really happened. Like a nightmare. Fairydust and faerie-queens.

I looked down at my skin and was surprised to find that I was unmarked; whatever had been used on me (taser? Some military-grade shock-baton?) had only made me feel like my skin had been torn off in one lightning draw. There were no signs of the assault at all, or at least not that I could see.

Random muscles spasmed.

I'd no idea how long I'd been out. I checked my datapad, but whatever had shocked me had fried its circuits. Out of habit I shoved it back in my pocket.

Lewinskiy was gone. The one tangible suspect, gone. Fair odds he was back at the prison now – or in some other secret hideaway with his friends.

I got to my feet, gradually summoned the strength to walk. I needed to get out of here – escape before Francis and his men got back. If I wasn't too late already.

My wet trousers chafed against my thighs.

The door – the keyhole was still smoking. The smell of cordite had faded somewhat, but it was clear that some charge had been put in the lock, then detonated. I smiled grimly. Good job the person who did this knew what they were doing. Could've killed me by accident.

Into the main security hall, walking slowly becoming easier. Still deserted. I checked the time – just past four.

Had to go home. Had to change, get some food, wake up. Home. Brain won't work properly. Home.

* * *

My door had been replaced. Scorch-marks still stained the walls. The longest part of my journey was that last section down my own corridor. What did my neighbours think of me? How could I be so clumsy, so careless? Just so damn stupid?

I stared at my new door for a moment, fearing…. Well, consciously fearing another bomb had been set up. Subconsciously? Fearing the future, maybe.

I touched the entry-reader and the door unlatched – and then I saw it – a box – a red light flashing on the jamb.

I stood there, staring, dazed, for a moment. My brain sent urgent messages to me muscles to get me to run, to dive back, to cover my head and wait for pain–

I didn't move. I felt fused, my feet iron, as if I were the android statue in the Comms Bar, a being cursed to remain immobile forever. A watcher never to react.

Just to die.

It's not a bomb, some part of me whispered. *It's not a*

bomb.

It was a radio. An old-fashioned radio transmitter, almost an antique.

I took the deepest breath and a tear slipped down my cheek. Oh, what an idiot I was. Another breath.

One muscle at a time I reached out, my brow still twitching from the tasering, and touched it. Leaned up close. No explosives, not that I could see. No suspicious wires.

I closed my eyes and pulled it free. Nothing happened.

There was a note on the back. *Call me at once. U.*

It could still be a trap. The battery-case could have been packed with gelignite or whatever else. I knew nothing of bomb-making.

I wish Gísladóttir was here, I thought, then immediately doubted.

I went inside. Standing in my main room, with its carpet still singed from the letter-bomb that had nearly killed Rampaul, I looked longingly first at the door to the bedroom, then to the kitchen. I was tired, so tired.

I raised the radio, pressed the transmission button. "H-hello?"

Silence. For a moment. Two.

"Mr Nordvelt." The voice was cracked and sandpapered but recognisable.

"Unity," I croaked.

"I have been trying to reach you for some time."

"I've been—"

"I need to see you immediately."

"Immediately?" My brow twitched.

"Immediately. At once."

"Unity, no. No, I'm not going anywhere right now. I need—"

"There's someone you need to meet."

"Unity, no. I'm tired, I ache – I've got to rest."

"Anders, I'm sorry but this can't wait. You need to meet this man. And you need to meet him now."

"Can't I just—"

"Do you know how long I've been waiting for you?" Her impatience came loud and clear through the airwaves. "I've been trying to get hold of you for hours."

"But... why?"

"Because there's someone you need to meet."

"Who?"

"My office. Now."

"Can't I just..." It was hopeless, I knew it. I let her drag me, whimpering, back out into the corridor.

* * *

Later, the three of us sat on a bench in an atrium and slowly my brain began to accept what I'd just learned. Unity knew me well enough to realise I needed silence; she chatted inconsequentially with Michael Nguyen, the young Vietnamese man whose office-cum-studio she'd led me to.

I sat leant forwards, elbows on knees, head in hands. Felt my hair, the first bristles of regrowth.

What Michael had shown me – it beggared belief. Almost.

My thoughts were scattered, couldn't focus. I needed a distraction. Needed to give my subconscious time to process.

So I picked up the news-sheet that'd been thrust at me by another Bangladeshi messenger. I read it again. And again.

Baurus Resigns!
Full representation for all citizens!

In an unprecedented move the Mayor, Ricardo Baurus, has formally relinquished his position as the head of the Executive Committee of Australis.

The march on his offices, led by Shakil Mithu and Benitez Ferraldi, initially looked to be meeting with resistance. Confronted by a squadron of security officers headed by Head of Security Albert Francis – and reinforced by Senior Officer Gísladóttir's UN peacekeepers – it seemed as if violence would be inevitable. Fortunately for all, wiser heads prevailed...

...Baurus finally emerged to meet the protesters and was met by a barrage of complaints. Appealing for calm, he invited Ferraldi and Mithu for private discussions...

...when they emerged some half an hour later the political map of the city had been completely ripped up. To tumultuous applause, Mithu announced...

...Baurus stepped down with immediate effect, to be replaced on the Committee by both Ferraldi and Mithu. Further changes are to be announced shortly; we anticipate that several members of the Committee will follow suit and be replaced over the next few days...

Speculation is that Professor Holloway and Chief Engineer Prashad will be forced out...

...after announcing the results of their discussion, Mithu gave this statement. 'I wish to personally thank all those who have given their time and energy to make this happen. I realise this has been a difficult time for us all. I can assure you all that I – and Mr Ferraldi – will do all we can to restore and improve everyday life here in Antarctica. We will reopen all shops, get workers back to their jobs and get the forums back up again as soon as possible.

"All citizens are invited to attend an address given by myself and Mr Ferraldi – tonight, in the main concert auditorium, at eight o'clock local time."

The announcement has been met with joy and relief...

Mithu looked every inch the statesmen in all the many picture that adorned the sheet. By contrast, Ferraldi was merely background. As was Kaiser and Mikhail and Collins – even Maggie got her face in there once or twice.

Lewinskiy claimed to have slept with Gísladóttir. Why did that bother me? What did I care?

"Okay..." I said slowly.

Natsuko and Nguyen looked round at me.

"Well?" she said.

"Michael – can you... can you demonstrate what you just showed me before a crowd?"

The young man blanched. "I can't go up on the stage. I can't talk, not in front of that crowd."

"I'll do the talking. I have to."

"So what...?"

"The concert auditorium has a big screen, doesn't it? You can set it up on there?"

"Oh – yes, yes, of course. That's what I do, right?" He gave me an eager look.

"Anders," Natsuko began, "you are...? You're going to show everyone?"

"I have to."

"They might not let you. They might not give you the chance. Do you think they'll just let you hijack their celebration? Besides, at least half of them won't believe you."

"So what do you suggest?"

She hesitated. "It would do no harm to have a little back-up."

She was right. "Okay. Michael, go up to the auditorium and prepare your material. You and I, Natsuko, need to go and rally the troops."

Thirty

It was a push. No comms, everyone had to be raised by foot. I slipped into the chamber and had to shove my way past all the other latecomers. The chamber was packed; people were standing all along the rear of the hall and down the steps on either side.

Bartelli, Ramswani and Finch were near the front, on the far side. I caught the sergeant's eye and gave him a nod. Gísladóttir, struggling to squeeze in behind me, gave me an inadvertent push and I apologised absently to the woman whose foot I'd just trodden on.

Timing? I'd had no real plans for that. It seemed that it'd be determined by how quickly I could ease my way to the stage.

The lights fell. The great buzz of conversation fell quickly. A spotlight cracked on and Mikhail walked out to the podium. He was smiling broadly.

"Friends," he began, arms stretched wide, "thank you and welcome! In a moment we'll be hearing from my good friend Benitez Ferraldi and then from Shakil Mithu. Before that, however, I just want to say a few quick words of thanks.

"We have achieved something quite remarkable here. Something unprecedented in the history of the Company. Here we have, for the first time, used the power of the people to enforce a change of government. Peacefully.

Without a shot being fired, without a single casualty. You should all be proud of yourselves. We couldn't have done it without you." He was beaming, white teeth shining across the audience. He met my eyes briefly and scowled – just for a microsecond, and then his public face was back on.

"And now," he said grandly, "let me introduce to you the people who've done more than anyone else to ensure good governance for the city – please, ladies and gentlemen, a big hand for Benitez Ferraldi and Shakil Mithu!"

The crowd erupted into wild applause – even cheers. I shook my head, straining to see over the heads of those in front of me, always pushing forwards. I was about halfway to the front now, Gísladóttir a reassuring presence at my back. On the stage Ferraldi and Mithu were coming out together, smiling almost as widely as Mikhail had. Benitez raised a hand to the crowd and was rewarded with another burst of noise.

Behind the two figureheads I saw Collins at the rear of the stage. And there was Kaiser, and Maggie.

Slowly the audience quietened. Ferraldi approached the podium, Mithu at his shoulder. Kaiser came forwards to stand at his father's side, gawping openly at the massed crowd.

Ferraldi smiled and glanced at his notes. The spotlight turned his shadow into some mutated vulture.

"Citizens of Australis," he began. The croak in his voice, the creak – it made him sound warm, approachable – wise, even. And his tone carried a smile. "I'd like to begin by thanking you – but it seems that Mikhail has pre-empted me. So let me return the favour by thanking him for all the work he's done on my behalf. A round of applause, please, for Mikhail Petrovic."

Mikhail smiled, his cheeks reddening slightly.

"Now," Ferraldi went on once the noise had subsided,

"this has been a difficult time for us all. A difficult, trying time. And now, finally, we can turn our attention to the future.

"A lot of you will be wondering what is to become of Baurus. No –" he raised a hand to cut off a chorus of boos – "no, let us not be too harsh. It is not the fault of our former Mayor that he was put in this position. Ricardo Baurus ran this city to the best of his ability. He was given certain tools, and it was not his fault that they weren't sufficient."

There were a few murmurs of dissent from the crowd, and I was cynical enough to think that they suited Ferraldi's purpose just fine.

"Baurus," Ferraldi continued, "will continue to assist – in an advisory capacity – until the end of winter. Then we will reassess. Once the land-trains are running again I imagine we'll see some change in personnel.

"Now, over the last few weeks we've witnessed some… horrific events."

Ah. This was it. This was my cue. I hurried down the aisles, ignoring the offended looks of those I edged out. Gísladóttir was still behind me, and I was glad of her presence. Although I still wasn't sure just how much I trusted her.

Had everyone forgotten about Guder's murder? Did nobody care?

"The very integrity of the Company has been questioned – and rightly so, if we're to judge by what we've seen." He drew a heavy breath. "The videos we've all witnessed – they're horrific. They are intolerable. They –"

"They're fake!" I shouted.

Everyone turned to me. I met no-one's eyes – couldn't, for fear of losing my nerve. I swam forwards, forcing my way to the stage.

"Mr Nordvelt," Ferraldi called cheerfully from the stage.

"I should've known you..."

"They're fake," I shouted over him, "the videos – they're fakes."

I was surrounded by a sea of muttering, the tide threatening to overwhelm me.

"Mr Nordvelt, this is hardly the place–"

"The people have to know! You all have to know. Do *you* know, Ferraldi? Do you, Mithu? How about you, Mikhail?"

Ferraldi knew. There was something in the eyes. A caution. A fear. A *fury*. It was only there for a moment but in that moment I *knew*: this wasn't an honest man taken in. This was a puppet-master.

Finally I burst through the last line, into the narrow space before the stage. I saw Bartelli and his little team – Ramswani and Finch, the conscientious objectors who'd resigned *because* of those damn videos.

I scowled because I was frightened. I was exposed, I was making a spectacle of myself. I stared up into the hating eyes of Shakil Mithu.

Collins moved forwards from the back of the stage to intercept me, but Mithu held out an arm.

"No," he said sharply, the word reverberating around the hall. "That is not how it is going to be. If we are to build a real community here in Australis we must kill this *now*. You say the videos are fake, Senior Sergeant?" he said with venom. "Then I'm sure you have proof?"

"I have proof."

"Then come up here and share it with us."

Ferraldi leaned over to him and said something too quiet for me to hear above the hubbub. He was shaking his head, whispering urgently.

No, Mithu said back, the shape of the words clear, *we kill this now*.

Gísladóttir boosted me onto the stage and hoisted

herself up easily. At the other side Bartelli held his little team back – waiting.

I scrambled to my feet and turned to the audience – and was immediately blinded by the spotlight.

"He's pissed himself," someone called. I gritted my teeth against the laughter.

Ferraldi was backing off uncertainly. Collins scampered over to him and together they held another whispered conference. Mithu was still at the podium, his son at his shoulder. The older man was smiling at me – or rather, he was showing me his teeth. Humour? Yeah, it was in my appearance, in my piss-stained trousers, in my wild, frightened eyes...

I gritted my teeth. "Nguyen? The footage."

Slowly, steadily, a giant screen unfurled from the ceiling. The spotlights faded; the house lights went down.

"Surely we don't have to see this again?" Ferraldi protested. "We've all seen–"

"Not this, you haven't," I barked. "Play it, Nguyen!"

...Static... A crackling, whistling roar... Vision slowly filtering – and then suddenly resolved...

A slum: the camera jerks around, shows you a forest of crude buildings. There is no order. The shacks fall into each other, rubbish litters the dirt streets. But this isn't a shanty. This is the descendant of a shanty. It is a palimpsest, a polyglot of styles, of years, of building, rebuilding; cannibilisation of a thousand different materials and styles. This is rubble and dust...

Everyone in the hall knew this. Everyone felt the prickling of their skin, the anticipation of horror. Voices raised in protest; they saw no need to witness it again...

"Nguyen, skip forwards," I shouted.

The picture jumped – another familiar scene. The Company soldiers, bulldozers at their backs, blue-cap before them, begging for more time, more time.

"Looks good, doesn't it?" I called. "You could be right there – where is it, Ferraldi?"

With the lights down all I could see was a shape. He said nothing. Collins stood at his shoulder.

"Undress it, Nguyen."

The first to go was the sky. That gold-orange-amber dust-haze went as if dragged away. In its place was a simple, shade-less, perfect green.

"Layer one," I said.

Then the bulldozers disappeared as if they'd never been present.

"Layer two."

And then the buildings disappeared.

"Layer three."

All that remained, frozen in their tableau, were a dozen men standing in a great green space. The Company soldiers, so menacing a moment before, now looked comical, all dressed up in their combat fatigues in an empty warehouse.

The crowd were muttering, uncertain, unsure.

"*You* could have faked all that," Mikhail cried from the rear of the stage. "You and Baurus, you–"

"Nguyen, move forwards!"

The screen went black for just a millisecond and then another freeze-frame appeared. The dervish, the mad-man with the sword – the peasant so casually gunned down in the street. This image was taken just after he'd been shot; blood was spurting from him as he began to fall.

This time Nguyen needed no prompting. The sky disappeared. The buildings behind him. Half of the peasants winked out of existence. Then the blood.

Finally his skin-colour changed – no longer Indian, now he looked more Latino.

No-one knew quite what to say, but everyone was saying

it at once.

"This proves nothing," Mikhail yelled desperately. "You! You could've done this. Why are you determined to ruin everything, Nordvelt?" He took two paces towards me and I turned to him slowly, too slowly, as if in a dream—

I felt hands on my shoulders, and then Gísladóttir had spun me aside. Mikhail froze – and I realised that the UN officer had a pistol pointed at my old colleague's chest.

"You will stay where you are," she said coolly.

I picked myself up. As I did so I met Kaiser's gaze. He looked... horrified. Furious. His mouth worked silently as if not sure – and then his father pushed him back behind him out of any possible line of fire.

Mikhail froze. Slowly he raised his hands, took half a pace back. He stared at me with undisguised hatred.

"Nguyen," I called into the chill of the aftermath. "The next video."

The court-room. Gonzales standing in front of the lectern, the bored judge towering over him. Steadily Nguyen undressed the scene. The background, all the Company insignia – gone. The chairs gone. Gonzales suddenly put on weight.

When he'd finished the scene really looked rather comical. Just two men and a woman putting on a silly school play.

The second scene was even more ridiculous. Just a group of men pushing a gurney around an empty warehouse. The machines seemed little more than papier-mâché lumps, more like bad outsider-art than instruments of terror.

I didn't ask Nguyen to show the final scene. That hadn't been tampered with, just acted out.

"There was no brainwashing!" I yelled, "no conditioning, no massacre! All this has been a fake, all a fake, right from the start!"

"No!" Mikhail yelled over the murmurs of the crowd, "no. Tell them, Benitez. It's all—"

But Ferraldi was gone.

And so were Collins, Mithu and Kaiser.

Thirty-One

Responsibility. All my instincts were to pursue them, but I had responsibilities. The hall was in uproar, arguments flying through the air, disruption, chaos – the potential for violence. The potential for a stampede, for loss of life.

I grabbed the microphone that lay unattended on the dais. "Nguyen, raise the house lights! Ladies and gentlemen, please, remain in your seats, remain calm."

Mikhail grabbed me by the shoulder. He mouthed something, could've been anything. He looked stunned. Looked to be on the edge of tears. "Anders… Anders, *what's happening*?"

I ignored him, turned back to the audience. "Ladies and gentlemen, we're going to have to clear the hall–"

"It's a plot!" someone yelled, "a fascist Company plot!"

"It's Baurus," someone else shouted.

Damnation. I waved to Finch, told him to hurry out and get Francis, bring in security. God knew where the boss was hiding, but Finch just nodded and burrowed his way out of the hall.

"Stay in your seats!" I snapped at the crowd. "We'll have to leave one row at a time."

"It's a coup! Baurus' coup!"

"You can't keep us here!"

"A piss-pants putsch!" some wag yelled.

I felt myself blushing, felt anger rise inside. Bodies were milling around on the stage; so many people, where'd they all come from? I was jostled from behind, turned sharply –

And there was Unity, expression unreadable – until she broke the moment with a microscopic smile. She indicated the microphone and, wordlessly, I dropped it into her hand.

"Go," she whispered.

She turned to the crowd, and I went.

* * *

It hadn't been that simple. It never was. But now I sat once more in a four-by-four racing out towards the prison. Gísladóttir was beside me, driving the vehicle with an expression of fierce determination. Bartelli sat behind me, Mikhail next to him. The man who I still thought of as a friend was... he was in a state. He was shaking his head as if denying the existence of the world. He'd insisted on coming and, though none of us really wanted him along, it seemed too cruel to refuse him.

Besides, he might be able to answer questions.

As for how we knew where Ferraldi was heading...

"I got one of my men to paint them in the auditorium," Gísladóttir had explained as we'd hurried off-stage, into the wings and into the passageways beyond.

"What?"

"Laser-pulse," she said as she fumbled with a type of datapad I'd never seen before, some military model. "Used in missile-guidance for decades. Totally harmless. Look through a rifle-site, take a data-scan, log it in the computer. They're painted. Ah, here we are – Ferraldi's heading for the garage."

Running off home. Running off, tail between their legs. "Come on," I'd said, and the four of us had sprinted after them, raced to drag on warmsuits. Except for Mikhail, of course.

"Surely they'd know we check the prison?" Bartelli said as the four-by-four finally cleared the city perimeter.

"I don't think they're running to a plan," I said. "Just trying to regroup and work out what to do next. They'll know they can't leave Australis – unless they've got some secret land-train hidden out in the wastes?" This last started off as an attempt at sarcasm but ended up addressed to Mikhail. For all I knew they *did* have some way out.

But he shook his head. "Nothing I know of," he mumbled.

"They'll come to terms," I said, trying to inject myself with a confidence I wasn't sure I felt. "They'll know they're trapped. They'll have to talk to us."

Gísladóttir called over her shoulder to Mikhail: "So, you knew nothing about these lies?"

He shook his head, an agonised expression on his face. "I – I *believed* him. I thought – I thought we were working for a better Company, a better city. I–"

"You didn't know the films were faked?"

"No, no – I swear, I first saw them as you did, on the forums in Australis. I was as disgusted as you – I *believed* him. Why would he do that? Why would he do that, Anders?"

"What was your brief when you came here?" I asked. "What did he say you were here to do?"

"We... we were, well, it's like you know..." He trailed off. "Look, he came to see me whilst I was recovering – after you nearly killed me, Nordvelt."

I felt the eyes of Gísladóttir and Bartelli upon me. "Go on," I said as stone.

"He – he said that he was concerned about... the way things were being run. The direction the project was going."

249

"He offered you a job?"

Mikhail nodded, staring fixedly at the back of Gísladóttir's seat. "He told me of advances in s-science that should've been introduced before the base was built—"

"The anti-freeze in the blood?"

"Yes. He trained me, helped me – he gave me a *purpose*, Nordvelt. You don't know what it's like, do you?" he said, face growing hard. "You don't know what it's like to have your life torn away from you. I'd worked my whole life as an oilman. I was one of the *best*. I played sports – you remember me telling you that, when we first met, Nordvelt? All that – gone in a second. Because of *you*."

I gritted my teeth. I took it.

"So yeah, I was happy to work with him. Happy to come here and expose all its many, many failings." He barked a laugh. "All *your* many failings."

"And the videos?"

"Ferraldi had suggested he knew of problems higher up in the Company, but I'd never imagined it'd got that rotten." He looked up at me, stared into my eyes. "I knew nothing, Anders. I promise you, I knew nothing."

I stared straight back at him. "Congratulations. Now you know how it feels to be used as a pawn."

Bartelli coughed behind me, stirred some of the tension around the vehicle. "So... What we going to do when we get to the prison?"

"We're going to get answers," I said.

"And if they refuse to co-operate?"

"They'll realise they have no choice."

"And if they don't?"

I didn't have an answer. At my side I saw Gísladóttir check her pistol was loose in its holster.

* * *

It was immediately obvious that something was wrong.

There was no radio check as we approached. No query. No request for ID.

No-one spoke as we slid the four-by-four silently through the great gates. The lights in the courtyard were already on – we'd seen them from several miles back.

A suited figure was waving to us from in front of the administration block, a smaller person at his back.

Gísladóttir slewed the vehicle to a halt – but even before we'd disembarked the figure was at the door, desperate to get in to us.

I threw my door open and had scrambled out before the engine was off.

"Dead, they're all dead," the man was saying, gabbling over and over again, "they're all dead..."

I hurried round the vehicle and took him by the shoulders. "Mithu? Is that you?"

"They'll all dead..."

"Shakil, it's Sergeant Nordvelt. Tell me slow and clear – who's died? What's happened here?"

I saw his Adam's apple flexing beneath the skin of his suit. He coughed shortly, cleared his throat. "We... we got back here – we argued – Kaiser was with Lewinskiy. I found him and dragged him out..."

"Why?" asked Mikhail.

"Never mind that," I snapped. "Shakil, what happened then? Who's dead?"

"We... we sat in the courtyard for a while, in the car... Then Collins ran out, he fled..."

"How did you know it was Collins? Didn't he have a suit on?"

"...no. No, he didn't."

"He had the surgery," Mikhail murmured. "He doesn't need a warmsuit."

"So I went back inside – and I saw – I saw..."

"What did you see?"

"The air hurt my eyes," he screamed suddenly. "Even under my mask! *It hurt my eyes!*"

"Okay, Mithu, calm down. We need to get you and – is that you, Kaiser? We need to get the two of you safe. Are you okay to get back to the city?"

"What? I can... I can drive, yes."

"I can do it if my father can't."

I turned to face the blank mask of the boy. He'd spoken clearly, maturely. "You're sure, Kaiser?"

"No, I'm fine," Shakil interrupted. "I'll be fine – just – just shock. I'll be fine."

"Okay. Okay." Deep breath. "You two get home. Drive slowly. Be careful. When you get to the city go straight to the medical centre–"

"What's left of it," Bartelli muttered.

If we hadn't been in masks I'd have scowled at him. I settled for ignoring the remark. "If your eyes were burning, you need them checked out. You'll make sure, Kaiser?"

The boy nodded.

"Good. Go!"

The four of us remaining turned to face the admin building.

"Something that burns the eyes even when masked," Bartelli said quietly.

The nerve gas that was installed as a security measure. We were all thinking it, I could tell.

"What about Collins?" Gísladóttir asked.

"Don't you have him painted?" I said.

"Ah! Ah, yes – of course." She took the datapad off

Bartelli and started to fiddle with it–

"Not now," I snapped. "We've got to check this out first."

"How d' we get in if there's gas?" Bartelli said.

"There must be masks – proper gas-masks, I mean," Gísladóttir said. "The security troops must have had access to them."

"Any idea where they'd be?"

She shrugged.

"Time to search, then."

Thirty-Two

Gísladóttir inched the door open, using the barrel of her pistol to push it wide.

Nothing moved.

Slowly we crept inside – Gísladóttir, the soldier, then me and Bartelli, and finally Mikhail. I'd never seen the big man so subdued, so scared.

I was too tense to feel proper fear.

The first body we came across was that of the young girl, the receptionist or secretary or whatever. The one who'd tried to steer us away last time we'd been here. She'd been hurrying for the exit, it seemed, when her body had just... stopped.

Gísladóttir kept watch, her gas-mask turning constantly, whilst Bartelli and I knelt by the body.

"No pulse," he wheezed through his mask.

We turned her over. No wounds. No obvious reasons for her collapse.

As if in slow-motion Bartelli looked up to the nozzles in the ceiling. Invisible odourless death.

We went on.

We found Ferraldi next. He lay on his back, in the same room where he'd announced his presence before. And there was Augustin, bent up against another door.

"How does this gas work anyway?" Mikhail asked. He was hugging his arms across his chest as if he were feeling the cold.

"Exposure up to thirty seconds – unconscious," Gísladóttir said. "Exposure over a minute – dead."

"Why would Collins *do* this? I mean… why?"

No-one answered. We went deeper.

Lewinskiy, gazing lifelessly up with a little twisted sneer still on his lips.

"These are my men," Gísladóttir said. "Fisher, Okur, Akineev."

"The ones who pushed me out of the vestibule." It seemed like a lifetime ago. It was for these poor corpses.

There was silence. Just the sounds of our own breathing amplified by the enclosing gas-masks.

"What about the prisoners?" Bartelli asked eventually.

"What?" For a moment I couldn't think of what he was talking about.

"Prisoners. The criminals, N'Gepi and–"

"The war criminals, of course."

"We need to check–"

"Okay, you're right. We need to do a full check here – but it's time we got Collins before he gets too far."

"But where can he go? It's fifty miles to the city," Gísladóttir asked.

"He can do that," Mikhail said quietly. "He is… incredible."

I thought of the way he moved, that sinuous smile. I believed him.

"Okay," I said, "Bartelli, you and – and Mikhail – you stay here–"

"I'm not staying here!" Mikhail interrupted. "I'm not staying here! I'm not staying… in this place. I want answers too! I can help you find Collins–"

"No," I snapped. "No you can't. You're still a murder suspect, Petrovic."

That shocked him into silence.

"You'll stay here – in the courtyard if you can't handle being inside. Bartelli, do a full search – I'm sorry, I know it's a shitty job, but someone has to stay here. Keep trying to raise help. Comms must come back on sooner or later. We'll send a team when–"

"Will you accept help from the United Nations?" Gísladóttir cut in.

I looked round at her in surprise. "Yes. Of course."

"Right." She pulled a radio from one of her many pockets.

"You have comms?" Bartelli asked.

"Of course. We are the United Nations. We're not slave to your Company systems." She tossed the mic to Bartelli. "I'll tune into your frequency from the vehicle. If you run into any trouble."

"Right. We know what we're doing. Agnetha? Let's go."

Thirty-Three

Gísladóttir drove. I sat beside her, scrutinising the datapad she'd handed me.

"He's left the road. About a mile to the south of it, twelve miles ahead."

"Twelve miles? In what — half an hour? That's not possible."

"Collins... he might be capable."

We fell into silence.

All the war criminals were dead. Bartelli had radioed through not long after we'd set out. Was it wrong that I felt sympathy for them? A lot of their victims would have begged for a fast, painless death like that.

With them had been N'Gepi's three nurses.

Another eighteen people I could've saved. Plus Augustin, Ferraldi — taking his secrets to the grave, or would Collins have the answers? — the girl, the four UN soldiers... and Guder.

I felt myself hardening, as if I was becoming part of the invisible field of ice-boulders through which we were passing.

Collins had twenty-six lives to answer for.

Why hadn't I looked further into Ferraldi's mysterious bodyguard? Who's to say he'd ever really been a bodyguard? What if Ferraldi had always just been the front?

"You scowl any harder, your face might stick like that," Gísladóttir said. I was amazed by her coolness.

"We need to turn south soon," I said, returning my attention to the scanner. "Can you find somewhere suitable?"

"Mm." She focused on her instruments. Not much point looking outside; the faintest of moon-silhouettes were all that could be seen by eye. I gave thanks that our normal every-day masks had light amplification settings. And that there wasn't a damn ice-storm out there.

"He's heading towards the city?" Gísladóttir asked.

"I think so. He's taking a few detours, but yes, he's heading west."

"Okay. No way off the road here, but we'll go ahead and cut him off, right?"

Another mile and we were through the boulder-field – or at least that's what the map showed us. I never felt quite at ease relying purely on maps. I wanted to *see*. I wondered idly what animal's DNA they'd use to fix that in the next batch of human upgrades. What the new gods would look like. How human they'd be.

Gísladóttir gently eased the vehicle up the ice-bank that had built up at the edge of the road. There was a brief moment when the four-by-four was on two wheels before the balance tipped and – calm as you like – Gísladóttir gently accelerated down a steep slope on the other side.

"How accurate's the map in this thing?" she muttered.

"It'll be good near the road. Less good further away. It'll have all the major landscape features logged in, but the smaller ones..."

She grunted, killed the cockpit lights and kicked the headlights on to max.

"Collins'll see us from a mile away with those on," I said.

"You'd rather break an axle on a fissure? Do you want a fifty-mile walk? Fine for Collins – not something I fancy myself."

"But—"

She grinned at me, a spark of... of bitterness? Anger? Lust? *Something* in her eye. "You want to live forever, Nordvelt?" she said. "Now – which way?

"Three and a half miles away. Just east of south."

"How far east?"

"About half a mile."

"Find me somewhere we can park this thing out of sight and still be within range of his projected path."

I bent to the datapad, wondering as I did so how giving orders could come so naturally to her. Trained to it, I knew – but I was a security officer, and had been for years. I hated telling people what to do – even when I'd been security chief it'd felt so unnatural.

"There's – a sort of basin – something... A valley. He'll have to cross it. If we park at the neck..."

"Show me."

The four-by-four juddered its way across the broken terrain, its big studded wheels finding grip even over the sheer ice. Impossible white showed the headlights: a white tinged blue by our lamps, shadows in the terrain so dark as to look like solid shards of obsidian streaking past us.

Half a mile from our target.

"He's going further south," I said.

"Anything on the map to explain it?"

"No."

Gísladóttir swore. "He saw the lights?"

I shrugged.

She dialled back the beams. "We'll have to slow. Keep watching him."

"If we go a little further west... Looks like he's heading into a... a canyon – don't know how to describe it – we can get him there."

"Show me," she said again.

We veered away, our speed varying between a crawl and maybe a dozen miles an hour.

Behind a massive rock outcrop, ochre rock sparkling with ice-frozen veins, Gísladóttir brought the vehicle to a halt.

She grinned at me. "You ready, cowboy?"

I didn't reply, just pulled on my mask.

"Keep hold of the datapad. I want my hands free."

"We want him alive, Gísladóttir," I cautioned.

"Please. What do you think of me?" Her expression hadn't changed. How much *did* I trust her?

Getting out of the four-by-four wasn't easy. We'd been totally isolated from the gale that was howling across the – well, as far as I knew from right across the continent. I had to shove the door with all my strength and slip out. The door thumped resoundingly shut and I staggered, struggling to keep my feet. Gísladóttir was swearing to herself again on the other side of the vehicle.

"This way," I called.

The wind was easier on the other side of the outcrop.

"He's over there," I said, pointing roughly eastwards.

"ETA?"

"Just a few minutes."

"Okay. You try and stop him. I'll have a gun on him."

"What? But–"

"You want it the other way round? You reckon you can shoot better than me?"

I gritted my teeth, took a deep breath. I turned away from her and dialled up the light filters in my mask. Then I took a good long look around.

It was like I was watching an old Wild West movie. Like I was seeing a black and white desert, slightly out of focus. The… the sheer endlessness of it all…

I got a grip. Nearer to me: we were standing atop a steep slope, the land falling away dramatically in front of me. Not a chasm; walkable, both up and down – but it looked to be littered with scree; lumps of ice like fists, or like cars, or like great slate tiles. The slope ran some quarter of a mile down before rising steeply on the other side. I knew it was impossible, but I couldn't help seeing some ancient river at the bottom, back in the early days of the planet, when Antarctica was a tropical paradise.

A few yards away Gísladóttir was setting herself on the break of slope. She lay down on the ice belly-first. From one of her pockets she drew out a matte-plastic item, which she proceeded to bolt to her pistol.

A stock, I realised. *She's turning it into a rifle*.

"Don't just stand there," she growled, attaching a sight to the body of her weapon. "Where is he?"

One last glance at the datapad before stowing it safe in a pocket. "Seconds."

"You going to arrest him, then, or what?"

I made my way carefully down the slope. The ice-scree wasn't too bad to walk on; it crunched under my feet, the grips on my boots providing plenty of traction, and the lumps themselves frozen in place. I moved to cover; a massive erratic boulder a third of the way down, then the huge shadow of an ice-slump. And then–

Movement at the top of the far slope. I ducked back and froze.

It was Collins. He hadn't seen me. He was doing as I'd been – jogging from shadow to shadow, moving confidently, quickly. It was a matter of moments before he was at the bottom of the incline and coming up to pass me some thirty metres further down the valley.

I waited until he was behind a big lump of ice, momentarily out of sight, and dashed as lightly as I could across the slope. Slammed my shoulder into solid ground as I dived to cover. Tried to keep my breath quiet. I was glad he wasn't wearing a mask; didn't have the advantage of the wind-howl being filtered out.

Silence. I got to my feet carefully, back to the block of ice. Where was he?

Had to risk a look. I sidled along the boulder and peered round.

He was barely five yards away. Bypassing the cover I was using, he was jogging steadily upwards…

As he passed I stepped out—

His reflexes seemed almost superhuman. I don't know what gave me away, whether I'd moved too soon, whether my feet were too heavy on the ice…

He spun round and was raising his arm – I threw myself aside just as a sharp *krak* shattered the silence, the sound echoing across the canyon. I rolled, raised myself to a crouch without pause and leapt again for cover.

I could swear I felt the second shot passing by my ear.

I landed heavily on my belly and crawled out of sight.

Where the hell was Gísladóttir?

I listened hard for any sound of Collins' approach. Couldn't hear anything above the beating of my own heart. My mouth was dry. I swallowed. Wished I had a weapon.

Where was he?

I dug out Gísladóttir's datapad but I'd cracked the screen when I fell. Couldn't make any sense out of it.

A few ice-flakes landed on my shoulder. I brushed them off absently – and then I looked up—

I threw myself aside just in time. The shot sent shards flying up from the stop I'd just been lying.

Collins was standing on top of the boulder I'd been hiding behind.

No time to think – even as he was moving the barrel of his pistol toward my chest I leapt up and grabbed the backs of his legs and used my whole bodyweight to drag him down. We both fell hard, but where I landed on my knees, he hit his back on the boulder and lay gasping for breath.

He still held the gun, and despite his obvious pain was again taking aim. I dived on top of him, both hands grasping at the weapon. His bare hands in my gloves – a shot ripped over the continent, safely into the Antarctic night. We wrestled together but even with his lighter frame he had the edge, the training. He freed a hand and stuck it, palm first, into my chest. The pain was immense, an impossible pressure knocking me back, forcing me off him. I kicked out wildly, caught the hand that still held the pistol. He let out a sharp yelp and the weapon flew into shadow.

He didn't need it to kill me. He sprang to his feet as I scrambled backwards. His stance was low, the whites of his eyes the only contrast. I was backed against a rock, used it to help lever me up straight – but then he was on me, dancing forwards and landing two heavy punches on my belly. I squirmed aside, made a dash for more cover, trying to circle back to where the gun had fallen. But Collins was in front of me in a heartbeat, throwing more punches; I leapt backwards, narrowly avoiding contact.

How the hell was I going to survive this?

Even as I thought that his foot snaked out, a glancing blow to my hip. Back again, back again.

But retreating only gave him time to draw a knife from his belt; a vicious-looking thing, short but wicked-sharp. The cutting edge looked almost golden in my filtered vision.

Aw, fuck.

I retreated again; what chance did I have now? Ducked back, vaulted another obstruction, turned and ran uphill. I didn't need to look round to know he'd be following. I jagged to the left, run around a boulder like a slingshot and dodged back the way I'd come. *Find the gun, find the gun... my only hope, my only chance...*

But he was a ghost, a phantom; he reared from a shadow at my right; with the strength of desperation I smashed my elbow down even as my body twisted. His blade nicked my suit but I felt no pain – just a sudden heat, then freezing cold.

But my elbow connected with his forearm, forcing him to stumble, the tip of the knife gouging the ice. I spun and hammered into the side of his head with my left hand, sending him down to hands and knees. As I advanced on him he slashed out again and I was forced to jump back lest my feet be severed.

He got to his feet in a single fluid motion and I gave ground again.

Where was Gísladóttir? Had she just abandoned me?

I began to panic. I couldn't beat this guy. He had training, athleticism, I'd never dreamed of. I skipped back to avoid another side-kick and stumbled on the irregular surface. It was all I could do to keep my feet. I turned and ran – and suddenly I was in the same shadow that the pistol had flown into. I paused; Collins hadn't followed my straight in. Would he be going round the other side? Over the top again? Out, away, from a different angle? I tried to look everywhere at once whilst searching with my feet for the gun –

The shadows shifted. I looked up from my crouch. Collins had gone over; and now he stood, white grin against the heavy black of the night sky. He held his knife point down, a massive shard of ice in the other hand.

He leapt on me.

A shot rang out as I threw myself aside.

Collins lay on the pack-ice, gasping, groaning in pain.

"Nordvelt," Gísladóttir shouted from... from God knew where. "Nordvelt, you okay? I got him, right?"

I couldn't answer straight. I was too busy trying to breath, to stem the tide of panic.

"Nordvelt?" she cried again.

"H-here."

"God, who are you?" Collins cried from the floor. He had an oddly high-pitched voice, almost squeaky. "Don't kill me, please, don't kill me! I know nothing, I saw nothing!"

I dragged myself to my feet, approached Collins cautiously.

"Collins, you're under arrest for –"

"Who are you?" the man yelled.

I opened my mouth but before I could speak Gísladóttir appeared, strolling easily down the slope with her rifle held over her shoulder. "So, I got him, then?"

"Who are you?" Collins moaned again. He was clutching his blood-splattered leg. "You're not Mithu – who are you? The mask – who's behind the mask?"

"God," Gísladóttir said to me, "you never told me he'd move like that. Like a panther, right? Took me an age to find the shot. Worried I'd be too late."

"Why would you think I was Mithu, Collins?" I asked after I'd kicked the knife out of his reach.

"Nordvelt? Is that you?" He almost sounded relieved. "Oh God, I'm sorry, I thought you were – I thought you were going to kill me!"

"Why did you think that, Collins?" I said stone-faced.

"I thought you were Mithu! I thought you'd come to kill me – like he killed Ferraldi and the rest!"

"*Mithu* killed Ferraldi and the prisoners?"

He stared up at me as if I was insane. "Who else? Who else could it've been?"

Thirty-Four

We dragged him, limping into the teeth of the wind, back to the four-by-four and restrained him in the back seat. My side was a dull cold – an itch, an ache, but there was little blood. Too cold for it to run freely. Gísladóttir applied a field dressing, then did the same for Collins' leg. He was bleeding heavily – the antifreeze in the blood?

He'd offered no further resistance. He seemed almost glad to be under arrest. Still, we were taking no chances. We searched him thoroughly and found no other weapons.

Was Collins a murderer or a victim?

I was tired. Dead tired. I barely spoke as Gísladóttir guided the vehicle back to the road and to the city. Only the need to be alert to Collins kept me awake.

That and the knowledge that I had no choice, now, but to speak to Francis.

* * *

The security centre was still quiet, but it wasn't deserted as it had been earlier. Jawad was at reception, giving instructions to some young officer whose name I didn't know. When we entered – Gísladóttir and I leading in the cuffed prisoner – their mouths fell open.

They said nothing, just gaped at us as wearily we

trooped past them towards the cells.

Francis was in his office. Once Collins was safely locked away I left Gísladóttir to speak to her people and trudged in to see my boss.

"What the...? Nordvelt?"

He'd been talking with Ramswani: she was standing stiffly in front of his desk as he frowned at her. I ignored them both for a moment and fell into a seat.

Francis scowled at me for a moment, then dismissed Ramswani.

He gave me a very, very long look. I didn't have the energy to fight it, just waited for him to speak.

"I hear you've been busy," he muttered eventually.

"Busy – yes."

"Are you a hero, Nordvelt?"

"What?"

"You might just have saved the city tonight, with your little display out there in the auditorium. Still not had time to change your pants, I see."

I was past caring. "Saved the city? What do you mean?"

"No chance of Ferraldi taking over now, is there? Discredited him good. And that fuc... troublemaker Mithu."

"Ferraldi's dead."

"*What?*"

"Ferraldi's dead. Lewinskiy's dead. The prisoners – they're all dead."

"Have you gone *insane*, Nordvelt?"

"Bartelli's there now. We need to send a team–"

"Where? Where's Bartelli?"

"At the prison. Augustin's dead. That girl..."

Francis stared at me again, trying to bore into my head. Then he got up and went to the door. "Jawad!" he yelled. "Who've we got available?"

I tuned out. Couldn't hurt to close my eyes for just a

second...

"Nordvelt!"

I snapped upright in my seat. "What?"

"Jawad tells me you've brought in the bodyguard, Collins. Now suppose you tell me what in all hells you've been up to?"

* * *

Gísladóttir was waiting for me when I finally got out. I gave her a weak smile as we fell into step.

"How was it?" she asked.

I shrugged. "He... I don't know. I'd expected more shouting. He just... listened."

"Did you tell him everything?"

"Not quite everything. I gave him the full story of what happened out there, though."

"So are you back on his team?"

I just shook my head.

"So what now?"

"We arrest Mithu. See if we can get one of them to confess."

"I meant right now."

I looked at her. Her grey-blue eyes were sparkling, a little hitch of a smile on her lips. "What do you mean?"

"Well, I don' know about you, but I'm feeling pretty pumped. Got the blood going, right? Make you feel alive, right?"

"I—"

"You were pretty good out there — kept him at bay long enough. Man, Collins can fight! The way he moved..."

"I know," I said with just enough weight to shut her up.

But she was still looking at me in that strange way.

She was walking very close to me. I was aware of the warmth of her shoulder against mine and it felt good. I could smell her skin, the incredibly human smell of sweat, could almost *taste* her neck.

"You want to maybe get a drink?" she said.

I hesitated, tempted. "The bar was smashed up. I doubt anywhere'll be open, not after all –"

"I've got a bottle of vodka in my room..."

I realised then how little I wanted to be alone.

We were silent in the elevator as it descended.

When the door opened at the bottom I turned to her. "Gísladóttir..."

She laughed. "I reckon it's time you called me Agnetha, right, Anders?"

"Agnetha – I can't. Not yet."

Her face fell and when she looked up again, her expression was hard. "Fine," she said with a toss of the head.

"I need to end this. This case, you mean."

"For real? It's all over bar the shouting, right? All you have to do is pit Mithu and Collins against each other. One of them'll break."

I shook my head wearily. "Maybe. Don't know if it'll be that simple."

She shrugged. "No reason we can't have fun though, right?"

God, I was so, so tempted. I just wanted to give in, to let myself be taken away...

But that had never worked out well for me. I just didn't have what it took to let myself truly relax, to truly be free. Not whilst there was still a job to do, at least.

"I'll see you tomorrow, Agnetha," I said with another attempt at a smile.

She stared at me open-mouthed. "You're kidding me. Are you not too pumped to sleep? Don't you wanna celebrate?"

I smiled at her, leaned forwards and kissed her gently.

Then I stepped out of the lift and went home.

Thirty-Five

Mithu and his son were in the middle of a bitter argument when we came to arrest him. I wished I knew Bengali. They were standing in the middle of their living room, faces red and startled as we walked in.

Bartelli was still asleep after spending the whole night in the jail. I had Alexandros and Finch at my back – small men both, but I didn't think Mithu would try anything.

"What is it?" Mithu snapped. "What is it *now?*"

"Shakil Mithu," I said, "I'm here to arrest you on twenty-six counts of murder. The Company will provide you with counsel if you–"

Mithu glanced at his son. "It was Collins," he said to me.

"We'll discuss that at the security centre."

He stared at me strangely; at once angry, thoughtful, evaluative. Then his face fell into an expression of great sadness. He sighed and looked over his shoulder to snap something at his son.

"Let's get this over, then," he growled at me.

Once again his son spoke and once again his father overruled him. Kaiser looked to be on the edge of tears; he turned on his heel and marched into his room, slamming the door behind him.

Mithu turned to face me. He held his hands before him, ready for the cuffs.

* * *

Later, in the interrogation room, Ramswani brought Collins through, set him at the table. Bartelli sat before him, slumped in his seat. His lids were almost closed, but I knew he was watching, aware for any slip that Collins might make.

I leaned against the door and weighed up the suspect. He still looked a wreck; pale, unsmiling, almost as slumped as Bartelli. "So tell us what happened," I said.

Collins kept his eyes on the table. "From when?" I'd forgotten how odd his voice sounded.

"After you left the auditorium."

"Mithu wasn't supposed to come with us." He swallowed, coughed dryly. "Benitez and me, we just wanted to get back to the prison. Everything had gone wrong! You'd seen to that! We just wanted away…

"But Mithu, he was so angry. He said we'd lied to him, betrayed him—"

"Which you had," Bartelli said mildly.

Collins waved away the comment, then winced and reached down to rub his bandaged leg. "He wanted it out with Benitez – wanted a fight right there and then. But we ignored him, went straight to the garage. Still Mithu followed us, that boy of his in tow. We got in a car, they took another… followed us right to the prison."

"And what happened there?"

"They were still shouting! Benitez lost it with him, really lost it. Lewinskiy took the kid out of the room, no need for him to see that, I just watched to make sure that Mithu didn't attack him."

"Did he?"

Collins shook his head. "Mithu marched out. Then a few minutes later he came back – you know how he walks, all upright and proud, always injured. He thought he'd got what he wanted, some kind of representation, some freedom for his people. But you took that all away from him."

"Why did he come back?"

Collins laughed bitterly. "Forgotten his son. Spent a few minutes looking, he was in the control room. That's when he must have turned on the gas."

"Why would he risk killing himself – and his son?"

Another dismissive wave. "He set it on *delay*. Didn't come on for another ten minutes."

I nodded. "So you didn't actually see him operating the controls?"

He shook his head. "Maybe it was all a plan. Give him an excuse to go in there."

"So – let me get this right. The four of you got back to the prison. You all went inside. Who else was there?"

"Augustin," he said immediately. "Fat little toad. Lizbet, his secretary. Lewinskiy, Fisher, Okur and the other one, Akineev."

"No-one else?"

He shook his head again.

"The war criminals?" Bartelli suggested.

"Oh – yeah, they were in their cells."

"The nurses."

"Nurses?"

"N'Gepi's nurses."

Collins shifted in his seat. "I didn't know about them," he said.

"So," I said, "the four of you went inside. You met all these other people–"

"They were around, we didn't talk to them, not really – too busy arguing. They kept their distance."

"Did Mithu make any threats when he was arguing?"

Collins hesitated. "No... Not threats of violence, at least.

He threatened to expose Benitez, to see him arrested, to give evidence against him..."

"What sort of evidence?"

Collins' head fell.

"Evidence that you and Ferraldi planned to destabilise Baurus?"

"Not me!" he squeaked, "not me! I'm just the bodyguard, I just—"

"That didn't stop you going to that meeting — with Lewinsky and Mithu and Oluweyu."

He squirmed again. "Yeah, look, I just did what Ferraldi told me."

"The two of you were working to undermine Baurus from the start."

"*He* was! I had nothing—"

"You hired Lewinskiy to cause trouble, didn't you? To start fights, to burn down the medical—"

"*He* did! Not me, not me!"

"Who took down the internal communications?"

"That was Lewinskiy and his gang. Heard they tasered you, right? Vicious bunch. They did the jobs like that, like, yeah, like burning the medical centre."

"Did Mithu know about the communications blackout? That Ferraldi planned it?" I asked.

Collins shook his head. "Ferraldi said it was a better story if they believed it was Francis setting up for martial law. Mithu really hated — hates — the Company, man. Easily manipulated."

"Okay." I believed him but we'd check it out. It fitted with the modus operandi — the incendiary grenade tossed into the main communications node. But it'd have to be checked. "Tell me about the videos."

"Ferraldi had them made in Brasilia. He knew all about the troubles that'd taken place here — he knew of Mithu, about Francis – all about *you*. He thought that they'd be the best way put pressure on Baurus."

"Why did you want Baurus out so badly?"

Collins shrugged. "I don't know. I don't really know. I think – someone above Ferraldi was rivals of someone above Baurus – they both wanted control of the project, I think, I don't know..."

"Politics," Bartelli grumbled.

"Yes – yes, politics."

"Why do you think Mithu tried to kill me?"

He barked a laugh. "God, you don't know *that*? I've been arrested by a damn idiot."

"Well?"

"Mithu hated you, man. He *hated* you. It wasn't just the Company, it was you. After the death of his wife, you know, his kid was going on about you, how his dad was going to take you down..."

"How did you get out of the prison? How did you know the gas'd come on?"

He hesitated open-mouthed for a fraction of a second. Then he gave me a weak smile. "When I realised where we'd be staying I made damn sure to read up on the security arrangements. Part of my job, you know? Had to. Ferraldi had sent me to check that the Mithu's had actually left – I'd never seen the boss like that, you know? Don't think he'd ever failed before. So I went back to reception, and I hear this 'click'. Set me on edge – knew something was wrong. Then the doors started to close and I didn't hang around. Just squeezed into the vestibule. I knew what he'd done straightaway –"

"You didn't try and save your boss?" Bartelli asked.

Collins looked down. "Knew what was happening. The plan was to find gas-masks and get back in..."

"Why didn't you?" I asked quietly.

He was staring fiercely into the table. "Because Mithu was right outside the door. He saw me and gave a yell – reached into his pocket for something. A weapon, I guessed. So I legged it – there's no-one faster than me, you know. It was only – only after I'd got out of the whole prison complex that I realised…"

"You'd taken too long."

He nodded. "I mean, it's not like I've not had clients killed in the past," he said. "It's a blow to the ego, you know? Bad for future references," he grinned, a little gallows humour. "But…"

"Yes?"

He shrugged and looked to the ceiling. "We worked well together, Ferraldi and me. I liked him."

* * *

The same table. The same set-up, Bartelli seated and me by the door – but this time it was Mithu in the suspect's chair.

He sat proud, back straight – but only as far as the shoulders, which were slumped, and his head, downcast.

"So what happened?" I asked.

He looked round at me. I didn't see the hatred that Collins said he nurtured for me – just a great weight, a sadness. "I don't know," he said.

"You don't know? Is that all you have to say?"

"They – they were all alive when I left."

I stared at his bowed head. "Let's back up a little. You followed Ferraldi and Collins from the auditorium…"

"Yes."

"Why?"

"Why?" He laughed, almost a cough. "You have to ask

me that? You know full well why."

"I need to hear you say it."

He stared at me for a moment, then dropped his gaze. "Because I was angry. Because I'd been used. Because I thought I was fighting for a better world, and it turns out we're just pawns in a Company game."

"So..."

"I wanted it out with him. I was furious – furious! I wanted..."

"What?"

"I wanted revenge," he said, voice little more than a whisper.

"You followed him all the way to the prison."

"Yes."

"Why did you take your son?"

His head shot up again. "Leave Kaiser out of this."

"I'm just asking."

He glared at me. "What else was I to do with the boy? He'd gone all the way with me – he..."

"Yes?"

"I wasn't thinking," he said. "I was just so used to him being with me, it never occurred to me to send him away."

I nodded. Paused. "So you got to the prison, you and Kaiser in one vehicle, Collins and Ferraldi in another."

"Yes."

"What happened then?"

"I shouted at Ferraldi. A lot."

"In the courtyard?"

"At first. Then inside." He smiled humourlessly.

"Who else was there?"

"The fat toad Augustin." The same description Collins had given. A shared insult? "And the girl, whatever her name was. The soldiers – Ferraldi's pitbulls."

"So what happened?"

He sighed. "I was yelling at Ferraldi. He started to yell back at me — telling me to back off and let him think. I told him to think hard, because no-one would ever believe anything he said ever again. He… he shouted something back, and Augustin was wringing his chubby little hands and the girl was crying — Lewinsky took Kaiser out, then."

"And?"

"I walked out. I was so angry — if you think you've seen me pissed then you've seen nothing," he said with a snarl.

"And then you went back in."

"Yes."

"Why?"

"To get Kaiser."

"Not like you, to forget your son," I said mildly.

He stared at me — a long slow look that gave me absolutely no indication of his emotions. "I told you," he said quietly, "I was angry. I wasn't quite myself."

"You went back inside. What did you do?"

"I asked the girl where Kaiser was."

"Why the girl?"

"Because she was the first person I saw," he said, temper suddenly breaking.

"And she said…?"

"Why do you want all these stupid details? Just end this charade!"

"We need a proper record," Bartelli mumbled from behind his moustache. "Need to know exactly how it happened."

Mithu eyeballed my partner. "She said Kaiser was in the control room with Lewinskiy."

"Did you see Collins? Or Ferraldi?"

He shook his head.

"So you went to the control room?" I asked.

He nodded.

"And Kaiser was there?"

"Yes."

"And Lewinskiy?"

He shook his head. "He'd gone."

"Where?"

MIthu shrugged. "For a smoke, for a beer, for whatever else a crooked soldier does with his free time. I don't know. Maybe he just wanted to be the hell away from me. Wouldn't blame him."

"Tell me what happened then."

He paused. "I told Kaiser to get in the car. And then…"

"Then what, *Signor*?" Bartelli asked.

"…I followed."

"So you were the last person to be in the control room before – before the gas came on?"

He looked at me for a moment before replying. "I suppose so."

"And you didn't turn on the gas?"

"No."

"Who do you think did?"

"I can only think it was Collins. He was the only other survivor."

"Why do you think he'd have killed his boss, his colleagues?"

"You'd have to ask him," Mithu snapped.

"We have done," Bartelli said.

"He says you did it," I finished.

Mithu stared at me steadily, slowly exhaling. "He would say that," he said finally.

"Must've been one of you," I said. "At the moment it looks like you have a motive, he doesn't."

He nodded, acknowledging my statement.

"So tell us. You're accusing him, he's accusing you. Why should we believe you? Give us a reason for his actions."

"I don't know. Everything – they'd betrayed us – Ferraldi, Petrovic, Collins – they'd betrayed us and they got caught out." He couldn't keep the bitterness out of his tone, even though he must have known that it just strengthened the case against him. "They'd been caught out and they'd lost whatever game it was they were playing," he spat. "Maybe Collins thought it best to wipe the slate clean. I don't know. I'm not psychic. Maybe Collins was in charge all along and he decided Ferraldi was a liability."

"Sounds pretty weak, *signor*." Bartelli observed.

Mithu shrugged. "Maybe it was Ferraldi himself, a way of getting free of us all. Then something went wrong. I don't know. Maybe it was Lewinskiy, trying to clear all evidence of his part in all this, and then he got caught up in his own trap. They were all alive when I left, that's all I know."

"When we arrived at the prison, Gísladóttir and I, you said you'd been back inside a third time..."

"I saw Collins come rushing out – rushing out, unsuited, he ran for the hills. That was enough to tell me something was wrong."

"So you went inside to check?"

He shrugged.

"Why did you go back inside, Shakil?"

He growled at me as I used his first name, but soon turned back to stare at the table in front of him. "I... I'm not sure, not really. I just... felt something was wrong..."

"You must realise how weak that sounds."

He sighed. "It's the truth."

"One more thing, Shakil. What did you do when you saw Collins run?"

"I – I don't – what?"

"You saw Collins come out of the building, yes?"

He nodded.

"What did you think when you saw him?"

"I... I don't know. Don't know if I thought anything."

"He wasn't wearing a warmsuit. You recognised him."

He nodded, again staring down at the table.

"You reached for a weapon."

"What?"

"Did you reach for a weapon? Did you try and kill him too?"

He shook his head as if he didn't understand the question.

I shared a glance with Bartelli. "Very well, Mr Mithu. That'll be all for now. I'm sure we'll have more questions later, but for now – Sergeant, will you do the honours?

Bartelli nodded and I slipped out of the room.

* * *

I went straight into the room next door and flicked on a viewscreen. I was immediately looking back into the cell I'd just left. Bartelli was getting slowly to his feet; Mithu sat, still hunched, as the sergeant pocketed his datapad.

The prisoner stood in response to a gesture and held out his hands so they could be cuffed.

"Tell me, Mr Mithu," Bartelli asked casually, "why do you hate my colleague?"

"What?" The handcuffs snapped on. Mithu dropped his arms and stepped away from the table.

"Sergeant Nordvelt. Is clear you hate him... I jus' curious why that should be."

Mithu looked up, but I couldn't read anything from his eyes. He shook his head. "I don't... We're never going to be friends. But I don't..."

Bartelli shrugged. He was good at shrugging. "The way

you look at him… your tone of voice. Is hatred, I think to myself."

Mithu shook his head, his face showing honest incomprehension. Bartelli grunted and led him from the room.

Thirty-Six

I couldn't have told you what I was thinking.

Time passed. Days. I was the golden boy, Baurus returned to power and all my colleagues slapping me on the back and telling me I'd done well.

I'd let twenty-six people die and still didn't have proof of the murderer. I didn't believe them, not for a second. That's if there was just one murderer; with his expertise in explosives and the testimony of Collins, current thinking was that Lewinskiy had killed Guder, crippled Jackson and sent Rampaul into hospital. And that Mithu had killed the rest. We might never know the truth of that.

It was remarkable how many people wouldn't look me in the eye as they shook my hand. I was only a hero because one was needed. At any moment I could slip to being the villain. Every time I had to fight the urge to tell them to go fuck themselves.

I was in the garden, on top of the administration building. Maggie's garden, the only speck of green for thousands of miles. I stood at one edge, leaning on the low wall and staring out into the night sky. The transparent sheet that kept in the heat the plants needed also filtered out the exterior lights from the buildings around me, and didn't reflect the lights from behind.

I stared at the black sky, hoping for a moon but all I could see was the occasional pinprick of a star. Or maybe it was a satellite.

The gravel crunched behind me. I didn't turn.

"Anders?"

"Mikhail."

The big man came and leant on the parapet next to me. "I just want to say..."

He trailed off but I didn't say anything, didn't turn my head.

"I just... I wanted – I wanted to say sorry."

"What for?"

"For – for – look, Anders, I want you to know that I knew nothing of Ferraldi's... that it was all faked. I – I was taken in. I was a fool. I'm sorry."

"I understand," I said quietly.

"He – he told me that... that you were Baurus' creature. That the Mayor covered for you, after..."

I said nothing.

"He convinced me that you were my enemy," he finished.

"I was never your enemy."

"I know that now."

We stood together in silence for a long time.

"What will you do?" he asked eventually.

"What do you mean?"

"I mean, are you going to stay here – in Antarctica? I was talking to Maggie... and Francis interviewed me, you know that? Got the impression he'd... he'd rather you weren't here. Everyone seems to think you'll be leaving."

I shook my head. "I've... not decided anything yet."

"I'm not staying," he said. "I – after all that's happened here, Antarctica doesn't hold particularly happy memories for me." Out of the corner of my eye I saw a bitter smile cross his lips.

"I don't blame you."

"First train come spring."

I nodded.

Silence fell again.

"I know...

"What?"

"I know you've not come up with a killer, but I can't believe it was Collins. I mean, I saw Mithu, I worked with them both – Collins worked well with Ferraldi, never gave any indication of being a – a..."

"And Mithu?"

He stared glumly out into the darkness. "Like I told Francis, Mithu knew how to hold a grudge." He sighed. "I thought – I thought I knew him. You know, all the hours we talked together, him and Ferraldi and Collins and the others... I never saw it coming. Guess I'm –" he broke off to give a bitter laugh – "guess I'm a really shitty judge of character, huh?"

I smiled at that, and he left, I think, feeling a little better about himself.

* * *

Next up was Francis.

"Nordvelt," he said gruffly.

I turned to see him standing a few paces away looking almost constipated, such was the awkwardness he was clearly feeling. The smart suit he wore, the polished shoes – they didn't fit with his surroundings, the grass on which he stood, the bowers, flowerbeds and trees rising at his back. His dark face haloed by his thinning grey hair. He almost looked comical, but I didn't smile.

He shuffled his feet. "Growing the beard back, I see," he muttered.

I shrugged.

"I just wanted to say – just wanted to say well done. You got your man. Glad to think that Mithu won't be troubling the city ever again."

"Has he confessed?"

He waved a hand as if that wasn't important. "He had a motive, Collins didn't. We'll have a full hearing, but we don't have a damn jury to convince, do we? Baurus' sent for a judge – he wants one from outside the city, someone who can be seen as truly impartial. Come spring, when she gets here, we'll go through the whole thing and I've no doubt she'll find Mithu guilty," he said with satisfaction.

"What'll happen to him?"

He shrugged. "That's for Brasilia to worry about. He'll probably be put into environmental reclamation for the rest of his life."

That meant forced labour in the most hostile, dangerous parts of the planet. Or beyond.

"Or he'll be the next inmate of the prison," Francis said with a vague wave out into the wastes. "There'd be something fitting about that, don't you think? He caused the Company a lot of embarrassment when he killed N'Gepi and the other criminals. Lost a lot of face with the UN, we did – we pledged they'd live out the rest of their lives in there..."

"Which, of course, they did," I said.

He barked a laugh. "Well, true, true." He sighed and became serious again. "I just – I just wanted to say – I know this's been hard on you. *I've* been hard on you. I just – take some time. If you – if you decide to leave Australis I promise you a good reference. If you want to stay I'm sure we'll find a way to work together." He tried to smile.

The mimicking instinct is hard to overcome. I had to look away so I wasn't obliged to smile back.

He shuffled his feet again. "Look – I'd best get back to the office. Take as long as you need. I've got things... things are under control. Take as long as you like, make your decision. Come and see me when you're ready."

I didn't reply. After a few seconds he nodded and left.

* * *

There was nothing left to do.

Still they kept coming: the well-wishers — friends, strangers, all the people who knew my name but whose I'd forgotten long ago. Was I really a saviour? The hero of the city?

They didn't realise that I'd failed.

I'd looked into Mithu's eyes. I'd spoken to him — many, many times over the last year. I'd never seen a killer there.

Was it so easy to accept Baurus back as leader after all the bad things that'd been said about him? The self-delusion of the masses angered me. People were *happy* that I'd helped re-establish him. Ferraldi's plans may have been ignoble, but Maggie was still being wasted under Holloway, Fergie and Dmitri under Prashad. Resentments hadn't gone away just because the figureheads, Ferraldi and Mithu, had fallen.

I was branded by this city. And I just wanted to escape.

Twenty-six deaths on my conscience, all because I hadn't seen a killer when he'd looked into my eyes.

I hid in a dark corner of a dark bar and made myself sip, not down, my brandy.

Comms had been restored. I put a call through to Jawad in security.

"Sir?"

"Jawad, where's the boy staying? Kaiser Mithu, I mean."

"One second..." I heard the tapping of his keyboard.

"He's still in his father's apartment – for now. He's old enough to stay there on his own, though, of course, as a non-productive he should be moved–"

"Has any assistance been provided to him?"

"He has a social worker – and – yes, a psychiatrist as well."

"He's being cared for?"

"As far as I can tell, sir."

"Thank you." I disconnected.

I was glad. Something, at least, was working – the boy would need a great deal of support.

I thought back to my own childhood, growing up in the shadow of my father. He too was a monster. Yes, I knew the damage that a murdered mother and a murderous father could do to a boy.

At least, with the second video revealed as a fake, I could trust my own memories. My own sense of self, such as it was, was mine and mine alone.

Cheers, me.

I'd have gone round and spoken to Kaiser myself, but the thought of the hatred in the boy's eyes was more than enough to stop me.

I knew all the facts. Still I turned the case over and over and over again.

Because I didn't want Mithu to be guilty. For all the fights we'd had in the year since we first met, all the times we'd found ourselves on opposite sides, there was something I saw in him. Something... admirable.

Or I thought there'd been.

But I just couldn't find any reason for Collins to have turned on his master like that.

Who else was there? Gísladóttir? Mikhail? Who else had the motive and the opportunity? I was still drawn to Lewinskiy as the killer, if only because then we could have everything wrapped up in a nice neat bow. He had the opportunity and the skills to have carried out all the killings. He was there in the control room when Mithu and Ferraldi were arguing.

But, try as I might to convince myself, that last move just didn't seem right. Yes, he could have set up the gas on delay, could have had something go wrong and died himself in the process, but I didn't see enough anger in him for that final act. Only someone with a real burning anger would have allowed the girl Lizbet and N'Gepi's nurses to die like that—

I went cold.

Oh dear.

Oh dear.

There was someone else, wasn't there?

I checked the level of my glass. How many had I had, now?

Too many – must be too many.

I must be wrong.

I got up and left the bar, left my drink, and went somewhere quiet to sober up.

Thirty-Seven

I sent Ramswani and Rampaul – only just back on duty – to pick up Kaiser. I had Mithu brought up from the cells. I needed the two of them together.

The boy looked nervous, and that was no surprise. He peered around the interrogation room, his eyes darting around every corner before settling on me. He gave me a look of undisguised hatred – and then he spun round as Bartelli escorted Shakil into the room. The older man gaped as he saw his son; and Kaiser threw himself at his father, crushing the man's cuffed hands against his belly.

Both tried to speak at once, a torrent of Bengali that meant nothing to me. Behind them Bartelli shut and locked the door.

"What is this?" Mithu asked. "Why have you brought me up? What's my son doing here?"

Kaiser once more spoke in Bengali, but his father waved away his words with a small gesture.

"Please, will you both sit?" I asked with a wave at the table.

Mithu frowned, glanced back at Bartelli who met his eyes without response.

"Sergeant, will you remove the cuffs, please? He won't try anything here."

Bartelli grunted and did as I asked. Mithu rubbed his wrists, ignoring his son's chatter as he stared at me. Reluctantly he took his place at the table. "What is my son doing here?" he asked again.

There was a chair for Kaiser too, but he chose to stand at his father's shoulder.

I stood as well, a few paces back from the table. "There are... one or two details I need to get clear with you."

"I can tell you anything you need to know. You don't need my son here."

Again Kaiser spoke, and this time Mithu snapped a word to shut him up. The boy looked twitchy, anxious – constantly shifting his weight, fiddling in his pockets, looking all around the room.

"Who would hate policemen enough to want to kill them?" I asked.

Mithu stared at me for a long time. "Collins was no fan of yours."

"Collins didn't kill these people."

Mithu and I stared at each other for a long, long moment.

Then he sighed and slumped in his chair. "How did you know?"

"You have the motive," I said.

"You killed my wife."

"Not me. Not even a real officer. But yes. You have reason for hating the security team." I leaned back against the wall. "Who would want to kill Ferraldi?"

"He betrayed me. We've been through this, Nordvelt. Look, Nordvelt – you're after a confession, right? Okay," he said, sweat beading on his brow. "Okay, I confess – I did it. I killed them all – that's what you want, right? I did it?" He was speaking quicker now, almost gabbling, a gesture cutting off his son as Kaiser went to speak, to put an arm on his father's shoulder.

"Who would gain from the deaths of the prisoners?" I went on.

"They were all murderous scum! They deserved nothing better!"

"Of course, it does no harm to you that their deaths embarrass the Company. But what about Augustin? And the girl, Lizbet? The UN soldiers?"

Mithu shifted in his seat, frowning.

"They –" Kaiser began, but his father snapped off whatever he was going to say with a single word of Bengali.

"I am sorry for the girl," Mithu said quietly. "It was... it was a mistake. I was angry, I can't tell you how I regret it – all the deaths. I'm sorry for her. Please, I did it – I killed them all, even the policeman at the beginning. Please –" he looked up at me, tears in his eyes. "Please, there's no need for Kaiser to hear this. Take him out, please, please–"

"You're lying, Shakil," I said.

"What more do you want from me? I've admitted everything!"

"Your confession's a lie."

"Why would I give up my life for a lie?" He was looking round constantly now, his seat, chest rising and falling faster than it should've been.

"Love."

Kaiser, too, was looking very uncomfortable. He'd never settled, never stopped moving. Now he spoke low and urgent into his father's ear. This time Mithu didn't try and cut him off, just listened, listened – and then shook his head sadly and said a few quiet words back.

"You've never hated me, have you, Shakil?" I asked gently. "Oh, you've disliked me. You've been furious with me – with the whole security service. You've a temper – I could see you trying to kill me, but only in anger, never as a pre-planned, orchestrated campaign."

"It was in anger that I – that I murdered Ferraldi." His voice shook, the merest tremble betraying him.

"But the explosion that killed Guder?"

He shifted in his seat, mouth opening and closing but no words falling out.

"That was an act of hatred. Hatred against me – and against the security service as a whole. Whoever planted the explosive didn't care if I was hit, or if it was another sent in my place. As long as it was a lawman."

"I – I meant it to be you," he croaked.

"No. No, you didn't." I looked in his eyes, saw my own sadness mirrored there. Whoever said that catching a killer gave any satisfaction? This was torture . "It wasn't you, Shakil. You're not a murderer."

The world seemed to be holding its breath.

"It was you, Kaiser."

The next few moments – seconds – happened in slow motion.

The words between father and son, momentary–

The boy pulling something out for his pocket–

Kaiser pulling back his arm, throwing–

A solid impact on my chest, a thump as Kaiser hit the floor–

The father's yell of panic–

Looking down to see a home-made grenade at my feet–

The boy shouting something, then the crash of a chair as Mithu hit the floor by his son –

And then nothing.

* * *

Nothing happened.

Bartelli righted the fallen chair. He took Kaiser by the shoulders, bewilderment on the boy's face and half-helped, half-lifted him into the seat. The cuffs went on as tears started to stream down the boy's face.

I looked over him at Mithu as he got slowly to his feet. "I'm sorry," I whispered to him.

Tears were running uncontrollably down his cheeks but he wasn't sobbing. I felt wetness on my own face too.

"What did you do?" Kaiser yelled. "What did you do? It should have – it should have..." He trailed off and rattled his cuffs forlornly.

"The reason," I said half to myself, "that we couldn't find the man who'd given the letter-bomb to Kaiser to give to me was that there was no man. He wanted it to sound like it was Lewinskiy but not close enough for us to be sure. What would you have said if we'd put him in an ID parade, Kaiser? Would you have fingered him?" I shook my head. "No. You'd have been happier to waste our time, wouldn't you? Besides, Lewinskiy was your source – of knowledge, and of explosives. Of the guest password that allowed you to access the forums anonymously."

Mithu sank slowly back into his seat.

"Did he give you the explosives," I went on, "or did you steal them? But I'm sure Lewinskiy told you how to use them."

"How did you know? How did you know?" Kaiser wailed as Bartelli started to lead him towards the door. "Why didn't it go off? *Why?*"

"We scanned you as you came in," the sergeant replied as if – well, as if he was talking to a child, not a multiple murderer. "As you were waiting, a low-level electrical shock – if you felt anything it was only a tingle – and the detonator was defused."

The boy subsided into tears and Bartelli escorted him out.

When they were gone – straight into the waiting arms of

Ramswani and Finch in the corridor – I let myself slide down the wall to the floor. I looked at the grenade. It was bulky, crudely wired with soldering cracking after its landing on the floor. A dangerous thing. Have to get that properly dealt with. But I couldn't see to that just then.

I looked up at Mithu. "I'm so sorry," I said. "So sorry."

Mithu stared numbly down at the explosive. "You – you should have let me take the blame. It should have been me, I should–"

"When did you realise?"

He shook his head, sniffed. "Not – not until we'd left the control room. I swear."

"How did you convince him to let you take the blame?"

"I'm his father. He is – he is–"

He is a good boy.

I shook my head. "I'm so sorry."

Epilogue

A few nights later, Maggie, Mikhail and the rest of the original crew took me out for dinner. We were in Abi's restaurant – of course – with the chef himself taking the time to come and eat with us. But it was… it was too soon, perhaps.

"Anders," Maggie sparkled, the smile never quite reaching her eyes, the embarrassment too set to displace. "Come, sit. It's so nice to have all that… unpleasantness behind us." She looked away as soon as decently possible.

And that set the tone. All the clearings of throats, the conversation desultory and pointless. Only Weng – silent little Weng – only she seemed unaffected, looking at me as if – as if I was some kind of hero. And that hardly helped me relax.

I took refuge in alcohol. We all did. Maggie with her wine, Keegan, Dmitri with beers – all except teetotal Abi. I did my best, I swear. I swear I tried to smile, to accept the unspoken apology with as much grace as I could manage. But… But the excellent food was picked at, the courses came and went until only glasses remained on the table.

Maybe it was time to accept that I'd spent my whole life on the edge. That circumstance, not affection, had linked me with these people.

I felt a sudden sadness – and a sudden desire to see Dr Fischer again, the original base doctor that I'd only seen once since she was brought out of her coma years ago. She, right now, would know exactly what to say. Or what not to say. She'd make me smile.

At my side, Fergie was relating some anecdote to Keegan, using volume to hide his uncertainty. "...and so I says to him, right, I say 'watch yourself with that drill, Graham – you'll have the whole roof on us. And then before he could say anythin' to me..."

"It is good to see you, Anders." Weng leaned forwards in her seat, flush on her cheeks from her small wine.

I smiled at her, raised my glass.

"Thank you," she said, low and urgent. She reached out like a cobra to seize my hand in both of hers. Her skin was cool and soft.

Out of the corner of my eye I saw Maggie conspicuously look away.

"Thank you," Weng said again.

"...took hours to dig him out o' there, y'know?" Fergie finished with a laugh.

Weng glanced to the pure white tablecloth, then looked up again coyly, shyly, as Keegan launched into a counter-story. "You know," she said in a low, low voice that I had to learn forwards, lean close to hear. "You know – you remember...?"

Maggie cleared her throat, then asked Max about her art, asked if she'd ever thought of exhibiting her statues.

"...you remember... in the old base... I said..."

"I remember, Weng," I said softly.

"You saved me, Anders. You've saved me again."

"I think I should go," Maggie said abruptly.

"Aye, me an' all."

For a moment I writhed in my seat, embarrassed, uncomfortable – and then angry. And the anger gave me the strength to do what had to be done. I stood, placing one hand on the back of Weng's, and then slipping my trapped hand free. Not for the first time they were all watching me. I stood.

"Weng – all of you – thank you. But let's not kid ourselves. After all that's happened… I know I'll – I'm bound to you. We'll always be – be friends. But this is too soon. Thank you all for the meal. And Weng – Weng, you told me not to change…" I made the mistake of looking in her eyes, seeing in them pain and confusion and the fear of humiliation and rejection, and nearly choked, could barely go on. "Weng, I'm not the same person now. I'm sorry. I can't be what you want me to be."

Silence.

"I'm sorry," I said. "But I have to go."

My mouth opened again, but I couldn't find any more words. I gave the table a weak smile and a shrug, and I turned away.

Agnetha Gísladóttir was staring at me across the room, crooked smile on her lips. She was wearing her blue dress again, leaning back against the bar. She tipped her glass to me in mock salute.

I felt an urge to look back at my… my friends, to share a word – but I resisted it. Conscious of their eyes on my back I took my beer over to her, ignoring their muttered words, ignoring Weng's single choked-back sob.

"Anders Nordvelt," Agnetha said as I reached her.

"Agnetha Gísladóttir."

"That's *Captain* Gísladóttir."

"In that case, it's Senior Sergeant Nordvelt."

She grinned at me, and after a moment I laughed. I couldn't help myself, despite the discomfort I still felt for Weng – for the rest.

"She what're you doing here?" I asked. "Are you waiting for someone?"

"Sort of. I came to see you, actually."

"Oh?"

"Mm." She finished her drink and turned to wave the empty glass at one of the bar-staff.

"How did you know I was here?"

She smiled and held up her datapad. "You think my men didn't think to paint you as well? I've been tracking your movements for days."

"That's kind of creepy."

She grinned again and her eyes fell to my glass. After a mere second I accepted her silent offer and ordered another beer.

"I like to keep track of... certain people," she said once the barman had refilled us.

"With good intentions?"

She shrugged, took a long draught. "I was talking with Unity."

"Unity? Why?"

"Well, she is my boss here in Australis. You know that."

She was still grinning, still teasing me. I sipped my drink, uncertain. Very, very conscious that I was still being watched by the old crew.

"She gave me some advice."

"Oh?"

"She told me to wait until you came to me. But... well, some advice I've never been good at taking."

"Why...?" I tailed off and covered my embarrassment with more beer.

"Yes," she mused, "Unity said you weren't the brightest."

I blushed and glanced back to the table. Fergie, Maggie, Dmitri – they were all watching me. Max was scowling at me, even as she comforted Weng. My blush redoubled.

"Want to go somewhere a bit more... well..."

"I've still got that bottle of vodka in my room."

"The same bottle?"

"Metaphorically speaking," she said unapologetically.

She led me out.

* * *

The night shift passed slowly. Kaiser was kept safe. He was cared for. I got back to work – I tried to – but I couldn't focus. There wasn't much to do anyway. The long night is the worst time for the security team, but, after all that'd happened, the riots, the revolution, it seemed that the troublemakers were contenting themselves with petty drunkenness. I didn't need to get my hands dirty, didn't need to get out of my seat. I was, after all, Senior Sergeant. I could delegate this sort of thing. Eventually I gave up and took leave.

But there was still business for me to attend to.

I knocked at the door, shifting my weight awkwardly. I had no idea how I was going to be received – violence wouldn't have surprised me. But this visit wasn't something I could put off any longer.

I waited for a minute, maybe more. I knocked again.

Eventually I heard a cough, maybe the shuffling of feet from inside. The door opened.

Shakil Mithu stared down at me, his mouth twisted in an expression of distaste. He didn't say anything, not straight away. I stared back at him – saw him unshaven, eyes red-rimmed behind his glasses.

After a moment he turned his back on me and went back inside. But he didn't shut the door in my face, and this I took as an invitation. I followed him into his living room. He fell into his chair as I shut the door behind me.

The silence weighed heavy in here. Just the sound of his breathing and the air-conditioning and nothing else.

"May I sit?" I asked. He didn't reply, didn't even look at me. He just fiddled with a much-creased piece of paper; one of his old news-sheets, I saw.

I sat opposite him, watching his long fingers tear a scrap off a corner and roll it into a tiny pellet...

"Shakil..." I began.

He didn't look at me.

"I just–" In the face of his silence I was losing my nerve. I didn't know what to say or how to say it. "I'm sorry, Shakil."

His eyes shot up to lock with mine, a flash of anger curling his lip. Then he returned his gaze to his fingers.

"I just – I wanted to see how you are."

"I am fine," he said in little more than a whisper. Another rip, another pellet. The small table next to him was covered in them, some spilled to the floor.

"I wanted to say sorry."

"For what?" His voice was hoarse, cold. "As far as I'm aware, you did nothing wrong."

"I'm sorry for – for everything that brought us to this. For Lata. For Kaiser. For–"

"And what could you have done?" he snapped, a little of his old anger boiling through.

Absently I wondered if he would actually try and hurt me. I wondered if I should provoke him into it, spark catharsis. I think I'd have been willing, had I been sure it'd help. "I should–" My voice caught. "I should have figured it out sooner. Before the damage was done."

"If I, the boy's father, didn't realise what he was doing then you had no hope," he growled.

Not using his name – some psychological trick to distance himself, to save him? I wish I understood these things better. "Nevertheless, I'm sorry."

Rip, roll, abandon... the news-sheet got steadily smaller.

"Have you... have you given any thought to what you'll do now?"

He shrugged.

"There will be changes. In Australis, I mean. Baurus – well, he may or may not stay on as Mayor, but there'll be an enquiry," I said. "Things will change."

"Why should I care?"

"I – I will – if you still want – I will make sure you get back to Bangladesh, if that's still what you want."

His eyes shot up, staring fiercely at me over the rim of his glasses. "You had the last year to get me home. Why so sure you can make it happen now?"

"Before I was pushing for an investigation into the way you – and your people – were brought here. Now I'll make sure it happens for you, and for anyone else who wants to go."

He stared at me for a long moment, then dropped his eyes back to his lap. "There is nothing for me in Bangladesh now."

"You want to stay here?"

No answer.

I took a deep breath. "Shakil – look, Shakil – in the last speech you made..."

"What about it? Want to rake over all my mistakes again?" He smiled humourlessly. "There's nothing you can say that would – that could hurt me more..."

"You said that you were prepared to stay here to work on making the city better for everyone."

"I think I have run out of credibility. No-one will listen to me now."

"I think you underestimate yourself," I almost whispered. "You're too smart to labour down the mines. You always were. I – I just want you to know that I know that

Australis could use you. I know you've always hated the Company—"

He snarled at the mention of the almighty Company. "Tell me, Nordvelt — after all you've done, after all you've seen — even if those videos were faked — tell me — do you still believe in the Company? In its benevolence, in its wisdom, in its ineffability?"

I hesitated. "You know..."

"Take your time. Take your time, boy. I'm not going anywhere."

I realised I was sitting with my mouth open and I closed it, swallowed. My throat was dry, my saliva rare and precious. "I believe..."

"Yes?"

"I believe that the Company is here and we have to deal with it. It's not perfect, and yes, my eyes are opened. I believe, now, in everything you've said. That corruption saw you transported here, that the Company is capable of great feats of inhumanity."

He opened his mouth to speak but I went on, rolling over whatever he was going to say. "But the Company, for better or for worse, is humanity. It's the only chance we have, now, of maintaining some global civilisation in a world where we've burned most of our natural resources and raised the seas. The old world is gone. We're left with the Company, which at least tries to feed and maintain all its citizens, and chaos. Which would you choose, Shakil? What's your answer?"

He sat back, an instant response dying on his lips. He considered, eyeing me steadily, but made no answer.

"We live in no utopia," I said. "This is not a perfect world by any means. But we do live. We live, for the most part, without starvation and without eating each other. We live. So no dystopia either. The Company is. For better and for worse, the Company is.

"And I think the Company needs someone like you."

He almost choked at that, laughter, disdain, amazement all overwriting themselves in his face.

"I know," I said, "I know – but who can make it better if not people like you?"

"Who put you up to this? Was it Baurus? Or Francis? If you think I can be *bought*–"

"No-one put me up to this. No-one knows I'm here. This is–"

"So I can bash your brains out right here then take a walk out to the prison, join my son in his cell?"

"If you don't want to work for the Company," I said, "I think the UN would be happy to take you on." Now it was my turn to smile humourlessly. "I'd give you a good reference."

Silence.

"Do you have anything else to say, Mr Policeman Nordvelt?"

"I – I just... I just want you to know... If you ever need anyone, I'm here."

"I have friends," he snapped. "Why on earth would I ever, ever turn to someone who embodies everything I hate in this world?"

I shrugged, helpless. "I just..."

"Just what?"

"I just wanted to make the offer. You know how to find me – if ever you need."

He looked back to his fingers. After a moment I realised he wasn't going to say anything more.

Heavy-hearted, I got to my feet and was about to let myself out when he spoke.

"What will happen to him?" Mithu asked in a voice that was barely more than a whisper.

I paused. "I'm not sure... I mean, he'll be held–"

"In a cell."

"–Until the judge arrives – until the summer, and then a proper board of enquiry will be launched. Then... well, his guilt is certain. An adult would be sent into environmental reclamation for a period of years."

"Environmental reclamation. Underseas, in the Pacific trash pile, or in space, or some other dead-zone." He snorted. "Tell me, Nordvelt, what's the life-expectancy of those in environmental reclamation?"

"I'm not sure. I'm sorry."

"I will never see my son again."

"That's what'd happen to an adult," I reminded him. "The judge might take his youth into consideration–"

"And what would that mean?"

"If it's anything like my own experience–"

"Ah, your famous rebel-leader father."

"–Then a long period of psychological intervention. Then slow integration back into the world, under supervision, then–"

"He becomes you."

I had nothing to say to that. I stood and stared at him.

"That video – the second one that you so ruthlessly dismantled in front of a whole auditorium of people – the mind alteration. That video may have been faked. But that's what's going to happen to Kaiser, isn't it? He's going to return a different person."

"Shakil, he killed 26 people. Some changes may be necessary."

He shook his head, sunk back in depression. "Get out, Nordvelt," he said softly. "Just leave me alone."

I hesitated.

"Get out!"

"I'm sorry," I said again, and I left.

* * *

Spring. The equinox first, then the slow countdown until the land-trains started running again.

Another Company investigator was arriving to tidy up Ferraldi's mess. The United Nations soldiers were leaving.

I stood with Gísladóttir as the train pulled in. Her soldiers – those that had survived Antarctica – were chatting idly, kit-bags at their feet or over their shoulders. A little down the way Baurus waited with Francis and the rest of the Committee. To greet the man who'd decide all our futures and the judge who would decide what was to be done with Kaiser.

Everyone was suited, of course. The days may have been warming, the sun actually peeking over the horizon, but it was still damn cold.

"So what are you going to do?" Agnetha asked, yelling as the engine roared to a halt.

"What?"

"What are you going to do now?"

"I–" The doors were opening. At the rear of the train squadrons of engineers and porters were diving in to get a fresh batch of supplies. Towards the front the Committee were taking it in turns to be introduced – to introduce themselves – to a group of figures that had emerged. Authority had arrived.

"I don't know," I finished. "I thought–"

"Hold there," Agnetha interrupted. "Form up, lads!"

Her soldiers came to something like attention. Then, after a wave from their commander, they grabbed their bags and lined up to embark.

Agnetha turned back to me. "You know you could come with me?" she said suddenly. "We're always looking for people."

"Don't think I'd be much good in the army."

"Oh, you'd be absolutely terrible. That's for sure."

"So what—"

"I meant the UN as a whole. Could get a job anywhere. Or if you want to stay in the Company — I spoke to Francis, he said he'd help if you wanted a transfer."

"I bet he would," I muttered. "Look, Agnetha... the truth is that I've no idea what I want. I just..."

"Yes?"

"I don't know. Maybe I'll take a holiday," I said half to myself. "Travel. I've been in Antarctica for a long time. Maybe... Maybe that'd do me good."

She nodded. Behind her the soldiers were trooping into their carriage. I was sure a few of them were mocking us and our relationship (whatever that was) behind her back — and I was sure Agnetha knew that too, and didn't give a damn.

"Well, senior sergeant, I reckon I'm due some time off too. Maybe, if you make it out of here, maybe we could... hook up?"

"I'd like that, captain. That'd be good."

"You know that captain outranks senior sergeant, don't you?"

"In the UN, maybe—"

"Silence! You, Nordvelt, take off your mask."

She was laughing at me again. I couldn't keep the grin off my own face as I unclipped the mask, revealed my face to the cold.

She unclipped her own, either oblivious to or ignoring the fact that her soldiers had stopped entering the train and were now openly watching their commanding officer. She shook away the tears that the cold had brought to her eyes and grinned at me.

"Now, do I have to give the next order, or have you the initiative to take control?"

I smiled. I took her in my arms, the suit's scales soft beneath my fingers, and I kissed her long and deep.

A sarcastic cheer went up from the watching soldiers. Behind Agnetha's back I gave them a cordial finger. That brought a further cheer, and laughter.

And then she was gone, just one final wink from the doorway.

I turned away to see all members of the Committee staring at me, along with the investigators from Company headquarters.

I was tempted to share my finger with them too, but I doubted they'd cheer.

I turned and strode back to the city, and still I couldn't stop smiling.

Acknowledgements

This novel, as all novels do, owe a huge debt to those who I am almost certainly going to forget to credit. So let me start by thanking you; if you've got this far, you must be worth a lot more than I can give. I hope you've enjoyed the story and carry only good things away from it.

Thanks to all my friends on Twitter, who have lifted me through a difficult year and have always been there for me with a smile and a word of encouragement. Especial thanks to Alex, for beta-reading for me when all felt lost, and to Tim, Dave, Robin, Geoff, Marissa and Tony: the Ab-FAG group, for help getting *New Gods* into publishable shape.

Siobhan Logan, and the rest of Leicester Writers', helped with the blurb and with last-minute jitters. Thanks be to you. And thanks, of course, to the wonderful Shellie Horst for creating such an amazing cover.

I'd be remiss not to mention Don D'Auria, Josie Karani and the rest of the team at Flame Tree Press. They took a chance on me, and I'm still hugely grateful for their efforts.

Finally – of course – I must thank my family. Sheila and Peter, Jen and Lyra; you're great, and I don't know what I'd do without you.

Printed in Great Britain
by Amazon